ALSO BY DAVID E. TALBERT

Baggage Claim
The People's Playwright, Volume 1

Love
on the
Dotted Line

David E. Talbert

A Touchstone Book
Published by Simon & Schuster
NEW YORK   LONDON   TORONTO   SYDNEY

TOUCHSTONE
Rockefeller Center
1230 Avenue of the Americas
New York, NY 10020

This book is a work of fiction. Names, characters, places, and incidents
either are products of the author's imagination or are used fictitiously.
Any resemblance to actual events or locales or persons, living or dead,
is entirely coincidental.

Originally published in hardcover in 2005 by Simon & Schuster, Inc.
First Touchstone mass market paperback edition May 2006

TOUCHSTONE and colophon are registered trademarks of
Simon & Schuster, Inc.

For information about special discounts for bulk purchases,
please contact Simon & Schuster Special Sales:
1-800-456-6798 or business@simonandschuster.com.

Designed by Paul Dippolito

Manufactured in the United States of America

10   9   8   7   6   5   4   3   2   1

Library of Congress Cataloging-in-Publication Data

Talbert, David E.
   Love on the dotted line: a novel / by David E. Talbert
      p. cm.
   I. Title
   PS3620.A53 L68 2005
   813'.6—dc22   2005041266

ISBN-13: 978-0-7432-9602-1
ISBN-10:   0-7432-9602-8

To my wife Lyn
I could love you for a lifetime . . .
and still I would want more.

*—*DAVID

One

SEX TO MARCUS was like eating a plate of ribs on the Fourth of July weekend. He didn't mind getting his hands dirty or his face messy. As a matter of fact, he preferred it that way. He was a sop-up-the-gravy-with-a-biscuit kind of man. An eat-two-helpings-and-come-back-for-two-more kind of man. A damn-a-towel, I'm-a-wipe-my-mouth-with-the-back-of-my-hand kind of man. This morning I was his barbecue. And the only thing missing would be that one slice of white Wonder bread and a tall glass of red Kool-Aid.

Buzzzzzzzzzzz!

I changed my position under the warm duvet, like routine, trying to catch a peek of the Benjamin Franklin Bridge, which through my tired eyes resembled a ribbon floating in the sky. The view from Marcus's third-story loft apartment in Penn's Landing was the next best thing to waking up to him each morning. The sun reflecting on the Delaware River through his large bay window and his Persian-style interior could almost make you forget you were in the heart of downtown Philadelphia.

In an almost unconscious state Marcus's elongated fingers tapped the alarm's snooze button and under the covers he went. He started at my ankles, licking them ever so gently. Slowly working his way up my calf, over my kneecap, and along the inside of my thighs, where an uncontrollable moan seeped from my lips . . . aaaaaaah.

Marcus was the kind of man that could keep you in the bed all the livelong day. Damn your job, your career, or whatever your life goals were. After a few nights with Marcus, your only aspiration was waking up next to his ass. Hearing the sound of the covers rustling, watching the imprint of his bald head slowly going lower and lower and . . . aaaaaaah. Another moan eased through my tightly clutched bottom lip. He was there again. Handling his business again. At the same bat place, same bat time, hitting that same bat spot again.

Buzzzzzzzz!

Again Marcus tapped the alarm as the swooshing sound of the sheets silhouetted his sculpted frame. He was in full stride now. He was good, getting to better, getting to best. He was a man of ambition, always seeking higher heights and deeper depths and . . . aaaaaah.

The alarm rang again. And then again and again until one long, drawn-out sigh signaled that I had ascended to heaven, whispered to the angels, and touched the hand of God.

Buzzzzzzzz!

Marcus and I met at a fund-raiser dinner for former city councilman-turned-Philadelphia mayor Clarence Amos. Marcus was there representing his investment firm, Strauss & Landing Capital Management, one of Philly's best, and presented a $50,000 check toward a scholarship fund. To me any man waving a check for $50,000 was worth some further investigation. I managed to negotiate an introduction from a mutual friend. After just a few minutes of conversation his charm overpowered his check. Marcus and I spent the better part of the evening huddled in a corner talking about everything from parties to politics. We were almost instantly inseparable. Except for his work-related nighttime social engagements and my seemingly round-the-clock trials and arbitration, we were almost never apart.

"So, my Mona Lisa, is there any better way to start your day?" he asked with a kiss. I love when he calls me that. Mona Lisa is a li'l nickname he gave me the first morning I woke up next to him. He said waking up to my smile the next morning was picture perfect. He refused to call me Mo like everyone else. He's too original for that. And besides, it was more than a nickname he had given; it was a symbol of security. A sign of sincerity.

"Not that I can think of," I whispered, returning a kiss from his still-moistened lips.

Marcus's six-foot-three-and-a-half-inch frame and my five-foot-six-and-three-quarters body fit together as perfectly as a pair of lambskin gloves. My head lay comfortably in the small of his chest in that good space between his right pec and shoulder bone. Most men give good sex, but Marcus gave good love.

Buzzzz!

Marcus leapt from the bed and glided his chocolate, chiseled, naked body to the shower for his routine ten minutes of morning exhilaration.

Still tingling with sensation, I caught a glimpse of my own cocoa brown body peeking halfway out of the covers in his cheval mirror. My freshly permed shoulder-length flip was in disarray. But I quickly adapted to that morning look, seeing that Marcus and his rhythmic stroke was the reasoning behind it. Even my haven't-been-to-the-gym-in-a-minute slight pudge didn't bother me as much as it used to. I knew he liked a shapely woman. From my thick legs to my voluptuous breasts, my overall size eight physique was to his delight. And he indulgently substantiated that over and over again.

From the corner of my eye I noticed the luscious bouquet of pink and white roses in a crystal bud vase sitting next to the clock. I sat up and reached over to read the attached note:

> *With the wisdom of a woman twice your age, and the body of a woman half your age, for you any age is a damn good age. I planned dinner for two tonight at our favorite restaurant.*
>
> > *Love,*
> > *Marcus*
> > *(The man whose bed you're sleeping in.)*

It was just like Marcus to remember even when I thought he'd forgotten. Especially since this is the first birthday since we've been together. But that's what made him perfect. Perfect in the sense that he was present. He was attentive. Aware. Without me ever having to say what was wrong, he just listened. Even after a long day's work, he took the time to listen. Even when I was going off about this case or that case, he just sat there and listened. And that mattered. A lot. For me, it just didn't get any better than that.

We were the perfect couple—he's now an investment banker at one of the largest private banks in the city. Responsible for close to a quarter of a billion dollars' worth of investment portfolios, stocks, bonds, and mutual funds. I'm not supposed to know the names of his clients, but he can barely keep a secret. At least, not one from me. His life was an open book. No hidden agendas. No double lives or split personalities. What you saw was what you got. And even if Marcus had some type of covert scheme lurking, it wouldn't be long before I'd uncover it. It's not often something or someone gets past my radar. Like most women, I have the innate ability to recognize and eradicate dirt from a mile away. Which is a good thing, considering my profession. I'm a contracts lawyer at Benson, Bartolli & Rush, one of the leading law firms in Philadelphia, and I spend all day every day dotting Is, crossing Ts, finding and filling the loopholes.

So we were both pretty anal all day, so in each other we looked forward to impromptu moments of romance. And if nothing else, an unconscionable supply of trashy, tribal sex.

Vrooooooooooom.

From inside my purse, I could hear my cell phone vibrating out of control. I slid out of Marcus's massive four-poster bed and quickly tiptoed over to the dresser, trying to make as little contact as I could with the freezing hardwood floor. I smiled while answering, already sure of who was lingering on the other end.

"Guess where I was thirty-four years ago?"

I knew it. It was my mother. Every year on my birthday, she called me the exact hour and minute that I was born.

"Momma," I said, half-groggy, trying to make her think I was asleep.

"I'll tell you," she said, barely taking a breath. "I was in Chestnut

Hill Hospital Women's Center giving birth to an angel. Giving life to my first and only child. You should know, because you are that angel. A gift from God. Oh, you should have seen the look on your father's face. That is, after he came to from fainting. He loved you so much. We both did."

"If he were here right now, he'd tell you, too," she continued, getting choked up. My father had passed away almost ten years ago from diabetes.

"I know he would," I said, trying to break her out of it.

"I know you know, baby. And I know he knows it, too, while he's smiling down on us even now. Gone 'head, baby, give your daddy a little wave."

"Momma," I said, hoping to move the conversation along.

"Anyway I've got a card from the saints at True Vine," she continued, still weepy. "Pastor Zachary had the missionary board chip in for a gift for you. They say they haven't seen you in a while and everybody misses you. I told them you're busy and that you always ask about them. He's thinking about retiring next year. He has the gout, you know."

That was my mother. She could go from one unrelated subject to the next without taking a break or skipping a beat. Without leaving room for an interjection, comment, thought, or reflection. I could lay the phone down and walk away and she'd never know. One time I did. I walked away for fifteen minutes and when I came back, she was still going. And going. And going.

"You know I tried you at home, but you didn't pick up. Are you at Marcus's house?" she asked, always hoping that a steady relationship meant she was one step closer to the grandchild she had long since wanted.

"Yes, Momma."

"Oh, that's nice. Tell him I said good morning. He's a good man, you know. He's not like Terrance, or Kevin, Calvin, Orlando, or Dalvin. Especially Dalvin. He was a mess. A train wreck waiting to happen from one end of Broad Street to the other."

"Train wreck, Momma? Don't you think 'train wreck' is a little harsh? We were in the third grade."

"Okay, so it was a choo choo train. But it was still a train," she said, now laughing at herself.

"Momma," I said in a voice that she knew all too well.

"I know. I know. Baby, I just want you to be happy, that's all. I just want you to find somebody like I found somebody. You deserve a man that'll make you pancakes on Sunday, just like the ones your father used to make me. I can hear him now, jumping out the bed, slipping on those raggedy pair of slippers that I tried to get him to get rid of for years, stomping down the stairs, then after a spell or two, he'd yell up the stairs, 'Baby, come on and get you something to eat.' I'd act like I didn't hear him, like I was still asleep, and he'd march up the stairs, huffing and puffing—lean over and whisper in my ear—'your pancakes are ready.' After all these years, I still wake up sometimes and I can hear him rumbling through the kitchen, clanging through the cupboard, fixing me pancakes. I just want the same for you, baby. That's all."

"I do, too, Momma. I do, too," I said, reflecting on my own memories growing up in a household filled with the fragrance of family, love, and pancakes.

"You tell Marcus he's got some big shoes to fill. I don't even know if they make that size anymore, but just in case they do . . . you tell him what I said, you hear."

"I will, Momma."

"I know you will, baby. And tell him any time he wants another piece of cake or pie, he's more than welcome. Like I always say, the nearer the bone, the sweeter the meat. I love you."

"I love you, too," I said, easing the flip phone closed, embracing the fact that since my father's been gone my life became her life, and, like it or not, we were going to be joined at the hip until she could usher me into the arms of a loving man who could rightfully take care of me. But even with all her quirks and crazy run-on sentences, she was my friend. She kept me grounded. I was thankful to have her in my life.

I scurried back under the covers, hoping for five more minutes to linger in his scent. There was no question in my mind. Marcus was the one. First there were all-night conversations, which turned into the occasional creepovers. Then the random weekend sleepovers, which quickly turned into me leaving a toothbrush here, a pair of lace panties there. I marked my territory on most of his apartment by strategically strewing feminine subtleties in all the appropriate hot spots. A box of tampons in the master bathroom. A bottle of pink nail polish on the floor behind his nightstand. And if neither of those thwarted the hoes, there was the always explosive, half-empty birth control dispenser in the front of his kitchen drawer. Like I said, I had covered all my bases. Not that I didn't trust my man. I just didn't trust his options.

In my mind, the only thing left was a key to his apartment. I had no doubt that was forthcoming.

What I did may sound a little extreme, but it all depends on what you're looking for in a relationship. For me a relationship is about commitment and trust. Plain and simple. And see, I'm not looking for a wedding ring. I'm not pressed to run to the altar. For what? It may seem like the most logical desire for a woman, but after dealing with family law and drawing up divorce contracts and prenuptials all day, to me it's almost unethical to walk down the aisle. Why pay thousands of dollars for one day when you can seal your relationship with the same level of commitment by a couple deciding to make a conscious effort to do so. A piece of paper doesn't define the validity of any relationship; the increasing divorce rate today is evidence of that. And just because my and Marcus's fidelity isn't sealed with a platinum band doesn't make me wanting commitment from him or any man any less vital. It's just that I have too much to lose in a marriage and too much to gain in life and in my career. Why take the chance of losing half of that because some fool wants to act up?

"Baby, could you pull out my blue pinstriped Hugo Boss suit from the closet and could you pick out a shirt for me, too, please?"

"Sure thing, honey," I said.

In the time that we had been dating, I had successfully gotten him to shift his fashion from drudging off-the-rack suits to fresh, custom-fitted and designer suits, ones more befitting a man of his status and earnings. Not that he didn't already have style, but I figured since we're going to be together for a while, I might as well give him a look that I liked.

Easing myself out from under the duvet, I began sifting through his large walk-in closet for the suit and shirt. I reached for the pinstriped blue shirt that I had picked out for him a few weeks ago. As I began to pull it down from the shelf, I noticed a strand from one of his cashmere sweaters caught on a button from another shirt. After undoing the snag, I placed it back in its original place. Folding, then tucking, and then . . . now what is this? Something not so soft and fluffy had brushed up against my hand.

"Could you pick a tie, too? I'm running kinda late."

"Sure," I said, now curious to explore.

"Thanks!"

I reached for the hard something, only to find it was a box. But not just any box. It was a rectangular jewelry box. A blue rectangular jewelry box. But not just any blue . . . *Tiffany blue!!* Oh my God . . . it's a—

"Sweetheart, could you hand me a clean towel from the cabinet, please?"

"Yeah," I said, then quickly covered my mouth with my hand.

"Thanks."

Opening it slowly . . . slowly . . . oh my God! A diamond-covered tennis bracelet. Why would Marcus have a diamond-covered tennis bracelet in his closet? Stunned by its sparkle, it suddenly became crystal clear that today was . . . today was . . . today was my birthday! Oh my goodness! It's mine! It's mine! Who needs a duplicate key, I've got some duplicate diamonds. What's next? The duplicate last name?

"Sweetheart?"

I closed the box and returned it to its hiding place. Rushing to the linen closet and then into the bathroom.

"Morgan," he said, standing naked as water dripped down his body.

"Yes," I said, trying desperately to cover my joy.

"The towel, sweetheart."

"Right," I said. I was so overwhelmed I forgot to hand him his towel. As he dried off I hopped in the shower, humming to myself, thinking that I couldn't wait to get to the office to tell my best girl-friend, Altima.

Two

STAYING AT MARCUS'S place made it convenient for me to get to work on time. It was less than fifteen minutes away from our down-town offices. I hopped out of the shower, slid into my business suit, and was off. The frigid air instantly turned my smile upside down; it was Old Man Winter at his best. Biting. Ruthless. Hopping into my second-generation handed-down hooptie, I turned on the car and began praying that the heater would swiftly kick in. Fortunately for me it did as I made my way, backfiring muffler and all, finally pulling into my office building's Benz- and Beemer-filled parking garage. Today I wasn't even affected by the sneers at the make and model of my father's beloved 1987 gold Buick. A car that I should have long since put out to pasture, but since it was the last thing my father gave me before he passed, it was kinda hard to let it go. Admittedly I was a daddy's girl and driving in his car each day was the next best thing to him being there. What can I say, I'm a habitual hanger on-er. Even if it meant risking life and limb to do so.

I strolled into the offices past Tess, the always friendly front office manager. In my usual upbeat mood.

I wasn't at all surprised that she remembered my birthday. Tess was the best. Full of the unexpected, sharp as a knife, alert, and always aware.

"Good morning, Morgan. Happy birthday."

"Thank you, Tess," I said. Never once breaking my stride, I spotted my best girlfriend, Altima, and I grabbed her arm as she came out of the copy room.

As we walked the hall I heard greetings:

"Mo, what's up?"

"Morgan, good morning."

"Morning, Morgan."

Chitter or chatter didn't matter. With a head full of steam, we made a bee line straight to my dormitory-size, one-day-I'll-graduate-to-a-real-office office.

Finally inside, giddy with excitement, I couldn't wait to blurt out the discovery of my gift.

"Mo, you lying!" Altima shouted. Even with the door closed, you could probably hear our screams all the way to Wyoming. "Platinum, too? See, girl, I told you. Didn't I tell you? I told you, right, didn't I?"

Altima's eyes shone almost brighter than my own. She was my ace boon. My ride or die. We've been girls ever since middle school, when she almost got expelled for beating down this bully who wanted to fight me over some boy.

Obsessed with Matlock and Perry Mason, she always dreamed of going to college to become a lawyer. But with a GPA somewhere between 2.0 and so-so-so in high school, the more practical choice was court reporting school. But with sculptured nine-and-a-half-inch nails, that didn't last for long. So, when I finally graduated from law school and got this gig, I finagled her a job at the firm in the copy room. I figured if she couldn't be a lawyer, she could at least hang with them. Besides, like Oprah says . . . it's never too late. She still has aspirations of going back to school and trying to be at the very least a paralegal. I always hoped my ambition and success would rub off on her. Unfortunately her love life is like every love song gone wrong brought to life. But she stays encouraged nonetheless, being the most hopeless romantic I know. With her being queen of the copy room, I had the inside track on whatever went on in the office via fax, memo, or any other form of written communication.

"That smothered chicken got his ass sprung, didn't it?" She laughed as she high-fived me. She was referring to one of the many, many meals she'd cook and I'd serve from my own pots, pans, and plates, pretending that it was my own. My mother always said that the way to a man's heart was through his stomach, so I figured an occasional home-cooked meal via a friend was a harmless strand of wool pulled over his eyes.

"The chicken wasn't the only thing smothered that he was eating," I mischievously replied with an eyebrow raised.

"Ooh, Mo . . . you nasty!" she said, feigning embarrassment. "Well, I hope you put some gravy on it!" We laughed even louder and harder. "I told you that he was the one, I told you, right? Didn't I tell you?"

"Yes, you told me. My mother told me. Oprah told me. It seems like the whole world told me. I guess I was waiting for him to tell me."

"Well, he sure as hell told you. His ass told you with diamonds. Girl, you 'bout to make me cry," she said, swelling with emotion. "We need to hug!" She grabbed me close.

Altima was an emotional outburst waiting to happen. I was the exact opposite. I guess that's what made us such best friends. We were the perfect balance. In life's everyday cloud of uncertainty, she was my silver lining. To her the glass was forever half-full.

"I haven't gotten it, yet. I don't want to get too excited."

"Who else could he possibly give it to, but you? Don't wait till the battle's over, Mo, shout now!" she exclaimed.

Taking her advice, that's exactly what I did as we let out belts of even more screams. We instantly shooshed each other. Just as we did, my office door swung open as we heard . . .

"Is this a law firm or a sorority sleepover? What are you two project princesses in here talking about now?"

It was Ophelia Clarke, the company killjoy. She was nosey, opinionated, and manless. She would usually sport some tired wig or a nappy snatch back accented with a dollar-store clip. She wore next to no makeup and although she always claimed to be on some diet, you could never tell if she shed a pound due to her two-sizes-too-big suits camouflaging her figure. She drenched herself in the kind of cheap perfume that stayed in your office hours after she'd left and to top it all off, she was knock-kneed. But Ophelia was smart. Sharp as a tack. Everybody in the firm knew it. Still, her candidness, even if it was the truth, made her unbearable to be around. She could have you depressed faster than the Save the Children infomercials.

The water cooler gossip is that she's bitter due to her string of dead relationships, either put to rest because of her humdrum appearance or the fact that she's smarter than most of the men she dates. Little more than a glorified paralegal, she's been a lawyer at the firm going on five years. She's given most of the trivial cases, occasionally handles depositions, motions, or status conferences, but has not yet tried a case. The partners have dangled the promotion carrot only to yank it away in midnibble. She's been passed up six times by younger and less experienced lawyers who have worked at the firm for a shorter period than she has. She once admitted to me, over a glass of egg nog around the holidays, that the real reason she stays at the firm is because in her mind, this is the best it will ever get. Her career slump, in addition to her relationship downfalls, sends her seeking comfort and liberation at the bottom of a glass. As much as she works my last nerve I sometimes feel sorry for her. Altima can't stand her, but as callous as she can be to everyone in her office, I think she has always considered Altima and I as her girlfriends, seeing we're the only people in the office that would tolerate her longer than five minutes.

"What are you two in here gossiping about now?" she asked, one hand holding a chocolate-covered reduced-calorie bar and the other packing an arm full of files.

"Was there some kinda sign on the door that said, 'Bitter, do come in'?" Altima shot back. "None of your business," she said, returning the air of unpleasantries.

"Was I talking to you, Maxima? No, I wasn't, so mind your business," she shot back. The bell sounded. The bout had begun.

"My name is *Altima*. You know it."

"I was trying to give you an upgrade, but you're obviously comfortable in your current make and model."

"This bitch is wearing a wig shaped like a helmet and got the nerve to talk about an upgrade," Altima said looking at me, and then turned to Ophelia, daring her to speak.

"Anyway," Ophelia said, rolling her eyes and giving Altima the hand. "I'll ask again: What are you two in here talking about?"

"Nothing," I said, quickly clearing my throat as a giggle slipped out.

"Oh, really?" she said. "Oh, really? Well, I could hear that 'nothing' from the partners' offices all the way to the water cooler."

"Really, Ophelia, it was nothing, just girl talk." I said again.

"Okay, . . . so why doesn't anybody ever want to share with me?"

"Why?" Altima glared.

"Yeah, why?"

"'Cause your ass always got something negative to say, that's why. You're like the monsoon of misery. Always raining on somebody's parade."

"No, I don't."

"Yes, you do. I heard a bolt of lightning the minute you walked in the room."

"So that's what you think?"

"Uh . . . yeah."

"Morgan, is that what *you* think?" she asked, looking shockingly oblivious.

"Uh . . . yeah," I affirmed, as that one last jab was more than I could pass.

"Well," she said arrogantly outdone. "I can't help it. I'm a realist."

"Well, can you realize your knock-kneed self out of Mo's office so she can tell me more about her diamond tennis bracelet?"

"A-ha!" Ophelia said as her eyes lit up. "What diamond tennis bracelet?"

Once again, Altima had let the screeching cat out of the bag. And, as usual, Ophelia was standing, net in hand, ready to catch enough evidence to bag her verdict.

"Damn, girl, I'm sorry. I did it again, huh?" Altima said.

"It's no problem, Altima," I said, poising myself for interrogation. "Ophelia, it's a gift from a friend for my birthday. It's nothing special. It's just a bracelet."

"Just a bracelet? I'll be the judge of that," she said, eyebrows raised. "What cut and clarity are these alleged diamonds? Princess, oval, baguette, what? Where is it? I want to see it. Show it to me." She dumped the files on my desk and stood perched and eager to personally inspect the goods. Fidgeting, I slowly responded.

"I can't," I said, turning away to shuffle a stack of papers on my desk.

"You can't?" she asked, her tone rising. "Why not?" I could feel the heat from her breath on my neck.

"'Cause she can't. That's why," Altima shot back in an attempted stall tactic.

"And why can't she?" Ophelia asked again, the pitch of her voice rising.

"It's a birthday gift for later tonight! Damn, are you happy? Uh-oh!" she said catching her mouth with her hand, realizing she had again said too much.

"A birthday gift? For later tonight? Ahhh, now, the picture is getting a little clearer," Ophelia touted like a trial lawyer on her first big case. "A gift for later tonight?" Grabbing her chin with her hand, she turned and began pacing around the room. Like Columbo at a crime scene.

"So," she said, still pacing. "Since it's a gift and you already know what the gift is, then one can assume that you picked out the alleged diamond tennis bracelet prior to your birthday."

"Yeah. Sort of," I replied, shrugging my shoulder. "See, what happened was—"

"Or," Ophelia interrupted, "maybe you showed this alleged friend of yours a picture of the alleged tennis bracelet, thereby leaving him no room for error?"

"Yeah . . . it was something like that," I said, now squirming, hoping to end her cross-examination.

"The box fell from underneath one of his sweaters this morning and she opened it. Damn!"

"Obviously," Ophelia shot back in a tone as warm as a Russian winter. "Morgan, you do realize that what you did was breaking and entering. Without a search warrant, that's a felony."

"Is it a felony if I break my foot off in your ass?" Altima quickly rebutted.

"Come on now, Ophelia," I said, shrugging off the lunacy of her assertion. "Don't you think you're taking this a bit far? It's not breaking and entering. It's a *gift.*"

"Objection!" she shouted. "That's speculative at best. But for the sake of argument, let's say that it is a gift. How do you know it's a gift for you and not for someone else?"

"Someone else like who, Sherlock?" I asked, shooting spear-size daggers with my eyes.

"Like whoever," she said, backing up.

"Ophelia, must you always be a cloud? Couldn't you just for once be a rainbow?" Altima asked, now undone by her negativity.

"I'm neither. I'm a lawyer. My job is to look at the facts, weigh the evidence, listen to the testimonies, and argue the case. And, having done so, and having prior knowledge of the party's propensity for swan diving to romantic conclusions only for her parachute to stall and spiral splat to the ground, I'm left with no other alternative but to deem the evidence inadmissible." The verdict is in, the gavel has fallen. Love overruled. *Bam! Bam! Bam bam bam!*

"Ms. Clarke?" It was the voice of Tess, ringing through the intercom just seconds before we commenced to give Ophelia an old-fashioned ass whipping. "Ms. Clarke, a call on line two."

"Well, girls," she said, thankful for an out. "Duty calls. I'll leave you two inner-city Cinderellas alone to fantasize about yet another glass-slipper-carrying, Range Rover–driving project prince on his way to save yourselves from yourselves."

Grabbing her files, she sashayed her big self out of the door, leaving us alone and outdone.

"I can't stand that hateful heifer. I swear, I want to punch her dead in her fat gut," Altima spewed.

"Maybe she's right. Maybe I am jumping to conclusions."

"Or maybe she's just big, bald, and bitter. Forget her. She's just mad 'cause they don't make glass slippers in a size fourteen. I don't care what she says, that tennis bracelet is yours. It's from your man who's gonna put it on your wrist, for your birthday, okay?"

"You think so?"

"I *know* so. Marcus only has eyes for you," she said as her right eye suddenly began twitching.

"Altima."

"Yeah, girl, what is it?"

"Why is your eye twitching?"

"Is it?"

"Yes."

"Oh, girl, that's just dust. That's all, dust."

"Dust?"

"Dust," she said, waving her hand in the air.

Three

I MANAGED TO SLIP out early from work to get a manicure, a pedicure, and some much-needed predinner downtime to prepare for the evening ahead. I wanted to do more than just look good. I wanted to feel good all over. It was more than just my birthday, it was the day that would transform Marcus from an ideal potential life partner to a definite.

I live in Center City, not too far from my alma mater, Temple University, and within the cultural arts district. The neighborhood itself is aesthetically appealing due to beautiful streetlamps and walkways. My complex is on a quaint side street in a cosmopolitan community. Although newly renovated, the historic architecture reminds me of old Philadelphia.

Before I could pull my keys out of my purse, I heard something. It was my next-door neighbor Andre, spewing his most recent and unoriginal pickup line. "What's up, Sex in the City?" he said with a smirk, eyeing my slightly loosened blouse.

Andre, a serial dater who's seen more women through his revolving front door than a Macy's one-day sale, was a looker, all right. With no less than a six-pack popping from an airtight abdomen, Andre was street ball cut, with triceps as sharp as a samurai sword and bulging biceps as round and hard as the Liberty Bell. He spent more time in the gym than any place else, so he had no qualms about wearing the least amount of clothing possible. To him any season was the perfect reason to sport a pair of loose-fitting linen drawstring pants and no shirt, never mind if it was the dead of winter. When I first moved in, he was in hot and heavy pursuit for a good week and a half. But gaining absolutely no romantic return our relationship took its more natural course and we formed a sort of dysfunctional brother-sister relationship. But I wasn't fooled for a moment that given the slightest opportunity he would quickly revert.

"Yo, you know what today is, right?" he said, moving his head slowly, smiling, revealing a gift-wrapped Nordstrom box from behind his back.

"It's not much. Just a little something to make you feel like more of the special woman that you are," he said in a surprisingly sincere tone. Though a womanizer, he was still cute. And for the most part harmless. Moments like this made me realize why he had no problem attracting women.

"Now Andre, you know you really didn't have to do this," I said, well aware of the bright orange "pay or quit" notice that graced his door on a bimonthly basis.

"I know, but you know, you're worth it. Open it up," he said, as his grin grew wider.

"Now?" I asked, checking my watch.

"No, right now."

"Okay. But then I gotta go," I said, putting my purse down and quickly unwrapping his gift as he proudly watched on. "Oh wow!" I said, sifting through the tissue paper. It was the prettiest dark blue . . . it was the softest, most . . . it was a dark blue . . . something. I had no clue what it was.

"Andre, was is this?" I asked gently, hoping not to hurt his feelings.

"What is it? It's a scarf," he said, seeming shocked that I had asked.

"A scarf?" I asked, looking at him like he had been smoking.

"Yeah. A scarf. What's the problem?"

"The problem," I said, dangling it between my index finger and thumb, "is that it's only about ten inches long. You got this at Nordstrom's?"

"Nordstrom's? Hell no, girl," he said. "I got the *box* from Nordstrom. I got the scarf from this Ethiopian chick I've been hanging with for the past couple weeks. She's got her own shop down on South Street called Scarves and Things. She's really good. She's got her own line coming out next fall."

"Of what? Scarves or things?" I asked, chuckling.

"Oh, now you got jokes," he said defensively.

"No, you got jokes. Andre, what happened to the rest of the scarf?"

"Well, see . . . what happened was we sort of got into an argument right when she got started knitting the scarf and she started, you know, tripping, talking about she never wanted to see my face ever again and how I wasn't this and wasn't that. And, you know, she stopped knitting. Next thing I know, I see a plastic bag at my front apartment door with my name written on with a highlighter. Had my workout clothes, my toothbrush, a few condoms. And this was in it. So, I thought I'd give it to you anyway, just in case, you know, we got back together and she wanted to finish it. Anyway, it's the thought that counts, you know. And you were the thought 'cause I was thinking about you. It's gonna be worth a lot of money one day. I'd hold on to it if I were you."

"Thank you," I said, barely able to keep from exploding with laughter.

"You're welcome," he said.

"Now, I gotta go."

"Gotta go? What about the hug?"

"What hug?"

"You give a gift, you get a hug. That's the rule."

"What rule?"

"When a brotha, that's me, gives a sistah, that's you, a gift, albeit a somewhat unfinished gift, that's this," he says, snatching the scarf from my hand, "the sistah owes the brotha a show of affection, i.e., a hug, that's this." He outstretched his arms. There was nothing else I could do but laugh. He got me. I should have seen it coming, but I didn't. For his effort, I would oblige.

"Okay, Andre, but that's it. I'll give you a hug albeit a short and incomplete hug in appreciation of your short and incomplete gift. No pelvic thrusts, no grinding, groaning, or moaning or any of that. A hug. And its a five-second hug. Read my lips Andre, a five-second hug."

"Five seconds? That's like a tap on the back. I can't do less than twenty-five, I don't do less than twenty-five. At least twenty-five."

"Okay," I said, turning to enter my front door.

"All right, then, damn! Twenty."

"How about five?"

"You act like I asked for a lap dance or something. Which, you know, I would gladly exchange for a hug. All right, then, damn—five seconds. But don't try to give me them short shits, either." He slowly approached me.

"Could you at least unbutton your coat?"

"Do you want a hug or not," I snapped, having wasted too much time on a gift that was way too short.

"Damn. Okay, come here, girl."

For the next five seconds he hugged as I listened to him making weird animal kingdom sounds in my ear.

"Andre, I said no groaning."

"Who's groaning, I'm growling. Girl, that's the mating sounds of the Lion King. *Rarrrrrrrhhh.*"

"Okay, time's up," I said, counting down the seconds in my head.

"Oh, snap!" he exclaimed, looking down at his chest "Now look what you did. You done made my nipples hard."

"No," I said, laughing out loud. "You made your own nipples hard. Andre, seriously, I don't have time to play with you anymore, I've got a dinner date."

"So, I'm just supposed to do what? Stand here in this state of erotic overload with my nipples bursting from my chest?"

"I'm sure you'll figure something out. Good night, Andre," I said, closing the front door.

"If you change your mind, I'm right next door!" he shouted through the door.

"I won't be changing my mind!" I shouted back through the door.

"You gone need me and I'll be right next door marinating!"

If nothing else, he was comic relief. Hopefully one day some woman would be laughing long enough to actually take him seriously.

Four

NOW, IT WAS ON to preparing for my night with Marcus. I've rarely inhabited the apartment since he and I've been seeing each other. Tastefully decorated with contemporary furniture and art by William Tolliver, my style was sophisticated but relaxed, with a mixture of things purchased in and out of my budget.

Wanting to feel sexy, I started the bath water, pouring my favorite jasmine-scented bath crystals into the rippling water. I struck a match and lit my favorite Victoria's Secret scented candle and put on some Marvin Gaye. Then it was off to my closet, where I tore through my wardrobe for just the right outfit. A pantsuit? Too businesslike. A gown? No, that's too much. A dress? An easy-access short dress. Oh, no . . . I got it. A black chiffon halter dress with a short black cashmere coat. The perfect outfit for accentuating my positives.

Easing into the white porcelain tub, I melted into the piping hot water, and for a half hour I soaked as Marvin serenaded, my thoughts vibrating through all of my being. I washed, rinsed, dried, lotioned, perfumed, painted my face, and, right on time, the intercom buzzed. He was here. It was Marcus.

"Mona Lisa, it's me. You coming down or am I coming up?" he asked through the intercom.

"I'm coming down," I said, quickly gathering my coat, squirting my favorite fragrance, Michael Kors, into the air. Walking into it, I was ready to go. Other than my watch and a very thin necklace, I was wearing as little jewelry as possible. I wanted Marcus to know that diamonds dangling from the wrist of his destined-to-be was the only accessory that mattered. Then it was downstairs and off we went.

Our favorite restaurant was Lacroix, an upscale French restaurant with a classic grand dome and a beautiful treetop view of Rittenhouse Square. As we entered the restaurant, I took a deep breath. It was as if the nine months we had been dating was the calm before the pending storm and, in just minutes, it would be raining diamonds. Be still, my beating heart, be still.

"Mr. Alexander, it's so good to see you again," greeted the maître d'. "For you and the lady, we have a very special table. Just this way, please."

Our waiter quickly arrived. "Good evening and welcome. Would the couple enjoy the usual selection of wine?" he asked politely.

Marcus was somewhat of a creature of habit. Once he found something he liked, you could pretty much bet on him ordering it again and again. His usual was a bottle of Ptolemy Monroche. A red wine that went well with his favorite cuts of red meat.

But tonight Marcus was full of surprises.

"No, tonight I want to try something different. Tonight we'll have a special wine for a special lady who, like the wine, seems to only get better with time."

Marcus was known to occasionally shoot a line that appeared to leap right out of a Colt 45 commercial. But his sentiments were sweet, and settled into a warm spot in my heart. "May I recommend a chardonnay?" suggested the waiter.

"Fine," said Marcus as the waiter walked swiftly away. "So," he said, reaching for my right arm, then working his way down to my right hand to hold it ever so gently. He zeroed in on my eyes. Uh-oh . . . here they come. Here come the diamonds. Trying to keep my heart from exploding, I sat still. Silent. Nearly frozen in the moment. Softly, he continued.

"Morgan, I don't know if it's the glow of the moonlight bouncing off your face or what, but you seem to have a special sparkle in your eyes tonight," he said as he slowly began caressing my hand. All the while I was thinking to myself, It ain't nothing like the sparkle you're going to see when you wrap those rocks around my wrist.

"I don't know . . ." he continued. "Maybe it's just a little birthday pixie dust. Who knows," he said as he uncharacteristically rambled on. I wasn't about to stop him. He could talk from now till Jesus comes as long as eventually we arrived at the diamonds. I sat content, gazing into his eyes, trying to appear unaware of the glitter that loomed.

"I feel like something really special is gonna happen this year. Neither of us is getting any younger. I'm no spring chicken, you know. I've been around long enough to know what's out there. But more importantly," he said, pointing to his left pec, "I've been around long enough to know what's in here." I started to feel badly about criticizing his Colt 45 commercial tendencies. That was the sweetest, most sincere thing he had ever said to me. It was bordering on the kind of conversation that started me thinking that I might be in for more than just some diamonds. I might get diamonds and the duplicate key. Either way, it was win-win and I was no doubt in-in.

"I've had a lot of relationships, you know. Some good ones, some bad ones. But Morgan, this one . . . this one feels like—"

"Mr. Alexander." Damn, it was the waiter. And he was just about to give me the bracelet.

"I didn't mean to interrupt," the waiter continued, "but I have the bottle of wine you ordered." Slowly Marcus did the usual pour a drip, spin the glass, sip a bit, then nod. Only this time it seemed to happen in slow motion as the anticipation of the bracelet grew stronger.

"Would you like to order?" the waiter asked.

"In a minute," Marcus said, relocking his eyes on mine.

Finally, the waiter left. Momentarily distracted, again Marcus reached for my hand and paused. He paused some more. Then even some more. It was like listening to a scratched album. I was duty bound to bump the needle.

"Marcus . . ."

"Yes, sweetheart."

"You were saying?" I said, raising my eyebrows for him to continue.

"Oh yeah, I was saying. I was saying . . . I seem to have lost my place. Where was I?"

"'I'm no stranger to relationships, but this one feels . . . this one feels . . .' That's where you stopped."

"Oh yeah. Thank you. This one feels like it's the place where I belong. More importantly, Morgan, this feels like it's where *we* belong. It's working for me. For real. It's like I've found the missing piece to a puzzle. I feel like . . . I feel like . . ."

Rrrriiiiiing.

It was his cell phone. Please don't answer it. Please, please, please don't answer it, I kept repeating to myself.

"I feel like . . ."

Rrrriiiiiiing.

"I'm sorry, Morgan. It may be an important business call. Do you mind?"

Do I mind? Do I *mind?* Are you out of your damn mind, I thought to myself, of course I mind! That phone couldn't have rung at a worse time.

"Of course I don't mind," I said. "It's fine." Somebody's playing an awfully cruel trick on me, I thought, as I sat in my seat with a plastered-on look somewhere between adulation and constipation. The phone call seemed to last for hours. His lips began moving in slow motion; his words began taking on the muted sounds of bad cell phone dropout. Still, I kept that half-smile/half-bewildered/half-aloof look waiting for a final farewell, good-bye, peace out, or anything remotely leading to the end of the call.

"So, I'm being rude. I'm at dinner with a very special lady. We can finish tomorrow."

Finally, the call had ended. Reaching for my hand, he continued.

"So, are you ready to order?"

"Huh?" I said, not realizing I'd blurted it out.

"Food. Are you ready to order? I'm starving."

"Sure," I said. "I'm ready to order, but you were in the middle of saying something." I said it gently, hoping not to appear too eager. "Don't you want to finish saying what you were saying before you were interrupted from saying whatever it was you were saying?"

Staring at me puzzled for a moment, he paused, then started laughing.

"Morgan, you are so cute. I like that."

Oh, swell. He likes that.

The waiter returned and we ordered the best cut of steak, had more wine, and more conversation that detoured further away from the road that led to diamonds. Glancing at my watch, I realized we'd been at dinner for an hour and a half and still nothing. My wrist was still naked, bare, unaccessorized. My hopes began to fade. I had only one choice and that was to prolong the evening. The longer we stayed, the more likely he would somehow return to his earlier moment of inspiration.

Motioning the waiter once, I ordered a second course of roasted black cod on a bed of mirepoix, ravioli of escargot, parsley ventreche, and ate almost a dozen of their gourmet chocolate desserts.

"I've never seen you eat so much," he said, noticing the inordinate amount of food I had begun to consume.

"If there's one time to let yourself go, it's your birthday," I said, stuffing my face with fork full, spoon full, and any other utensil that could fit in my mouth.

He shot a half smile and watched the never-ending cycle of fork plate mouth. Spoon plate mouth. Knife plate mouth. By now I was as fat as a tick. If I moved one inch from my seat my stomach was sure to explode. Still, I stalled for more time, consumed more food, guzzled more wine and—still no gift.

By now, the more than occasional glances at his watch was a sign that he had long since been ready to leave. Thank God, a burp. I could continue. One dessert tray after another rested on the table. There were apple tarts, crème brûlée, carrot cake, and three flavors of sorbet.

"Morgan, are you sure you're all right?" he asked again. "I don't think I've ever in my life seen one human being, man, woman, or animal consume that much food at one time."

I could only shrug my shoulders for fear that the strain of anything audible would cause my already bubbling stomach to erupt. Another half hour went by and I felt nauseated. Still no diamonds. Something had gone god-awful wrong. But what? What was he waiting for? Had he hidden the diamonds in the dessert and I had mistakenly eaten them? I had given up and given in. Obviously, he was planning the gift for some other time.

Slowly, I pushed away the last tart from my edge of the table.

"Check, please," he said, raising his finger quickly for fear I would order again.

The waiter rushed to the table, obviously eager to reap the rewards from his several dozen trips from the kitchen to our table.

While we stood awaiting our coats, a woman draped in a full-length mink walked in.

Marcus immediately turned away.

"Marcus?" she said, lifting her right penciled-on brow.

Slowly turning, he manufactured surprise.

"Cynthia?"

"Marcus," she said again, this time with a tone too familiar.

"Cynthia, what are you doing here?" he asked, seeming slightly unnerved.

"I was hungry. A better question is, what are you doing here?" She shot me a look that let me know she had either *had* my man, *wanted* to have my man, or was currently *having* my man.

"I'm having dinner with Morgan. It's her birthday. Cynthia, this is Morgan. Morgan, this is Cynthia."

I could sense the claws slowly emerging from her palms. Oh, yeah, she had definitely *had* my man and from the look in her eyes, she had every intention of being back by popular demand. Thinking myself to be the bigger person, especially since I was going home with Marcus and she wasn't, I extended my freshly polished French manicured hand to hers. She glanced at Marcus and slowly extended hers. Our eyes locked, but I wasn't going to be the first one to blink. Marcus stood by silently, letting the moment play itself out with absolutely no intervention.

We were still gripping our hands when out of the corner of my eye I caught the glare of a sparkling something, which slid farther and farther down her wrist, the glare looming brighter and brighter in the midst. A prisoner of my own curiosity, my eyes slowly shifted lower and lower, nearer and nearer and . . . please tell me it wasn't. It couldn't be. It was. She was wearing my bracelet. Slowly, I turned to Marcus, who by now sensed that something other than a simple cat-fight was brewing. Slowly I released her hand as she stood there with every intention to make her position even more clearly known.

The maître d' returned with our coats.

Again, the silence screamed.

"Well, I guess we should be going," he said. "Cynthia."

"Marcus," she said softly as she stood flinging her hair, gloating on the obvious. Marcus's awkward silence screamed with guilt. As she shot me a look and I shot her one back, Marcus and I walked from the restaurant and out to the valet, never uttering a word or even stealing a glance. Out of the lot and onto the streets and still there were no words. Passing the exit leading to his house, still no words, no radio, no nothing. Finally, reaching my apartment, he pulled to the curb and turned off the car.

"Well," he said, "I don't know about you, but I had a very nice evening spending time with you on your—"

"So, who is she?" I asked, not wanting to hear the shit he was saying.

"She who?" he said, feigning a look of confusion.

I quickly shot him a look that would no doubt jolt his memory. He inhaled, exhaled, and then spoke.

"She's . . . a friend."

"A friend?"

"A friend."

"That's it?"

"That's it," he said, matter-of-factly. He'd obviously already convinced himself of the legitimacy of a man's all-encompassing interpretation of the word "friend."

"Marcus, I saw the bracelet," I said. I was beyond ready to cut the crap and get to the truth.

"What bracelet?" he asked, losing at least three levels of bass from his voice.

"The bracelet that bitch was wearing on her wrist."

He was speechless, so I continued. "It fell from behind your sweaters this morning while you were in the shower. And stupid me, I thought it was for me. Why would I think it was for me? Oh, I don't know, maybe because it was my birthday and I was practically living with you. I don't know, maybe you can tell me why I thought it was for me. Tell me, Marcus—why did I think it was for me? More importantly, tell me why it's for her."

"I don't know what to say. I'm sorry."

"You're sorry? About what?"

"About what happened?"

"What did happen, Marcus?"

"What happened was . . . look, Morgan, I never said you were the only woman I was seeing. Did I ever say that? I didn't, did I?"

"No, you didn't," I said, frozen by his smugness. "But fucking me every night for almost a year said it for you."

Again he paused, searching for the words. "So . . . maybe I should have said something sooner, but with your birthday coming up and all, I just didn't want to rock the boat, you know. Cause a whole bunch of drama. Like this."

"You didn't want to rock the boat?" I was baffled by the insanity of his words. "Marcus, I'm damn near living with you. We were in a committed relationship. At least I thought we were."

"We were in a committed relationship. When I was with you, I was committed to you. When I was with you, I never made you feel like there was anybody but you, did I? No, I didn't. If you hadn't been snooping in my closet you would have never known the difference. Ain't no reason why anything needs to be any different than it was. You want a bracelet? I'll go to the store and get you a bracelet. Will that make you happy, Mona?"

"Don't Mona me, and this has nothing to do with the bracelet."

"Shit, then what does it have to do with? So, I'm seeing another woman. So what?"

"So what," I replied, barely believing my ears.

"Yeah. So what?"

"Fuck you, Marcus, that's so what!" I said as I pulled on the door handle and started rising from my seat.

"Mon . . . Morgan, I'm sorry, okay? I never intended for you to find out like this."

"What you really mean is that you never intended on me finding out at all!" I slammed the door, almost yanking it from its hinges as I raced in the door of my apartment building and up the elevator, thinking.

Five

THE NEXT MORNING, I stood outside the door to my office building, taking a moment to collect my thoughts and compartmentalize my emotions. I had piles of contracts to review and even more to create. The perfect substitution for recent romantic meltdown. The doors swung open and I made it past the receptionist, holding it together, not once giving any indication that today was different from any other day.

"Good morning, Morgan," Tess said with her usual bright smile, oblivious to my grief.

"Good morning, Tess," I responded, bright-eyed and full of life and vigor. I continued past the water cooler.

"Hey, Morgan, good morning."

"Good morning," I shouted, waving, jovial, enthusiastic.

And then past several open office doors.

"Happy belated. Looking good, Morgan."

I was my usual cheerful self. My day was full of back-to-back meetings, which for me was just what the doctor ordered. One, it allowed me to shift focus and two, it allowed me to avoid contact with Altima and Ophelia. By now it was a little after 5:00 and I had just about made it through the day without having to face the music of last night's madness when just as I was returning from the conference room, rounding the corner, was the one person I feared running into the most . . . Altima. I stopped. She stopped. My half smile slid off my face and turned right side up into a momentary full pout. Quickly, I retrieved it. It was too late. She returned a full pout of her own and that was all I needed to send me rushing to my office, closing the door behind me, hoping that she would just pass on by. Barely seconds later, she burst in. With my back to her, I attempted to fix my face as I rummaged through the mounds of paperwork piled high.

"Hey, Mo. I left a message last night to see how your dinner went, but when I didn't hear from you I just figured you were with Marcus. And then when I didn't see you all day . . ." She continued rambling as her eyes wandered to both my wrists, hoping to catch a glimpse of glitter. "So, how was your dinner last night?" she asked tentatively.

"Dinner?" I said, feigning puzzlement.

"Yeah, dinner. The dinner you had last night with Marcus. Remember?"

"Oh, dinner. Dinner. Dinner. Yeah. Dinner was . . ." I paused, scrambling for the words, and then finally finding some that fit: "Dinner was enlightening. It was a feast fit for a queen. For dessert, I must've sampled almost every tart, pie, and cake they had. We had a two-hundred-dollar bottle of white wine that melted in your mouth. He usually orders red, but last night we had white. He said he wanted to make the evening special. And that it was," I said, amazed at myself for holding it together.

"That sounds great!"

"Yeah. It was," I said, hoping that she would abandon the subject. But I could tell by her silence that the question I feared the most was on its way.

"So . . ." she said, inhaling, "what about the bracelet?"

"The bracelet?" I responded, not having taken time to prepare a public response. The bracelet. What about the bracelet? "Well, I was right. It was a gift." I could hear her exhale.

"It just wasn't a gift for me." Taking pause, I manufactured a giggle as I continued. "Could you believe it was for another woman? Yeah. I know, I couldn't believe it myself. Turns out that he's been dating another woman at the same time we were dating. And last night, right after dinner, she just happened to show up at the very same restaurant with the bracelet dangling from her mink coat-covered arm. Now, who wears a long mink coat when they've just been given a diamond tennis bracelet? I don't even have a mink coat, but even I know that. Anyway," I said, finally raising my head to connect with her now watery eyes, "I've got a lot of work to do, so I guess I'd better get started."

"You need a hug?" she asked softly, motherly, lovingly. Almost frozen in the same spot where she hadn't moved the entire time.

"No, I'm a big girl. Thanks, but I'm okay."

"You sure you don't need a hug?" she asked again, moving a half step closer.

"Girl, I'm fine. It's all right, really. Thanks, though. I just have a lot of work to do."

"Well, can I have a hug?" she asked. She pulled me into her arms and hugged me close.

"Thanks, girl, but really, I'm all right." I wanted no part of a public meltdown.

"I know you are, girl. It's okay, you can let it out."

"There's nothing to let out, really. I'm fine." But I wasn't fooling anyone—not even myself.

"I know, girl. It's all right."

"No, really, I'm all right. I'm . . . ahhhhhhhhhh!!!" I said, bursting into a loud moan as I stood weeping and wailing in her arms. Each time I moaned louder she squeezed tighter, stroking my back and rubbing my arms. "Just let it out, girl."

"I . . . I . . . I . . ." I was babbling like I'd just gotten one of Grandma's good extension cord whippings. "I didn't even see it coming."

"We never do."

"But . . . but . . . but I should have seen it coming. I'm a lawyer."

"But you're a woman first. That cancels out everything."

"No, see, me being a woman is exactly why I should have been able to recognize his bull . . ."

"Girl, love makes you blind. You remember Rodney? The love of my life? With three kids and wife. You see? Love. Blind. He had a stroller in the trunk, a child safety seat in the back, and could only talk past midnight. And I still I didn't see it. Why? 'Cause I was in love."

Just as the therapy was getting good, my office door cracked slowly and then opened and closed. It was Ophelia. Altima and I released each other quickly and I turned to wipe my face so I could remove all trace of what was happening.

"I could have sworn the door was closed," Altima said, annoyed.

"Well, now you can swear that it's open," Ophelia retorted, cocking her head and raising her brow. "Good afternoon, Morgan," she said with her usual look of unspoken inquisition. How could I forget? Braceletgate.

"Good afternoon, Ophelia," I said with my head now buried into the stacks of paper on my desk.

"Okay, so let's get it over with. Let me see it."

"Let you see what?" Altima responded, knowing full well that the cover-up was on.

Ophelia was like a foxhound. It would take more than a simple misdirection to throw her off the scent.

"The bracelet that you spent the entire morning yesterday cackling about. Show it to me and prove that there is still hope for the single among us to find a man of our own willing to douse us with diamonds. Now, stop playing around and give up the goods—I've got work to do."

"Well, get to it then. Nobody asked you to bust into the office anyway."

"I can't get any work done. I could barely sleep last night in anticipation of seeing thealleged gift. Now, quit stalling. Where is it?"

"She ain't wearing it, that's where it is. Is that all right with you?" Altima shot in my defense.

"Now, that just doesn't make sense. What woman wouldn't be wearing a diamond tennis bracelet the day after she received it? Maxima, move out of the way, please."

"It's Altima!"

"And you say that with such pride. Morgan, may I see it?"

With my head buried in my desk, I could still feel the piercing look of Ophelia nearly singeing the hair on my neck.

"Unless, of course," Ophelia said, pausing for dramatic effect, "there is no bracelet. Which would probably explain why she isn't wearing one."

We were busted. After a moment, Altima could take it no more.

"Ophelia, why don't you just mind your damn business, okay? Could you do that for once? Damn. You always got to be starting something."

"So, I am right! There is no bracelet. I knew it! I knew it!" she said gloating, sparkling, her eyes twinkling.

"No, heifer, you were wrong, okay? There was a bracelet; it just wasn't her bracelet, all right," Altima blurted out. "I mean . . . that's not what I mean. What I mean was . . ." she said, hoping to retract it.

"And the plot thickens," Ophelia said. "So, if the bracelet didn't belong to Morgan, then who did the bracelet belong to?" she continued while pacing the room.

"Ophelia, isn't it preseason? Don't you got a tryout for the Cowboys or something?" Altima asked, hoping to distract her from her incessant line of questioning.

"Oh, sure . . . talk about my weight if you want. I'm big. But I know I'm big. See, I'm not in denial professing to *be*, or more specifically, to *have* something that I don't."

"Ophelia," I said, just wanting this to end, "I don't have the bracelet because it was a gift for another woman." Immediately Altima rushed to give me another hug.

"Another woman, huh. Well . . . looks like the monsoon of misery was raining the truth. Marcus ended up being like the glove in the O. J. Simpson case. All hype, no payoff. Well, the gavel has fallen. *Bam!* Love has once again been thrown out of court. *Bam!* Affection overruled. *Bam, bam!* Emotions dismissed! *Bam, bam, bam!*"

"You know what, Mo . . ." Altima said in half stride, pulling the Vaseline jar from her purse. "I'm 'bout to *bam* this bitter bitch upside her head."

"Altima, it's okay."

"It's gonna be okay after I beat this bitch down."

"Altima, it's all right," I said, grabbing her arm, almost yanking it from its socket. "It's all right. And she's right."

"Naw, but she gonna be right when I get finished with her."

"Altima, would you grow up," Ophelia said pointedly. "I'm not the one you should be fighting. I'm not the enemy. And if the truth be told, neither is Marcus."

"What the hell are you talking about?" Altima blurted.

"Yeah, what are you talking about," I said, just seconds from delivering my own verbal assault.

"What I'm talking about is that it's time women embrace the reality of what *is* and stop living in the fantasy of the is that ain't. Your man was no different from my man when I had one, or any other man, for that matter. We're always so quick to want to call them dogs when they do something we don't like."

"What are you talking about, Ophelia?" I asked. "He was dating at least two women at the same time. He *is* a dog." I continued feeling the fresh sting of a still-open wound.

"And maybe he was, but whether he was or not really isn't the issue."

"Then what is the real issue, Dr. O-Phil-ia?"

"The real issue," she said, rolling her eyes at Altima, "is clarity and communication. The problem is how we interpret the things that a man actually says versus what we want to believe that he said."

I paused, allowing her room to expand.

"For example, when a man says, 'I want you to spend the night,' we hear him saying that he wants us to move in. Why? Because we're looking for security. But he simply wants sex. When a man says he loves spending time with us, we think he's saying that he'd love to spend more time with us. But that's not what he said. He said he enjoyed the time he spent—regardless of how much or how little."

By now even Altima seemed intrigued, willing to add her two cents to the theory.

"That's just like when I used to visit Dewayshawn at the correctional facility and the guard said our time was up, he asked if he could have a hug. But what he was really saying," she said, as she began getting emotional, "was 'I wish I wasn't locked up in here so I could be with you and love you like you're supposed to be loved.'" She took the tissue I had extended to her.

"Thank you."

"You're welcome."

"Are we done taking a stroll back down penitentiary lane?" Ophelia asked.

"Be nice, Ophelia," I said, holding Altima close. "Go on."

"Say we catch our man red-handed, cheating on us with another woman. We go all crazy, yelling, cussing, and screaming. Finally, after all that, he passionately and sincerely pledges that he's sorry and that it will never, ever happen again. We hear him say that he won't do it again. But what he actually meant was not that he won't do it again, but that he'll never, ever get caught when he does do it again.

"Then, if and when we catch him again doing what he never once stopped doing in the first place, we reward and condone the behavior by romanticizing ourselves into thinking that the indiscretion is an isolated incident never to rear its ugly face again. And then when he does it again and again and again, still we do nothing because by then we've got too much invested in the relationship. We've told too many of our friends and relatives. Got too many pictures in our wallets, on our nightstands, our living rooms, as screen savers on our computers. We've marked up and resold his original package to the entire free world. To anybody who'll listen, we've given our man added value, made him appear bigger, faster, and stronger than he ever was. And now it's too late. We have no choice but to deal with it. We find a way to cover it up and sweep it under the rug. Why? 'Cause we never read the fine print. We're so ready to believe what we wanted to believe, we overlooked the clues. Which brings me back to my original point—lack of clarity and communication."

"So, what you're saying is that it's our fault?" I asked.

"Really, it's nobody's fault. He was only selling what we were buying. Men just play the game better than we do. 'Cause they make most of the rules. The way I see it, it's time we stopped hating the players and began learning how to play the game better."

"But what if you know what you're buying but it still don't work. You still need some kinda insurance," Altima said.

"Like a warranty," I said.

"A get-out-of-the-relationship-free card. A coochie-back guarantee. Something," Altima added. "Then what do you do?"

Looking at the stack of papers piled on my desk, I suddenly knew exactly what to do.

"We do this," I said, grabbing a stack of papers in my hand and holding it in the air.

"We hold our hand in the air?" Altima asked.

"No," I said, moving from behind my desk. "We create a contract. Then all of a sudden there's no room for miscommunication or lack of clarity. Why? 'Cause it's written in black and in white."

"A contract?"

"A contract?"

"Yes, my sistahs . . . a contract. I figure that the only way you'll guarantee that a man acts right after you've given him some is if you make him sign something forcing him to act right before you've given him some."

"I don't know about that, Mo. You can barely get a man to open your car door before giving him some, let alone expect him to sign a contract," bemoaned Altima.

"Right, but if you have him sign the contract before you gave him some and you made that one of the conditions, then you wouldn't have to worry about whether or not he would open up the door for you, would you?"

"I guess not. But then it's not love."

"Sure it is," I said. "It's love on the dotted line."

"But the contract only works if it benefits both parties," Ophelia added. "A man needs some incentive."

"Ophelia, what's between our legs is all the incentive he needs. We get what we want—security. And we give him what he wants—sex."

"Shit, I want sex, too," Altima blurted.

"Me, too," Ophelia added.

"Then put it in the contract. Now we have the two basic components that make up a contract—conditions and considerations."

"Yeah, but what if he signs it just to get some and then changes his mind the morning after?" asked Altima, still unconvinced.

"That's why there's the third and probably the most important component of a contract," I proudly added, "consequences."

"A penalty," Ophelia offered. "Something that would make him think twice about his offense."

"Just like over in the Middle East," Altima chimed in, "when somebody stole something, they chop off his hand. Now, he may steal again, but not with that hand, he won't."

"Right," I said. "But, Altima, we can't cut a man's wrist off in this country."

"Yeah, but we can tax that wallet!" Ophelia proclaimed.

"Attack his account!" I added.

"Cha-*ching!* Cha-*ching!*" Altima shouted.

"A contract!" Ophelia roared.

"A contract!" Altima exclaimed, with a soul fist held high in the air.

"Yes, my sistahs, a contract. A legal and binding document enforceable in a court of law, full of conditions, consideration, and more importantly, consequences! The way I see it, the only way a woman can guarantee that she wins is by giving a man something to lose."

"Sounds good to me," Altima said.

"Me, too," Ophelia agreed.

Altima and I looked at each other in shock of her compliance.

"Well, okay. Me three. A contract."

"Excuse me." Again, it was the receptionist chiming in the room. "Ms. Clarke, you have a call on line three."

Now there's no doubt Altima just wanted to cheer me up by taking my mind off my lingering pain. And I guess for Ophelia, deep down, she was using my misfortune to compensate for her own hurt.

A contract? A contract? I thought. Yes, my sistahs . . . a contract. As the words still rested on the tip of my tongue, Ophelia stormed out of the office, huffing and puffing about yet another under-whelming bit of legal busywork. Altima followed behind her and alone in my office for the next half an hour I finished my work for the day. It was now almost six o'clock and the day had just about winded down. As I was finishing up in my office, Altima stuck her head in the door.

"Mo, what you doing tonight?"

"Going home."

"Going home?"

"Yeah, going home."

"Let's hang out, have a drink, and empower ourselves."

"I don't know if I feel like it," I said, my mind still frozen on Marcus.

"Girl, come on. It'll do you some good. And besides, I'm buying," she said. "Well, I'm buying the first round at least. Since you're paid and I'm not, all the other rounds are on you."

The look on my face must have been pretty pitiful, because Altima went on to say, "Come on, girl, what you got to lose? You'll feel a lot better, trust me. And even if you don't, you'll be drunk as hell so it really won't matter."

"All right," I said. "Cool. It'll be just like old times, just you and me."

"And me," Ophelia said, barging into the room.

"And me, hell! You ain't going with us," Altima huffed.

"Why not?"

"'Cause you weren't invited, that's why?"

"Well, I just invited myself, how 'bout that?"

"How 'bout not," Altima said.

"It's a free country. I can go anywhere I want to."

"You could if you knew where we're going, but you don't."

"Oh, please. You're going where you always go. The Copa."

"See, that's where you're wrong, okay? We're going to Palmers. Ha!"

"Ha, yourself," Ophelia said. "I'll meet you there. See ya."

Immediately she left for her office as Altima stood deflated, having once again been bested by Ophelia.

"Why does she always do that to me," she said.

"It's okay. Ophelia isn't that bad, Altima."

"No, it's not okay. This was going to be me and you time. And besides, you know she can't handle her liquor. After one drink she'll be telling us all her business."

"You think?"

"I know."

Six

"THAT WAS SOME of the best loving I ever had in my whole entire life," Ophelia shouted, taking the last gulp of her fourth drink. "Marvin was his name. Starvin' Marvin is what I used to call him. He went down like he had just ended a hunger strike. He used to wear my thighs like they were earmuffs. And I used to grab his ears like they were little steering wheels. *Varroom! Scrreeeeetch. Varroooom!*"

Altima and I both stared at each other with our mouths to the floor.

"Now, that was some good loving," she continued. "Waiter! I'll have another, please. And this time, no ice!"

"She's not driving, is she?" I whispered to Altima.

"Yes, why?" Altima asked.

"Because one more drink and she won't make it alive."

"In that case," Altima said, signaling the waiter, "make it a double! And I'm paying."

"It's okay," I said, cutting my eyes at Altima. "I'll drive her home."

"Thank you," Ophelia said, now beginning to slur her words. "That's kind of you. Especially since I don't really like you that much." She grabbed the mixed nuts tray and dug into it, putting almost the entire handful in her mouth, save a few nuts that fell from her mouth to the floor.

"Mo, you haven't said a thing all night. We're supposed to be here for you. You gotta let your hair down. Relax. Exhale."

"I think Ophelia's doing enough exhaling for us all."

"No, I'm not," she shouted, her words slurred. "Everyone has to exhale for herself."

"At least have one drink," Altima urged, as the waiter returned to the table with a cocktail glass filled with green liquid for Ophelia.

"She's drinking enough for us, too," I said as I watched Ophelia down it in a single gulp.

"Wrong again," Ophelia said. "Every woman has to get drunk for herself, too."

She turned to the waiter, "Bring her one, too."

He returned quickly with the drink. "One Incredible Hulk for the lady."

"What's in it?" I asked.

"Hennessy and Hpnotiq. You'll love it. Whatever's hurting you, after you drink that, I guarantee you, it will not hurt anymore. That's a promise," she said.

"I usually only do the light stuff," I said.

"It's a special occasion," she said. "It's not every day someone gets dumped on their birthday. Cheers!" she said, lifting her empty glass in the air.

Figuring I had nothing to lose, I lifted my very unusual-looking drink in the air, clinked with Altima's Heineken, and began drinking. Soon after, I had another one. Then another and another. Ophelia was right. Whatever was hurting was no longer hurting. And even if it was, I was now too drunk to notice. For hours we all rambled, sharing stories of relationships past. Altima shared her struggle being in love with an inmate. Ophelia shared her wild sexual escapades. And me, how happiness had most recently eluded me by way of Marcus, the dream slayer.

"Girl, do you realize what time it is? It's almost eleven!" Altima said.

"I gotta get home," Ophelia said.

"You cannot drive home, Ophelia. You'd kill yourself."

"Oh, please. It's not like anyone cares," she said, pulling out her money from her purse.

"Don't be silly. Of course, somebody cares," I replied.

"Who?" she asked. "The senior partners who drive me like I'm a

Ford truck? The men who run in and out of my life like they're on an Olympic relay team? My family who hasn't one time given me credit for being the first one in the entire family who used her brains instead of her brawns to earn a living? So, come on—if you know so much, name me one person who cares whether I live or die?"

We both paused for a second. We had never heard Ophelia be so down on herself. Actually, we had probably never had a real conversation with her outside work. Altima and I both paused at a loss for words.

"You've had a little too much to drink, Ophelia," Altima said, breaking the silence. "Mo, I'll take you home first, then I'll drop Ophelia off."

"I'm fine. Just drop me back off by the office and you can drop her off. I'll hang out there till my buzz has buzzed itself out."

"Are you sure?" Altima asked.

"Yes, I'm sure. Let's go."

"Yeah, let's go," Ophelia said. "Let's go before I say something that would incriminate myself."

"Girl, it's too late for that," Altima said, holding both our hands as we all three barely made it to the car.

Altima dropped me off at the front door of our building, and somehow I stumbled into the elevator, into my empty office, and finally into my chair. A stream of light from a streetlamp outside shot through the window and bounced off the one picture of Marcus that sat on my bookshelf. Damn, he was fine. We were so perfect together. We should've had a contract, I thought. If we'd had a contract, maybe things wouldn't have ended up the way they did.

My mind was spinning. My emotions raging. And thanks to the number of Incredible Hulks I'd just thrown down my system, I was all of a sudden dead set on constructing the first one ever.

Seven

POWERING UP my computer, I opened a new Word document and began pecking away. Filling the blank canvas, creating the backdrop for a picture-perfect relationship. I was drunk and heartbroken. Not a good combination for a lawyer trying to create a contract. Especially if you're the man having to sign it. Unaware of the constant tapping on the door, in midpeck, I saw it slowly open.

"Anybody home?" It was Michael Sampson, the most recently elected and only black partner at the firm. He was a closet revolutionary who never allowed the color of his skin to affect his ability to navigate his way through the color-blind big-city boardroom where the only cooler that mattered was green. Never once losing his blackness to blend, never once shucking, jiving, cooning, or buffooning to fit in.

"Can I come in?"

"Sure," I said, feeling the buzz from the bottles of Hpnotiq slowly starting to fade. Being alone in a room with Michael was enough to jolt any artificial stimulant and replace it with a more natural one. If he did have a woman, she would be at best his mistress, because law was clearly his lady.

"I hear they're thinking about converting the conference room into a two-bedroom condominium. Should I put your name on the list?" he said with a smile. "Just think of all the gas money you'd save."

"Very funny," I said. "I guess I have been burning the midnight oil lately."

"You're past burning oil," he said, looking at his watch. "You've moved on to wood and twigs. What are you working on anyway? The Johnston case?"

"Yeah, uh, I'm just cleaning up a contract I was working on for them," I said, hoping he'd leave it alone and prevent me from drowning deeper.

"I'm impressed. I'm senior partner and I don't want to be here this late. I had an appointment, but if you need some help, I guess I could stay a little while and help you finish up."

"Actually I'll be done soon. I wouldn't want to hold you up. But since you're here . . . maybe you could help me with something."

I couldn't believe I was about to talk to him about this. But if it was to bite me in the butt later, I could always blame it on the alcohol.

"I have this friend who asked me about working on a 'certain' type of contract for them."

"What kind of contract?"

"You know," I said trying to generate an artificial giggle, "if I told you, you'd probably laugh."

"Try me."

"It's a dating contract," I said proudly.

"Oh, a prenuptial?"

"More like a pre-prenuptial."

"A pre-prenuptial," he said as a chuckle raced from his lips.

"Really, and you're considering helping your friend do this?"

"Actually, yes," I said, now myself convinced of its importance. "I think it would be good to create a contract to guarantee that a woman would never be sidelined by love, lust, or any other word masquerading itself as commitment."

"And you're serious about this?" he asked with both eyebrows raised and face twisted.

"I am. A contract decreases drastically any misunderstanding when it comes to what men and women want and what they're willing to give in order to have it. I'm doing myself . . . I mean, my friend, and the entire dating world a service. When I'm finished everyone will know exactly what they're getting themselves into and, if for some reason they change their minds, how to get themselves out."

"Not that I'm an expert or anything, but I always looked at two people dating as each being a starter house set on an oversize lot. Over time as you grew together you could then build, expand, and add on. This seems to have more of the track house feel to it."

"You ask any woman if she'd prefer to walk into a home already decorated to her taste and she would say yes."

"And you ask a man if he'd feel trapped without the freedom to create and expand, and he would say yes."

"My point exactly!" I said. "Thus a need for a contract. You get the houses, we get the home. But when it's all said and done, what you see is finally what you get."

"I see," he said, heading to the door. "Happy decorating and tell your 'friend' good luck. Judging from your taste, I'm sure you'll accessorize to perfection. Good night," he said, exiting as the fragrance of his cologne filled the room.

A good night, indeed, I thought to myself as the fuming funk of heartache instantly replaced Michael's lingering scent. Back to the business at hand—the contract.

First I had to come up with the conditions. What it was I wanted from him. After almost an hour of type and delete, backspace, type and delete again, I narrowed it down to three things that I needed— that every woman needed. Not just needed, but deserved. Honesty. Fidelity. Security.

Honesty to me means being upfront, forthright, and forthcoming about your feelings at all times. And should they alter, digress, regress, or became hazy, unclear, or unfocused, we want to know that, too. That way we have the option of working to inspire a relapse or leave you the hell alone and move on. Even if what you're feeling isn't really what we want to hear. We still want to know.

Second was fidelity. Since the dictionary is gray on the subject, I made my own definition of fidelity: Cheating is any action or inclination that's romantic, sexual (oral included), thoughtful, intimate, sensual, physical, lustful, kinky, erotic, exotic, sinful, sleazy, dirty, freaky, or flirty directed toward any other woman.

Third is security. Meaning, you will not hide me from your family or friends as if I only exist in your secret world of romantic fantasy. You will invite me to your mother's house for dinner and conversation, reminiscing, strolling through the high school yearbook, scrapbook, and baby pictures. You will make sure I get to know your close friends. Your boys. Your homies. When introducing me, you will not use generic terms such as "a friend," "my buddy," "my boo," or "my one." You will introduce me as "my lady," "my woman," or "my girlfriend."

Those were the conditions. Next thing I needed was the consideration. What I was willing to give to him. That was easy. I will offer what every man dreams of. Meditates over. Fantasizes about every moment of his life—sex. Not just sex, but good sex. Actually, I'd give him more than just good sex. I was willing to give the best sex ever. I will at no time withhold, leave you without, or cause you to doubt that I am eager to engage in any and every sexual act that does not compromise me physically, morally, or spiritually. I will be uninhibited, unencumbered, inventive, and explorative. I promise to be headache-free, bad-back-free, and will give you a three day's notice of cramps, strains, pulls, pains. And I promise that when I say it's that time of the month, it will actually be that time of the month.

Secondly, men often complain about women being needy. I included a provision for that, too—I agree to not be needy. To not call excessively, question without logic or reason. I will not whine, whimper, cry, weep, moan, wheeze, wail, or waffle around or about an issue. I will not hop, skip, leap, or bungee jump to conclusions before giving you the opportunity to exercise section 1 (A), the honesty clause.

Lastly and probably the greatest thing that drives a man out of his mind, I will not snoop. That clause reads as follows: I will not play mind games, catch you in a word trap, tap into your cell phone, break into your e-mail, sift through your pockets, rip through your wallet, tear through phone bills, or check two-way pager messages. I will not key your car, slash your tires, show up at your job unexpectedly, at your home unannounced, or *69 unknown numbers, unless, of course, all signs clearly lead to your intent to breach the honesty clause.

I rummaged through every contract I could find, looking for just the right template, just the right structure, and the right language for what remained—the consequences.

What happens if he breaches the contract and fails to live up to the conditions? How should the punishment fit the crime? After another bout of backspace, type, and delete I came up with a two-tier punishment plan. Because any woman that's ever been hurt knows that one tier is one tier too short. For breach of the contract, fifty thousand dollars or 25 percent of the annual income. And since, depending on the financial status, cash might not be enough, the second tier is a noncash penalty. At the expense of the offender, ten billboards and fifty bus bench advertisements will be strategically placed throughout the offender's residential and business areas. On this billboard will be a picture of the offender, with the words written across his chest in bold neon letters: BEWARE. This advertisement will serve as a form of caveat emptor—let the buyer beware.

Driving my passion was the desire to never again be blindsided because of miscommunication or flawed interpretation. I wasn't trying to trap a man; I just simply wanted to know. Number one has got to know she's number one and number two has got to know that, too. I'm a grown woman who understands a man is gonna be a man. I just want to know when the transformation is about to begin so that I can make a decision to either stay or move on. So, from now on, I'm not just giving my love freely. From now on it's gonna have to be reduced to writing. My affection will be a result of a mutual document bound by more than just emotions, but word and a signature.

For the next several hours and then several more days and several hours more, I cut and paste, whittled and shaped my way into what would become my very own dating contract. There was no doubt that my mission was complete. My place in history secure. I had fulfilled my purpose. Clutching the contract in hand, I was convinced I had done it. Beyond the shadow of a doubt, I was sure it would work. And to prove my theory, I knew the perfect lab rat.

Eight

ON THE DRIVE home that night my car started to sound like a twenty-one-gun salute. My days with that muffler were definitely numbered. I stood in front of my door jingling and jangling my keys from my purse. Like clockwork, I was greeted by the patented mating call of my neighbor Andre.

"What up, sexy?" he said, this time dressed in official Los Angeles Lakers uniform, sneakers, shorts, tank top, and all. "So, how was it?" he asked, leaning against the wall, poised for an extended conversation.

"How was what?" I said with a half sigh.

"Birthday sex. Ain't birthday sex some good sex? It's even better than makeup-to-break-up sex. Say I meet a woman within a month from her birthday. Shoot, that's better than hitting the Pick Five lottery. And as difficult as it may be, if it's that close to her birthday, I make sure I walk the straight and narrow. I don't say or do anything close to pissing her off—until, of course, the day after her birthday. Yeah, there's something about the day you came into the world naked that gives you the freedom to be just that—naked."

"Andre, are you serious?" Even for him, this lunacy was hard to believe.

"Hell yeah," he said.

"I didn't have birthday sex," I said, embarrassed to admit it.

"Why not?" he asked, looking perplexed and confused.

"Because on the night of my birthday, we broke up."

"On your birthday!"

"On my birthday."

"What kind of dumb ass breaks up with a woman the night of her birthday before they had sex?"

"One that has another woman."

Confused, he paused for a moment and then blurted out, "So?! What's that got to do with you? I mean, unless of course it was her birthday, too. Then all three of y'all could have hooked up. Even for me, that would have been a first," he said with his eyes brightening. "So, was it the other woman's birthday, too? 'Cause now you got my nipples hard."

"Good night, Andre," I said, baiting him as I turned toward my apartment.

"Sexy, wait. Wait. Hold up. Wait a minute, now, don't go. That was insensitive of me. I'm sorry. For real. I know I joke a lot, but I do have real feelings too, you know. I'm not just one giant-size overly endowed hormone. Seriously, I'm sorry to hear about you and your man. For real," he said, looking uncharacteristically sincere. "I never met him or nothing, but if you were digging him, he had to have been all right. You accept my apology?"

"Sure," I said, not really caring one way or the other.

"Cool. Now, let's hug so we can move on."

"Andre, please!"

"I'm serious," he said. "This is a straight-up and for real moment I'm having here. These are the times when roommates need to be there for each other."

"We're not roommates," I said, looking at him like he had really lost his mind.

"As thin as these damn walls are, we might as well be. Now stop playing and hug me, girl. Shit, why I gotta fight to cheer you up? This ain't for me, this for you."

This being Andre, there had to be a less than honorable motive seconds away from rearing its head. But why not. Though he was an unemployed, near-homeless, womanizing dog, he was at the very least harmless. And his absurdity kept me amused. And besides, after the last few all-nighters, a manly embrace was maybe just what the doctor ordered. Even if it was coming from Andre.

"Okay," I said. "Five seconds."

"This ain't for me. This is for you. Twenty-five."

"Ten."

"Twenty."

"Fifteen."

"Damn. All right. Fifteen."

We hugged. And actually it felt good. So good that I even continued past fifteen seconds, moving onto twenty.

"See that . . . is this that bad? No. See, I can be serious."

"Thanks, Andre. I'm surprised. Pleasantly surprised."

"It's cool. I'm often misunderstood. I just want you to know I'm here for you."

"Thank you."

"You're welcome," he said. "You know, though," he said, now slowly rubbing my arms, "I was wrong about something I said earlier."

"What was that?" I asked, suspiciously.

"About birthday sex."

"What about it?"

"It really ain't the best sex. There's one other kind that's got it beat by a looooong shot," he said, waiting for me to ask him to elaborate.

I figured what the hell. "What kind is that, Andre?"

"Sympathy sex. Also known as consolation coochie. You usually have it with a friend. Someone you've known for some time. A no-strings-attached deal, 'you ain't got to hug me in the morning, I'm just purging myself emotionally,' kind of one-night stand. Some-body you ain't got to worry about trying to spend the night or noth-ing 'cause he like, lives next door. A no-holds-barred, do-not-pass-go, do-not-collect-two-hundred-dollars, you-come-in-my-room, damnit, bring-a-lunch kind of sex. Some Adam and Eve, naked-to-the world kind of sex. Some before-there-was-cable-television-and-we-didn't-have-shit-else-to-occupy-our-time kind of caveman sex. Some undisputed heavyweight champion, I shook up the world kind of sex. With a friend," he continued, now bring-ing his voice down to a whisper. "With a friend who will understand. Sexy," he said, pulling his face back, staring me eyeball to eyeball. "I'll understand."

"Andre . . ."

"Yes, baby," he said.

"How can I put this?"

"Just put it, baby. Put it anyway and anywhere you want it. And if it don't fit, we'll force it."

"HELL NO. And that's putting it the only way I can think of."

"You're hurting right now," he said as he loosened his embrace, not for a second affected by my response. "I'll tell you what . . . if you change your mind, you know where to find me. If you could though, give me at least forty-eight hours' notice so I can rearrange my schedule to fit you in," he said with a smile as he turned toward his apartment.

Just as I was about to step into my apartment it occurred to me it was time to put the viability of the contract to test.

"Andre," I said in a sultry tone.

"That was fast," he said with a grin and one eyebrow arched.

"Andre, I want your opinion on something."

"Opinion about what?"

"Relationships."

He looked around his shoulder to make sure I was talking to him and not someone else.

"You want to ask *me* about relationships? Andre Thompson.

Gladys Thompson's son, Andre? You are in pain, huh. I'm like the poster child for the antirelationship. I kiss and tell all my friends. I make a woman sleep in the wet spot. I got a framed poster of Bishop Don Magic Juan on my headboard. And you want to ask me about relationships? You sure all he did was break your heart, and not hit you on your forehead with a two-by-four?"

"Andre, I'm serious."

"So am I!"

"For real. Why are you the poster child for the antirelationship? Why is it that you can't find someone to be in a committed relationship with?"

"The problem ain't *finding* one, it's picking one."

"Okay, so why can't you pick one?"

"One?"

"Yeah, one."

"Shit, I don't know. That's a tough one. Can I sleep on it?"

"No. For real. Why can't you pick one woman?"

"I guess because one hasn't really given me an incentive to."

"But what if she did give you an incentive?"

"What kind of incentive?" he asked curiously.

"Like what if it was a crime not to pick just one."

"Girl, what the hell are you talking about?" he asked.

"What if there was a document created to insure that a man had just one woman and only one woman. One woman that was all that he ever wanted or ever needed. And if for some reason he was unfaithful to her, broke her heart, cheated on her without cause or provocation, he'd be hit with financial repercussions."

"Shit, they already got that. It's called marriage," he said.

"I'm not talking about marriage. I'm talking about a document for single folks that want to date other single folks."

"Oh, I get it. A coochie contract?"

"No."

"Well, that's what it sounds like."

"Think about it, Andre, we have health insurance, right? Car insurance. Homeowners insurance. We have insurance on superficial things. Things that can be replaced. Why can't somebody have a deductible on his or her heart? Something that cannot be replaced."

" 'Cause the premium would be too high. And no man on earth would be willing to pay it. That's why."

"My point exactly," I said, now feeling validated. "If the premium was high, then it would ensure that you would be more careful about how you handled it. So, would you sign one?" I asked, feeling as if I had made an adequate case.

"Hell no!" he said, eyebrows raised, voice racing two octaves higher. "For what? Not me or any other man in his right mind would. You must be out of your got-damn mind! You know what . . . you need more than a hug. You need some therapy. Sign a pre-prenup? I wish a woman would . . ." he continued mumbling and muttering to himself.

"What if she wouldn't have sex with you until you did?" I asked, instantly snapping him back.

"What you mean, wouldn't have sex?" he said in midbabble. "Now that's against the law."

"What if the only way you could have sex with her was if you signed one?"

He scratched his head.

"I just wouldn't have sex then," he said.

"Andre, you have sex almost every night. You'd just stop?"

"Hell yeah, I'd stop. I ain't signing shit."

"You'd stop having sex?"

"I'd stop having sex."

"Well, that's a shame," I said, taking a half step closer toward him. "Because I just happen to have a contract in my purse," I said, pulling out an envelope. "Signing it could have been the only thing standing between you and a very long, hard night of romantic indulgence. A tour de force of sexual fury. A night of uninhibited pleasure," I said, taking a half step closer.

"Uninhibited? That's like—whatever is clever kind of sex?" he asked, starting to stutter. "You didn't say whatever is clever kind of sex."

"A night of uninhibited, unbridled, and unrivaled sexual exchange. Some *Tarzan the Legend of Greystoke*, swinging from the vine kind of sex. Some don't-stop, get-it, get-it, pop-locking, bed-rocking, till-the-cops-come-knocking kind of sex . . ." I said, now right up on him. "Between a man . . ." I said, rubbing my finger over his lips ". . . and a woman." I placed the same finger in my mouth, licking it from side to side. "A promise for you to have the best sex ever. "

"B-b-b-b-b-b-best sex by whose definition?"

"Yours, of course."

"Mine?" he asked, licking his chops.

"Yours."

"And afterward," he asked. "Afterward we wouldn't have to talk about whether it really *was* or *wasn't* the best sex ever? 'Cause really just having the aspiration alone to me is enough to make it the best sex ever."

"You wouldn't have to say a word. So, you would sign it?"

"Right about now I'd sign a stack of anticivil rights legislation."

"Then there's only one thing stopping us."

"What's that, baby?" he asked, now in full heat.

"A pen."

"Shit, that ain't no problem," he said. "I got a razor blade in the house. I could cut myself and sign it with blood."

"Wrong color. And besides, it would smear the paper," I said, turning and walking to my apartment. "Maybe some other time," I said, entering my door and closing it shut.

"Some other time? It's a Rite Aid right around the corner," he said, shouting through the door. "What kind of pen you want? A Bic, ballpoint, Magic Marker, a crayon?! Sexy! Sexy!!"

Nine

NEARLY THREE WEEKS had passed since my birthday dinner with Marcus. Knowing him as I do, life had no doubt returned to the basics of selling stocks, buying bonds, and plotting portfolios. By now our relationship had been labeled as a stock whose value had bottomed out. In his mind I was just another bad investment. An ill-advised transaction. These were the thoughts that raced through my mind as I lay wide awake at night, trying to put Marcus behind me. It was almost 11:30 and the TV wasn't doing it for me. I had flipped through this month's *Essence* magazine so many times I could almost quote the articles by memory. And it was at least two hours before *Oprah* was on. God, if I could just make it to *Oprah,* I would be all right. If I could just lose my hurt in the guaranteed hurt of one of her guests, then at least I would know that what I'm going through isn't as bad as what the rest of the world is going through.

But tonight, I wasn't gonna make it to *Oprah.* Tonight it was calling my name. Better yet screaming my name. Haunting me. Wanting me. Drawing me near. Thoughts of our past sexual escapades had pitched a tent and camped out in the forefront of my mind. I was in bed driving myself crazy. Rubbing my feet against my calf, against my thigh, grabbing my pillow, squeezing it tight. Damn, it was like that man had the superpower of telepathy and he was sending me messages. Just tap the match on my thigh and it would burst into flames. And then I started thinking . . . maybe I could just, you know, call him to say hey. We're adults. I mean, what happened happened. We've both moved on and there's no reason why we can't at least be cordial. I mean, we did have a lot of good times. Going on trips together. Going over to his house watching scary movies on the weekend. It's not like he was a sniper or something. He was just a man. A man with needs that I was obviously not filling. Damn, I wonder what he's doing.

I turned over on my side and there it was. It was staring at me. I'm going through it. I need some help. Some moral support. The sweat was pouring from my face as I reached for the phone and quickly dialed Altima's number. I know she'll say something to snap me back to the realm of reality and good sense. The phone rang twice before she answered.

"Hello?" she said.

"It's calling me, girl."

"Mo?"

"Girl, it's calling me. You gotta help me."

"What's calling you?"

"It."

"It what?"

"It."

"Marcus?"

"Yes."

"Marcus called you?"

"No, girl, it called me."

"It?" she said, now totally baffled. "Oh . . ." she said. "It. It."

"Yes, girl. Late at night I hear 'Mo . . . Mo. What's my name? Who's your daddy, Mo? Whose is it? Whose is it?' What do I do?"

"Stop answering it. That's what you do."

"I can't help myself. Girl, I'm getting weak. I'm gonna call him."

"Mo, don't. Don't you call that man. Girl, you're tripping. It's an illusion. A mirror. A smokescreen. Don't call that man."

"Girl, you got to come over here 'cause I don't trust myself."

"Mo, you scaring me. I'm on my way. But don't call him. As a matter of fact, unplug all your phones and take the battery out of your cell phone and throw it out the window. I'm on my way. Okay?"

"Okay," I said.

"Okay, girl."

"Okay!" I said.

"Don't call him."

"I won't. 'Bye."

"'Bye."

I instantly hung up the phone and then . . . I called him.

"Hello," he said huskily into the phone. Damn, his voice sent ripples through my body.

"Hello," he said again.

"Marcus. Hey," I said, acting like this was something other than the booty call it was intended to be.

"Mona?" he said in a soft and inviting tone. "Mona Lisa?"

"Yeah. Look, I was just dropping off some papers to a client of mine who was staying at the Doubletree downtown, so I thought I'd call and see what it—I mean, what you were doing," I said, biting my lip and holding my breath.

After several moments, he answered.

"I just got finished doing a little work myself and I was about to go to bed," he said, now fully aware of exactly where this conversation was going.

"Well, if you're not too sleepy I figured since I was downtown, I could come by so we could . . . talk," I said, in the midst of packing a backpack, toothbrush, pajamas, spare panties, and a pack of hot cocoa for a night of some stress-relieving, climax-achieving, damn, he-won't-be-believin'-how-good-it's-gonna-be kinda sex.

"If I was sleepy, I'm not anymore," he said as his voice gave every indication that he, too, was more than looking forward to our "conversation."

"I'll see you in a few minutes."

"Make it as few as possible," he said.

This is all Oprah's fault, I thought, as I dialed Altima.

"Hey, girl," I said in midyawn, feigning my slumber. "Girl, I'm tired. I'm okay."

"Mo . . ." she said.

"What?"

"Girl, if you're gonna get some, then just get some and leave. I can't be mad at you for that. But just don't be going over there catching feelings because you already know the deal. Get some and leave. And be careful. Okay? I love you."

"I will," I said. "And I love you, too."

I sped all the way downtown to his loft. Not believing that I was actually doing what and doing who I was about to be doing it to. Morgan, what is wrong with you, I said to myself, as by now common sense was catching up to my raging hormones.

The front apartment door buzzed open, and I headed for an even quicker route to his apartment by way of the stairs. With each step upward I thought to myself, Morgan, you shouldn't be doing this. I sprayed one squirt of my perfume over my body. Up the next flight of stairs, Morgan, you should get in your car and go home to your heartache. I pulled out my compact to check for any last-minute glitches in my grille. By the time I got through the next flight, I had just about mustered up enough strength to abort this entire mission, when suddenly the door swung open and there he stood framed in the doorway, wrapped in a thick burgundy robe, holding two glasses of wine—his favorite, red. Maybe he had finally reverted back to himself and abandoned the white wine and the other woman that had obviously staked her claim. Just get some and leave. That's all. Get some and leave, I kept repeating to myself over and over and over.

"Mona Lisa . . . Damn, you look good," he said.

Get some and leave, Morgan.

"You know I missed you, right? You know that," he said, now stroking my hair with his hand.

Get some and leave, Morgan . . .

"I can't tell you how many times I started to call you . . . how many times I wanted to call you," he said, taking my bag from my hand, kissing my ear . . .

Get some and . . .

"I just wanted to touch you and feel you. I wanted to smell you."

Aw, damn, he was rubbing his hand down my breasts, down past my waist into my thigh.

"Baby, what happened should have never happened," he said, now unbuttoning my blouse. By now my mind was numb, my thoughts and sensations tingling as he undressed my emotions first, disarming my anger and hurt, disrobing my doubts. Damn, I missed this man. Regardless of whatever went wrong, three weeks really wasn't that long. By now my clothes were off, inhibitions faded into the scent of a wood-burning fire, and the sound of popping flames flickered as he led me to his bed. He entered more than my body. He entered my soul, stroke after stroke. He entered my heart, and with another stroke, my mind. The tears began streaming down my face. He was making love to every crevice of my being, touching every spot, every space. With each stroke he went deeper and deeper and deeper, penetrating, relegating any notion of what was to what is. It was like he was making love to not just my present but also my past and my future.

I could hear the drums of our ancestral passion beating and throbbing. He had shifted my equilibrium. Altered gravity. Every-thing was all of sudden slightly bigger, my breasts seemed fuller, as the thrust of his . . . aw, damn, every part of my body dripped and dropped, oozed salaciously down his coated body. He was fluid. He was—aw, aw—my head began spinning, I was short of breath, I couldn't—I couldn't breathe—I—squinting my eyes, gaining a sense of time and place and—

"Are you all right?" he asked, softly stroking my face with his hand.

"Yes," I replied, still groggy. "What happened?"

"I don't know," he said. "I think you passed out."

Damn. Marcus had just fucked me unconscious. I had it bad. But it felt good as we together lay embracing each other. All of a sudden I could hear Altima's voice saying, Get some and leave. But leaving was the last thing on my mind. I wanted to prove her wrong, prove myself wrong. I wanted to give Marcus a final chance to make it all right. The now faint flames cast a glow on his face. I wanted to give him a chance to undo what had been done.

"That was the best ever. You know that, right?"

"You weren't too bad yourself," I said playfully.

"So," I said, resting on his chest. "So, what do you think?" I asked, in an open-ended tone to give him room to fill in the blanks.

"What do you mean?" he replied cautiously.

"About us?" I said, still snuggled in my favorite spot.

"About us," he replied in a familiar tone. "What about us?"

"About what just happened?"

"What just happened was you called me because you wanted something. I invited you over because I wanted the same thing. I never stopped wanting it."

"What about Cynthia?"

"What about her?" he said.

"So, nothing's changed."

"What would make you think it did?" he asked, still holding me close in his arms. It was suddenly clear to me. It was over for real. I rolled from under the sheets and got dressed.

"You're going home?" he asked.

"Yeah. I've gotta get up real early to prepare for some new clients," I said. I took one last look at his apartment and then kissed him on the lips. "Thanks," I said.

"If you're ever in the mood to 'talk', I'm always willing to 'listen.'"

"I'll keep that in mind," I said. As I walked out of his apartment and into the crisp night air, I thought to myself, If I hurry I can still catch the last few minutes of *Oprah*.

Ten

WHEN I OPENED my eyes the next morning, I decided right then and there that I would recover from the emptiness of last night's escapades and move on with my life. Time to let the past be the past and the future unfold as it should. I even tucked the dating contract I had so tirelessly prepared into the bottom drawer of my nightstand. I was going to open myself to what good the day would bring.

I opened the windows of my apartment, letting the new air in and the old funk out. All the negativity, ill will, broken dreams, empty promises, and anything else unhealthy that lingered was out.

Whooooooo. Damn, it's cold outside. That window thing lasted as long as I could keep the arctic breeze from stiffening every joint in my body. Okay, that's enough. In the shower I melted away even more layers, steaming away what leftover vindictive vibration still lingered. I was oh so fresh and oh so clean. Ready for a new day and introducing a new me. Exiting my apartment, nothing or no one could remove me from the joy of the day.

"Hey now."

Not even Andre.

"Good morning, Andre," I said, never breaking a stride. "Goodbye, Andre," I said, walking down the stairs and reaching outside. I was in good space by far. Thank God that nothing or no one could stop me, not even my . . . uh-oh.

Turning the key in the ignition, it sputtered and sputtered and nothing.

I stopped for a moment and tried it again. Again it rumbled and grumbled and almost . . . almost . . . almost . . . nothing. "Come on, baby, come on," I said, pounding on the pedal, shaking and shifting the key in the ignition. "Come on baby, not today. Not on Tuesday." Especially not the first Tuesday of the month, which was our official board meeting at the firm. The one chance I had each month to stand out, to impress, to plant the seeds that hopefully would grow into first a salary raise, then a promotion, then . . . the holy grail— senior partner. No doubt, not a good way to introduce the new and improved me to the workplace. Turning the key once again with my fingers, toes, and thoughts completely crossed, I turned the key and—nothing.

I made an executive decision to call a cab and deal with the car later. After a few moments, one arrived and off I went to the office. We were on a good pace to make it in time until . . . my worst night-mare, an accident. A three-car pileup that had all lanes, even the car-pool lane, moving at what couldn't be more than two to five miles per hour.

"Excuse me," I said to the cabdriver, who seemed to be in any-thing but a hurry as the only thing moving faster than the traffic was the meter on his dash. "Could you exit the freeway and take a back road?"

"Which one?"

"Any one that's faster than the one we're currently on. I have a meeting that starts in twenty-five minutes that I can't be late for."

"The shortest distance between two points is a straight line," he said. "I think we should stay on the freeway," he continued. "Always stay on the freeway," he offered, expressionless, neither moved, fazed, nor affected by the traffic or my dilemma.

"Excuse me?" I said, not believing that the cabdriver was now attempting to offer a philosophy on my dime and my time.

"I said, the shortest distance between two points is a straight line. Most people think by exiting the freeway it's gonna get them there quicker. But it's an illusion. All you're doing is moving faster on a path that's now farther," he continued, as still the car moved at a snail's pace. "But you're the boss," he said. "If you want me to exit, that's what I have to do. Do you want me to exit?" he asked.

"Yes, please," I quickly replied.

Instantly obliging my request, he exited, taking the next off-ramp into an even greater pile of stop-and-go traffic.

"See what I mean," he said, never once blinking or glancing in the rearview mirror. "It's an illusion."

For the next hour we weaved our way through the side streets, back streets, up a residential street, over the railroad tracks, finally reaching my building. Afraid to glance down at my watch, I slowly pulled back the sleeve of my coat to reveal—oh my God, I was forty-five minutes late.

Nearly pressing the buttons off of the elevator, I thanked God there was no one else waiting, given the fact that the firm was on the forty-fifth and final floor. The elevator door opened and, just as it was to close, what seemed like every employee in the building piled into the elevator, pushing every other button on the wall, making me that much later than the lateness I had already managed on my own. By the time I walked through the doors of the firm I was now fifty-two minutes late.

"Hey, Tess," I said, pausing for a quick damage check. "Did they start on time?" I asked, hoping they had been delayed or postponed or something.

"I'm afraid so," she replied, nodding her head.

"Thanks," I said fixing my face with a plastered-on smile, and then making my way into the boardroom. When I reached the doors, the lawyers were in midstride, voices raised, tempers flaring, papers flying across the room. It was the perfect time to enter unnoticed.

When I stepped inside, a hush immediately fell over the room. In what seemed like one collective motion, every lawyer and assistant glanced at their watches, then at me, then back at their watches, and then resumed. Two hours later, it was over. I quickly rushed out of the room, hoping that my lateness had been lost in their lawyering.

"Morgan, can I talk to you for a second?" It was Michael Sampson. I could tell by the look on his face that my tardiness was in the very forefront of his mind.

"Sure, about what?" I asked, looking aloof.

He gave me a look that made it clear I wasn't fooling anyone but myself.

"Let's talk in your office," he said, leading the way.

On the way to the office I prepared my opening and closing argument, not wanting the lashing to last any longer than necessary. Especially since I was starving. We entered my office, and Michael closed the door.

"Michael, I have a very valid excuse for why I was late."

"Morgan, there is no excuse."

"No, really, there is. My car wouldn't start."

"Then buy another one. You make enough money. Morgan, look, as color-blind a world as we'd like to believe we're living in, the reality is that we're not. As black professionals navigating our way through corporate America, we have to remember that we're one excuse away from first losing our credibility, one more from losing all hope of possible promotion, and finally one more from scanning the classifieds looking for a gig. You're a good lawyer with a very bright future ahead of you. Excuses only dull your glow. I'm on your ass because I care, Morgan."

"I'm sorry," I said. "You're right. And thank you."

"You're welcome. "

"Now, stop being cheap and get you another car."

"Okay," I said. "Okay."

"When?"

"Soon."

"When?"

"This week."

"When," he asked again with a fatherly, I've-had-enough-out-of-you look.

"Today."

Shooting me a half smile, he exited the office.

I immediately rang Altima's extension for some help looking for a car. I figured since she was named after one, she had to have some kind of insight into finding one. Moments later she entered my office with the classified ads and we began combing through them, looking for deals.

"How 'bout this one, girl? Or that one?" Altima pointed, but most were out of my price range.

"Maybe you should just go to a dealership," she said. "At least that way you get a warranty just in case something goes wrong." Just as the words rushed out of her mouth, we both did a double take, reflecting on our several weeks ago obsession over contracts, warranties, and guarantees. We both started laughing out of control.

"Oooh, I got it," Altima said, her eyes lighting up. "I was up last night watching old *Martin* reruns and I saw this commercial for Sealant Auto. And the brother that owns it is fine. That's where you should go get you a car."

"Yeah, I think I've seen the ad. But should I go because of how well his cars run or because of how good he looks?"

"Both," she said. "It's called a package deal. Being around all those cars, he got to know how to work his stick. How to get an engine roaring," she said. "*Varrroom.* How to back it up, pull it in, slap it on cruise control, and let his engine do all the work, girl," she said, high-fiving me.

"You are crazy, you know that?"

"I know that."

"And anyway, you know how these advertisers are, it's probably just some good-looking, out-of-work actor that they're using as a spokesperson in hopes of getting the attention of some unsuspecting female buyer."

"Well, they sure as hell did a good job, 'cause I don't even have a driver's license and I wanted to get me a car. Especially if he came with it."

"Do they sell used cars?"

"Yeah. But I think they call them 'preowned.' I don't know what the difference is, though."

"There is no difference," I said.

"Just get your car towed there. It's got to be at least worth a little something."

"Yeah, you're right." We hopped on the phone, found a reasonably priced tow truck company that, once I faxed them proof of registration, agreed to have my car meet me at the dealership by five o'clock, leaving me two hours to find just the right car that fit. The day rolled on. Seconds seemed like hours, hours seemed like days. Finally it was 4:30. I headed out of the building and into the cab that waited out front.

I was headed to Sealant Auto . . . where their word is their bond.

Eleven

THE LOT WASN'T anything like I had expected. No pushy salesperson rushed to harass me. There were no neon closeout, end of the year, red-light special posters. And, though the cars were being advertised as preowned, from the outside it was impossible to tell the difference. I remembered the words of my father, who always said to never judge a car by its coat of paint: Whatever you want to know, just look under the hood. I guess in many ways that was the nature of my job as a contracts lawyer. In a sense we were always looking under the hood, checking for cracks, leaks, and faulty wiring, a blown piston here, a fried spark plug there. I was rarely taken by the flash, or shaken by the flare of the outer coat. Surprisingly, though, it seemed like most if not all those senses were dulled when it came to the heart. Why else would I be so oblivious to what should have been obvious? But that's another topic all together.

My mission was finding a car that met my criteria of price first, dependability second, and aesthetic value third. Having done my due diligence, I had Altima pull a sample used car contract that I had reviewed in the cab ride over.

"Good afternoon, ma'am, Manny McPherson is the name. I'd like to help you make an educated and informed decision on the purchase of your next car," he said in a welcoming tone. He was the first salesperson to approach me, white, midfifties.

"Here at Sealant Auto," he continued, having obviously reduced to memory the standard Sealant Auto speech, "our word is our bond, and for over twenty years, it has been our bond with a five-star customer rating for quality, care, and customer satisfaction. Here at

Sealant Auto we stand by our product. We have the finest selection of preowned automobiles in the entire state of Pennsylvania, like this preowned Lexus over here," he said, motioning me to follow. "Showroom quality," he said. "Garage kept, low mileage, navigational system, and it still has the original warranty. A steal, no doubt. Or if you're a SUV kinda gal, there's this metallic blue Lincoln Navigator. Now, this is a beauty. One of the best-looking vehicles on the lot. It's got everything you need to make you feel safe and warm. It's got heated leather seats, and it even comes with a rear headrest DVD player for the little ones," he continued, never once mentioning anything other than the fluff and flash. Never once uttering a word about anything that really mattered. Having heard enough, I decided to cut to the chase.

"What about the engine? What's the cubic inch displacement? The horsepower rating? Is it turbo-charged? What kind of torque does it have? The mileage per gallon? Is the vehicle equipped with four-wheel disk breaks? The transmission—is it electronic overdrive or a standard overdrive transmission? What about the suspension? Is it individual four-wheel suspension? And the mileage? Do you have any supporting documents to support the mileage? A maintenance history report would be fine," I continued. By now his eyes had become glazed. I might as well be speaking penguin. He had tuned out, checking his watch, looking for a way to exit stage left.

"You know . . . I have a call that I was expecting, why don't you look around and if there's something that interests you, I'll be right inside." Cracking a brief smile, he swiftly entered the building, never to be seen again. Five minutes later there was Ted. Then Ahmed. Dan. Bob, and finally Trevor, a young black man, who had no doubt been dispatched for a soul sistah soft sell.

"My sistah, my sistah," he said, with a flair of the Nation of Islam. Giving him absolutely no Nubian love in return, just moments later he, too, retreated to the black hole of broken and battered salesman, pimp walking into the dealership himself, never to be seen again. Checking my watch, it was nearly two hours since I had arrived and still I was no closer to transportation than before. Staring at a sea of cars, I had almost given up when I heard a voice from behind.

"I've heard that a woman of discriminating taste is like an apple martini. Disguised by its beauty, its color, its candy-coated flavor, by the time you realize what you've actually consumed, it's too late, you're under its spell." As I turned, I noticed an outstretched, freshly manicured hand which led to a freshly laundered monogrammed shirt with a glistening S-encrusted cufflink, which led to a custom-made midnight blue suit with soft blue pinstripes, which led up a broad shoulder to a soft pink silk tie, which lead to a firm chocolate neck, a chiseled chin, to a set of fully moist, pillowy soft lips, then over the terrain of a well-groomed charcoal black mustache to a pair of light hazel brown eyes, thick eyebrows up to a buttery smooth forehead, to a low-cut naturally curly, you-know-I-had some-white-folks-in-my-family crown of glistening black hair.

"Sealant. Charles Sealant," he uttered—articulate, heavy voiced, calm, and confident.

"Chase. Morgan Chase," I said, extending my hand, all of a sudden realizing I had missed my latest appointment for a manicure and had at least three nails chipped and one or two hangnails. Not the best first impression, so instead of the soft, ladylike, check-out-my-manicure shake, I opted for the firm, all-business, I'm-every-woman grip, shifting the attention from my femininity to my assertiveness. Finally pulling in all the data into one clear image, I noticed that he had a striking resemblance to the actor in the commercial for Sealant Auto. Noticing my bewildered look of wanting to ask the obvious, he offered, "Contrary to public opinion, I'm not an actor. I'm the owner. I figured since you had sliced, diced, and skill-fully sifted through almost every sales associate in the entire dealership, I figured it was time—"

Cutting him off, I said, "You figured it was time you sold me yourself."

Taking a pause for a brief moment of inner amusement, he continued.

"I'm not here to sell you anything, I'm here to serve you everything. You're obviously a woman who knows what she wants, and how she wants it. So, once you communicate that to me, it's my job, my duty, and my joy to give it to you exactly how you want it and then make sure it arrives exactly where you want it," he said with a smile, knowing full well the meaning behind the meaning of his words.

"Well," I said, now feeling drawn in by his exchange and, after the last couple hours, more than eager for some mentally stimulating banter of my own. "What if I tell you exactly what I want and in clear and precise detail exactly how I want it, only to find that once I've been given it, it wasn't what I had thought it would be?" I said, not believing my own words as they effortlessly oozed from my mouth.

"Well," he said, "I suppose that means I'll just have to try . . ." he paused, taking one step closer, harder and harder, digging deeper, and deeper and deeper, "until—I've discovered what gives you the most intense and ultimate satisfaction," he said with his eyes, now locking firmly into mine. My lips quivered, my panties moistened, and beads of sweat grew beneath my nose resting on the rim of my lip. Damn, he was sharper than a number two pencil.

The moment marinated. I wasn't about to move for fear I would faint.

"Why don't we take a seat in my office?" he said, as he noticed by now the sunset casting its auburn glow on the sea full of cars. Slowly catching my breath and finding my footing, I followed him into the dealership, noticing a slight limp in his walk. Into the dealership past a floor full of every make, model, and size of mid-to-moderately priced cars, all in showroom shape.

From the corner of my eye I could see the salesmen peering, whispering, more than aware of not just whose name was on the dealership, but why his name was on the dealership. He was good. He was charming. But it was going to take more than charm. It was going to take one hell of a good deal to get my signature. His office was huge. Plaques, trophies, medals, and framed sales certificates covered his muted walls and on his cherry wood desk were an assortment of pictures of him and women, smiling, playing, laughing. I couldn't really tell whether they were family or friends, or women he had frequented.

"You have a very nice office," I said, finding myself uncharacteristically comfortable. "Obviously a family man," I said, dangerously close to crossing the line as my eyes led to the pictures on his shelf of even more gleefully gorgeous women, all in what seemed to be a consistent state of bliss.

"Actually, no. My family's in D.C.—" he said, rising from his seat and walking toward the shelf, taking a glance at the several photos while pausing in midreminiscence. "No, these are simply pictures of some of my very satisfied customers."

"They're all beautiful," I said, having fully digressed from my purpose.

"You should have seen them when they got here," he said, still glancing at their pictures. "These pictures inspire me. Each day I walk into my office they remind of what my real purpose is," he said pausing, tempting me to catch the dangling words, either finish his sentence or be lured into a request that he finish. He was poised. Relaxed. And in no rush.

"And that purpose would be?" I asked, feeling vested in the moment.

"To inspire beauty," he said effortlessly, without pretension. With the ease of a man in touch and in tune with himself. "Pleasing them pleases me," he said, then took his seat behind his desk. Pulling out a monogrammed Mont Blanc pen, he rolled his chair snugly inside the nook of his desk and continued. "Now, how may I please you?" he asked. Intent. Focused, undressing me with the suggestions of his words. His intentions seemed honorable. His desire sincere. His aspiration to please me was a welcome change from my most recent past. His ambition alone sent ripples through my body and for the next hour I melted in my seat as he pampered me with paperwork, massaged me with makes and models. He was a master craftsman of his words, a technician of his crafts. Obviously a well-traveled, well-educated man, he held court, in total command, as I sat captive, hanging on to every word, every gesture, every movement of his body as he circled his prey.

Right about now I would have signed a five-year lease for a skateboard. He answered all my questions, acquiesced to all of my issues and concerns. The fact that I was willing to take less didn't seem to defer his willingness to give more. He was wholly and completely serving my needs. Adding this option here, that reduction there, he was like a chef at Benihana slicing and dicing, gashing and slashing the prices, the payments, down until, finally, as the night air whistled through the showroom door, and the half moon dangled peacefully in the air, I had reached the height of satisfaction as he slid the contract across his desk, holding my hand, opening it, then resting the pen in my palm. I couldn't wait to sign on the dotted line.

Each page I signed stroking the pen, then another page and another, I glided that thick black Mont Blanc in my hand, as he turned the page. We had found a rhythm. I knew where to sign without even looking as we gazed into each other's eyes, then, finally the last page he reached for my hand, moving it to the final highlighted X as together we stroked.

I was now the proud owner of a fully loaded, 2001 champagne-colored Lexus in near-perfect condition. Like clockwork, an associate entered with a camera and a key.

"Would you be so kind as to give me the honor?" he asked, motioning me to join him for a photo. His right thigh rested slightly against my hip as the camera flashed. And no doubt days later I would join his bevy of beauties. His collection of very satisfied customers. I hopped into my car and drove from the lot. I felt good. I was safe, secure, and without ever once shedding one single strand of pride or clothing, I had been completely and ultimately satisfied.

Twelve

THE NEXT MORNING on my way to work I couldn't believe how many heads I was turning. On the surface it was good knowing I still had it, even though deep down inside I was clear on the fact that it probably was the sparkling look of my *preowned* car, combined with the fact that I still had it. But whatever the reason, heads still turned, cars screeched, and whistles blew. And the ride to work seemed not to take as long, and the traffic all of a sudden didn't seem so bad. I circled my office building a few times, making sure I was seen smiling, waving, pulling into the parking structure in my brand-almost-new Lexus coupe.

When I reached my floor, Tess was smiling as usual. But something was up. Everyone was peeking out of their doors, looking like they knew something that I didn't. It couldn't be the new car since they hadn't yet seen it. When I reached my office, I opened the door to the scent of . . . sitting on my desk was the most beautiful arrangement of exotic flowers I had ever seen. There were multicolored orchids, lilies, birds of paradise, and other flowers that I didn't recognize that were gorgeous, colorful, and vibrant. Just as I reached for the note the door swung open.

"Gurrrl, who is Charles? And why is he sending you flowers?"

"How do you know they're from Charles?"

"How else? I read the note," Altima said unapologetically, looking as if there was nothing wrong with snooping through my note.

"You read my note?"

"Yes," she said. "I read everybody's notes. I work in the copy room, remember? Now, who is he?"

"He's nobody."

Again the door swung open. It was Ophelia.

"Nobody doesn't send you flowers from one of the most expensive florists in Philadelphia."

"Good morning, Ophelia," I said, having missed her morning greeting.

"Good morning, yourself. Now who is he?" she asked.

"He's the guy who sold me my car," I said, shrugging it off.

"Wait a second!" Altima said, as her eyes lit up. "Charles Sealant, the owner? He sold you the car? So what does he look like?" she asked. "Do he look as good as the man on the commercial?"

"Actually, he *is* the man on the commercial."

"What commercial?" Ophelia asked.

"The commercial for Sealant Auto . . . 'our word is our bond.' Shiny black hair, pretty brown eyes—that man is fine! He owns the used car dealership where Mo got her car."

"It's not a used car dealership," I blurted out.

"It's not?" Altima replied.

"It's not?" Ophelia joined in.

"No. It's preowned," I said. "Cars that have been handpicked from the finest selection of imports in the world. There's a difference, you know."

"I guess," Ophelia said. "Come to think of it, I have seen that commercial. You're right, he does look good," Ophelia added, by now her own eyes lit up. "Wait. I wonder if it's the same Charles Sealant that used to play for the Seventy-Sixers. The one that had a huge contract, and then tore up his knee after his third year."

"It could be. he's tall enough to be a basketball player."

"So it is him," said Ophelia.

"It sounds like him," said Altima.

"I guess it is," I said.

"Well . . ." said Ophelia.

"Well . . ." Altima continued.

"Well, what?" I asked.

"Well, do he look like the commercial? 'Cause on the commercial, he is fine."

"He looks better than the commercial," I said, "but so what?"

"So what?" Ophelia asked. "These flowers are so what. That's what. Are you sure a preowned car was the only thing you drove home last night?"

"He sent the flowers because he's a nice guy. That's all."

"That's all?"

"That's all."

"Okay, then, let's review the facts. A fairly attractive woman—"

"Fairly?" I asked.

"Okay, moderately—" Ophelia continued.

Cutting her off again, I asked, "Moderately?"

"Okay, an attractive woman shows up one late evening to a dealership looking for a car. Instead of being helped by a generic salesperson, she's greeted by the owner, who then makes a sale. Upon closing the sale, the next morning, out of the blue, out of the kindness of his heart, because he's nice, pulls out his credit card and spends a hundred and fifty dollars to send flowers across town. Because he was nice."

"Yes," I said. "He's just being nice, that's all."

"So, tell me something," Ophelia asked, "is the yellow brick road really yellow or is it mustard or golden or sunflower, 'cause you are obviously used to spending most of your time in Oz. There's nothing nice about a man you just met, who, quiet as it's kept, already got what he wanted from you. These flowers are an invitation for him to take you out on a test drive. See how well you grip the road, if you know what I mean. Check your rear suspension, get under your hood, test your engine, and sample your four-wheel drive. See if your high beams flicker when the road gets a little bumpy," Ophelia said.

"Well, I think it's romantic," Altima said. "He's a throwback to the days of chivalry."

"Chivalry?" Ophelia said.

"Yes, chivalry."

"Are we that starved for romance that all a man has to do is send flowers to our office and we're almost ready to order a gown?" Ophelia was always the realist.

"Yep, pretty much," Altima said.

"See, that is just sad," Ophelia added.

"Well, Mo, if he's as nice as he is fine, I think you two are gonna make the perfect couple."

"Altima, we're not a couple," I said.

"At the very least you can get a free tune-up and oil change every ten thousand miles," Ophelia added.

"We're *not* a couple," I said again.

"You can get in free to all the car shows," Altima continued.

"And that's usually where you find a lot of men, so maybe he could get me a free pass," Ophelia added. "You think he can get me a free pass? Because those car shows are expensive."

"Hello! We are not a couple. We're not dating. We're nothing." My tone started getting louder.

"Then what would you call it?" Altima asked.

"Yeah. What would you call it then?" Ophelia chimed in.

"I wouldn't call it anything. They're flowers. That's all. Flowers, not a ticket to Tunisia. Flowers. That's all. I'm probably never going to hear from him again. Why? Because it was a gesture. A good business practice. A way to say thank you for four years worth of payments, that by the time I'm finished making them, I could have bought the car three times over. That's all. Nothing more and nothing less. That's it. So let it go, okay?" I said, not wanting to hear about it anymore and move on with my day. "Just let it go. All right?" I said, looking at them both, still looking unwilling to let it go. "Let—it—go!"

"Morgan . . ." Tess chimed in, "you have a call on line two. It's from a Mr. Charles Sealant." My heart dropped as we all hurried and scurried around the office.

"What does he want?"

"You know what he wants," Ophelia offered, making hip gyrations.

"Whatever he wants you'll never know," Altima chimed in, "because if you don't hurry up, he's gonna hang up. Whatever he wants, keep calm and relaxed. Calm and relaxed."

"Ask him about the car show," Ophelia blurted.

"She ain't gonna ask him about no car show, you selfish cow. Mo, pick up the phone."

Calming myself, gaining my composure, I answered the phone.

"This is Mo—I mean Morgan," I said nonchalantly.

"Morgan, this is Charles," he responded. His voice rattled into the receiver while both Altima and Ophelia crowded my ear, trying to listen in. "From the dealership," he continued. "We met yesterday." Attempting to shoo them away was no good, as they were like a growth on my ear. "I sent you some flowers. Did you receive them?"

"Yes, I did, thank you. I wasn't expecting them. But then again, I'm sure you do this for all of your customers," I said, hoping in my heart of heart that my words were distant from the truth.

"Oh, I don't," he said. I covered the mouthpiece of the phone, and tried calming down the cheers of Altima.

"Well, why me . . . ?"

"It was my way of inviting you to dinner. If you're not busy. This Friday night I have a business associate coming to town and I wanted you to join us for dinner around six. And then afterward we could maybe catch a movie or grab some dessert by ourselves."

"Friday night for dinner? I'd have to check my schedule first, can you hold?" I said, slowly putting down the phone, pressing the mute button, then letting out a loud scream.

"What did he say?"

"Yeah, your ear is too big; I couldn't hear a word he was saying," Altima shouted at Ophelia.

"He wants me to go to dinner on Friday night with him and an associate of his."

"He's seeing if you blend. What time?" Ophelia asked.

"Around six."

"Tell him seven-thirty is better for you. A woman should never be that available at first," Ophelia countered.

"This is not a game," Altima said, glaring at Ophelia.

"Oh, grow up, Altima. It's all a game. You either play it or it plays you."

Counting to ten slowly, then picking up the phone, I said, "Friday night is fine. But seven-thirty works better for me." I crossed my fingers and held my breath.

"That's fine," he said. "I'll pick you up then. I look forward to seeing you."

"Me, too," I said, putting the phone back in its cradle as both Altima and Ophelia stared with an I-told-you look.

"He's still a nice guy," I said thinking to myself that Friday couldn't get here fast enough.

Thirteen

WEDNESDAY CAME and went with cases, contracts, and clients one after another. But still my focus was on Friday. Thursday began, and it was pretty much more of the same, only now it was one day from Friday. Finally Friday was here. It seemed like every client who's ever had a case called wanting conversation or seeking clarification. I thought the day would never end. Finally five o'clock arrived. I managed to ease past the several offices without even a stir. Past Tess, into the garage, and into my car. The traffic on the way home was abnormally light. Racing up the stairs and into my apartment, I silently turned the key into the door, hoping not to alert Andre. Once in safely, I quickly ripped off my clothes, made my bath, lit a candle, and eased into the tub for half an hour to relax and reload.

By 6:30 I was flipping through my closet. I wanted just the right outfit that didn't say or show too much. I wanted a sense of intrigue, of chase. And given that it was a thousand below zero outside, whatever outfit I chose would also have to be wrapped in grizzlylike outerwear. Once dressed, I reached for my thickest, woolliest, heaviest coat. The cold and I were not the best of friends, and I did everything I could to avoid direct contact. Every woman understands that sometimes you have to stick a pin in fashion to avoid turning frigid. And any man that's dated a woman that's put on layers of clothing understands the thrill in unlayering what's been layered en route to getting to the good part. I slid my designer knit hat over my hair, making sure that once I removed it, it would be close to the way it was before I slid it on. It was now 7:30 and I was ready.

The apartment door buzzed. Oooh, a man that was on time. Impressive. Like a tightly wrapped penguin, I waddled over to the intercom.

"Who is it?" I asked in a sexy tone, acting like I had no clue who it was.

"What you trying to sound all sexy for? It's me, Andre."

"Look Andre, I don't have time to fool around with you. Goodbye," I said, releasing the intercom and trying to swallow my disappointment.

Before I could take a moment to primp in the mirror, the intercom buzzed again. I took a deep breath and once again tapped into my sexy tone that Andre so irritatingly interrupted.

"Who is it?"

"It's me, Andre. I locked myself out. Let me in before I'm out here to greet whoever it is you waiting for."

Busted. Pushing the intercom button, I buzzed him in.

Seconds later it rang again. Okay, now he was getting on my nerves. Frustrated, this time I was going to be anything but sexy.

"Don't you have anything better to do than harass me?" I blared. "See, I should let you freeze your little narrow ass off. 'Cause knowing you, you're probably damn near naked," I continued as the heat of my attitude melted into the outer air.

"Actually, I've got a long wool overcoat on. But still, it's pretty cold out here," a voice replied. A voice that sounded like . . .

OH MY GOD, that's not Andre! That's Charles, I thought, praying that maybe it wasn't Charles, but really Andre playing one of his tricks.

"Charles?" I asked, making a 180-degree shift from stank to sweet.

"Yes," he replied, his baritone voice almost vibrating the screws to my intercom loose.

"Hey."

"Hey. Did I catch you at a bad time or is that how you usually greet your dates?" he asked with a lighthearted tone.

"No, I'm sorry. That wasn't meant for you. It's a long story," I said.

"I can't wait to hear it."

"I'm on my way down," I said rushing and grabbing my purse, exiting my apartment door, racing past Andre, who just as I had expected was standing shirtless in baggy jeans with Joe Boxer peeking above his waist.

"Morgan, you know I was just thinking . . ." he said, as I didn't once stop to even acknowledge his presence.

"Not now," I said, not even waiting for the elevator but choosing the stairs that led to the lobby level two flights below. Finally, I had reached the lobby where he was waiting.

"You could have waited in the car," I said, realizing how cold it was.

"I was thinking about it," he said, ushering me to the Towncar where a driver stood waiting to open our door. "But for fear of an even greater verbal lashing, I decided to wait," he said with a smile. "Hop on in. There's a slight change of plans—my friend couldn't make it for dinner, so instead of joining us, I was hoping we could join him."

"Oh, that's fine," I said nonchalantly, hopping in the car as it idled in park. "He's still coming to Philadelphia, right?" I asked.

"He's not coming quite that close actually."

"Oh," I said, thinking that maybe because of the weather he was in a neighboring city. "So where are we headed? D.C.?"

"Wrong direction," he replied.

"New York?" I asked. "Is that where he is?"

"You're getting warmer."

Noticing the puzzled look on my face, he bailed me out.

"He's in Paris," he said, not once skipping a beat.

"Paris, Texas?" I asked, in a half-nervous, half-is-this-brother-out-of-his-flippin'-mind giggle.

"No," he said, himself now laughing slightly. "Paris, France."

"France?" I said, now thinking this man had completely lost his mind.

"Yes, France," he said.

Instantly the lights on my internal terror alert began peaking. Slowly I slid my hand on my cell phone, rubbing my fingers over the numbers 911, planning any moment to call for emergency assistance.

"My friend is one of the top automobile buyers in Europe. He supplies a great deal of the foreign cars that I sell. I think he might have even sold me your car. At any rate, he'd been wanting to discuss broadening his business and was supposed to fly in. I just got a call that instead he's chartered a plane and wants me to fly to France for a morning meeting," he said.

I paused, looking at him and then around the car, waiting at any moment for someone to start laughing or blinking, or screaming, "Surprise, you're on Candid Camera" or something. From the rearview mirror I noticed the driver never batted an eye. And Charles, aka Cool Hand Luke, sat expressionless as if he just suggested that we drive to the King of Prussia Mall. After bursting out with uncontrollable laughter, I managed to temporarily gain my composure.

"Charles, you're kidding, right? I mean, about the France fly-away-for-a-day thing and all."

"No," he said, still with a straight face. "I'm serious. I'd love for you to join me, if you feel up to it."

"Do you know how crazy that sounds? I mean, do you know how much that would cost?"

"It wouldn't cost a thing. My friend has already chartered the plane. Whether it's one passenger or twenty, it's the same cost to us—nothing."

"But what would I do once we got there? I'm not dressed for France."

"Have you ever been there?"

"No."

"Then how do you know you're not dressed for France?" he asked, noticeably making light of the moment that was close to becoming heavy. "Besides, that's not a problem; my friend owns a clothier that I'm sure would have more than enough outfits in your size. It is the fashion capital of the world, you know. You'll be fine. Trust me."

"Trust you?" I asked. "I don't even know you. Charles, I just met you a few days ago. Do you know how crazy this sounds?"

"Of course I do. But what better way to keep life from being predictable and routine?" he offered. "It's just a day. And if for some reason it doesn't go how you would have wanted it to, you've still got three hundred sixty four more to try it again."

"Not if you're a stalker, I don't. Or better yet, a mass murderer? Or a rapist?" I said, now being consumed with every crazy negative and deranged thought I could pull into my mind.

"Have you checked the crime rate in Philadelphia lately? That's much more likely to happen to you in Philadelphia than in France," he said.

"Charles, I don't even know you."

"I don't know you, either. So we're even. And besides, what better way to get to know me than during a six-hour flight there and back? I figure since it's an eight-hour difference, if we leave by nine we can get there by noon. Do a little shopping, meet and have lunch for an hour or so, and then off for a little sightseeing. And we'll be on the plane before midnight and back home before sunrise."

"When you do a first date, you really do a first date," I said, as the insanity of the moment started to settle in and the absurdity seemed less and less absurd.

Wait. What am I thinking, I thought to myself. No. Hell no. I don't even know this man. Damn, but a trip to Paris in a private plane. The farthest I had been was Atlanta to visit my cousin during freaknik. No, hell no. He is out of his flippin' mind.

"If you're not comfortable, I can understand and it's no problem. There'll be other times for us to get together."

"Other than a once-in-a-lifetime field trip to France?" I asked as through the rearview mirror I noticed the warmth of a smile begin to form on the face of his driver.

"That's why they call them once in a lifetime," he said, smiling. "Sometimes it only happens once."

"I'd have to let my girlfriend know where I was going and how to get in touch with me," I said. As crazy as it sounded, I was actually thinking about going.

Instantly, he handed me the phone in his car. I paused, looking at it for a moment and then reached for it, dialing Altima's number.

"Hey, girl," I said into the phone, not giving any sign of any trouble.

"Hey, Mo, I thought you were on your date with Charles?" she said.

"I am," I said. "He's right here."

"Oh, then why are you calling me?" she asked.

"I just wanted you to know where I was going just in case you were trying to get in touch with me. I'm going to Paris," I said.

There was silence. Then a burst of laughter.

"Mo, what are you calling me for? I'm trying to watch the *Hair-*

show bootleg. And you know you got to really concentrate because whoever recorded it had a cell phone that was going off during the whole movie."

"Altima, I'm serious. Charles and I are going to Paris for the day. I should be back by the morning."

"Paris, Texas?" she asked.

"No, silly. France." Still there was silence. "Altima? Altima?"

First she began crying and then proclaimed, "That is soooooo romantic. Oh my God, it's like right out of a movie. Have fun, girl. And call me when you get back. Oh, and get me a T-shirt or something. I love you. Good-bye!" she yelped still crying.

"Altima. Altima?" She hung up. Charles glanced at his watch. "One more," I said, dialing the number and then waiting for the pickup.

"Hey, Mom, it's me."

"I know it's you. You're my one and only child. How could I not know it was you? I was just on the phone with your Aunt Elna. She's got the gout, too, you know. Feet swole up the size of a cantaloupe. I was thinking about going down there to visit her and stay for a week or two maybe, to help her clean the house so she can get off her feet. As long as I'm back for the third Sunday service. You know Pastor Reid from Baltimore is coming up for a revival."

Knowing my mother, she was off on one of her run-on rants for the next half hour without ever letting me get one word in edgewise. Catching her in between a breath, I cut her off. "Momma, I'm calling to tell you something."

"Well, go right ahead, baby. I've been on the phone for five minutes; if you wanted to tell me something all you had to do was just say so."

"Momma, I'm going out of town for a day."

"Oh, that's nice. You should get out and enjoy yourself more. You work so hard at the office. You know, it's one thing you young folks don't do enough and that's take time to see the world, smell the roses. When your father was alive, he used to always take me on trips. We'd go up to Reading, Pennsylvania, almost every year on church trips and we'd shop and we'd—"

"I'm going to Paris, Momma."

"That's nice, I hear Paris is beautiful this time of year. You know you got a third cousin in Texas. Aunt Ethel's son Jeremy had a daughter with another woman who lived in Texas while he was married. I think he was on an Amway tour selling door-to-door soaps and house cleaning fluid."

"I'm not going to Texas, Momma. I'm going to France. Paris, France," I said.

"Baby, are you okay? Is there something you're trying to tell me?" she asked, her voice now becoming noticeably rattled.

"I'm fine. I'm going to France with Charles Sealant. I'll be back in the morning."

"Morgan, I've seen this on television once or twice before. Now, just give me a code or some kind of sign to where you are and I'll call the police and they'll find you. Name a street a store or anything."

"Momma, I'm all right."

"Or I'll call you back on your cell phone with the police on the other line and we can trace where you are from the telephone. Lord Jesus, Lord Jesus."

"Momma, I'm okay. Really. I'm just going for a day. I'm okay."

"You're okay?"

"I'm okay.

"You're okay?"

"Yes, Momma, I'm okay."

"Well, if you're okay, then let me speak with somebody there with you."

I pulled the phone to my stomach.

"Charles, my mother thinks I'm being kidnapped and she wants to speak to someone here with me. Do you mind?" I asked.

"Of course not," he said, taking the phone.

"Hello?"

"Hello, who's this?" she asked, as usual, screaming into the telephone.

"This is Charles. I'm taking your daughter with me to Paris for a day and I guarantee she'll be back before sunrise Sunday morning." He paused. "No, ma'am, I've never been to jail . . . yes, ma'am, I go to church . . . no, ma'am, I'm Baptist . . . yes, I have a job, I own a pre-owned automobile dealership . . . no, ma'am, it's not a used car lot . . . Sealant Automobile . . . yes, ma'am, I own it all by myself . . . no, ma'am, that's not an actor, that's me . . . yes, ma'am, that is my real hair . . . no, ma'am, there's no Indian in my family that I know of . . . it was good speaking with you, too. Here's your daughter."

"Momma—" I said.

"Oh, baby, he's a good-looking man," she said, cutting me off. "He's got a good job and good hair, too. And he's a church-going man. Now, he could really be the one. Just be careful and take things slow. You remember what I said, now, okay? Now, you be on your best behavior and bring me back something. A T-shirt. Bring me back a T-shirt and a magnet for my refrigerator. And call me the moment you get there. And then the minute you get back."

"I will."

"I love you, Morgan. From the moment I laid eyes on you when the doctor cut the cord, I knew you would be the one. I'll be praying for you, too. Close your eyes while I say a quick prayer . . ."

"But Momma—"

"Lord Jesus," she started, "watch over my daughter as she travels the highways and skyways. Be her copilot, Jesus. Protect her and cover her and at the appointed time give her a safe return home. Amen."

"Amen. Momma, now I really have to go. Love you. 'Bye," I said. "Bye-bye."

"So," Charles asked, "did I pass the test?"

"With flying colors."

"Thank you," he said. "So, what will it be?"

"Well, I'd better go back inside and get my passport."

I ran back in my apartment as fast as I could, contemplating if I had time to grab anything else I might need other than my passport. But I didn't want to keep him waiting another second. I snatched my passport from out of my travel bag and hurried back before he changed his mind.

I got back in the car, taking a deep breath and smiling. He returned the smile and motioned to the driver to continue. Ready or not, I was on my way to Paris.

Fourteen

WE REACHED the private airport quickly and after rounding corner after corner, hangar after hangar, we finally pulled up to one marked 87. The hangar doors opened slowly and out came a silver and blue plane with the word "Destiny" inscribed on its side in fancy blue lettering. The driver hopped out and opened our doors.

"We're here," Charles said.

"We sure are," I said, not believing I was really doing what I was about to really be doing.

"Still game?" he asked, being thoughtful enough to give me one last opportunity to Michaela Jackson moonwalk my way back to my apartment and into my bed like this was some dream that never really happened.

"You only live once," I said, resigned to throw rationality, logic, and common sense hurling into the wind.

"And if you live it right, once is more than enough," he said, rising from the car, reaching for my hand as we were greeted by a tall, fair-skinned man who had naturally curly, pepper gray hair.

"You couldn't have picked a better day for flying," he said. "My name is Watts. I'll be your date for the next thirty-six hours. I fly a pretty mean bird, but when we get to a comfortable cruising altitude, I'll whip you up the best martini this side of the heavens. So, if you're ready, she's all gassed up and rarin' to go."

Taking one last glance at Charles, I was greeted by a smile that said all that needed to be said. Together we walked up the stairs and into the plane. Momentarily I turned for one last look at life as I knew it. So long, Philadelphia. So long, apartment. So long, cheesesteaks, 76ers, Iverson and McNabb. It felt like I was headed to the moon, one giant step for all of mankind.

"Be careful there, little lady, she's ready to close," the pilot shouted.

Ducking my head into the plane, the deed was done. The cabin doors were sealed. We were headed to Paris, France. Home of the Eiffel Tower and a bunch of other places that I couldn't remember the names of but had seen all of my life in books, magazines, and movies. All I know is that if it's anything like I always imagined it to be, it's gonna be beautiful.

I leaned back into a seat more comfortable than my couch at home. There were about ten high-backed seats in the plane and each fully reclined into a twin-size bed. A full-size bar, a three-seater leather couch, a forty-two-inch plasma television screen. Suddenly it was clear to me why rich folks spend all their energy to not just get rich, but stay rich.

"If the wind stays friendly we'll be there in about six and a half hours," the pilot's voice rang through the cabin.

"Would you like a cocktail?" Turning, I noticed a flight attendant comfortably dressed in black slacks and a black fitted top. She had obviously been hiding out in the back, waiting to reveal herself once we had liftoff. I could only imagine who else and how many more would soon begin popping up. "My name is Pamela," she said.

"I'm Morgan," I blurted. "I'm a lawyer in Philadelphia. At Benson, Bartolli and Rush. 1342 South Broad Street. Suite 305, extension 18."

"Morgan," Charles said, leaning to whisper into my ear. "You're not a prisoner of war. Relax," he continued, then held my hand and rubbed it slowly. He was calming, reassuring, and easy. Okay, I thought to myself, Morgan, exhale. You're already on your way there, so hell, you might as well enjoy yourself.

"That's my wife," the pilot's voice again rang through the intercom. "I keep trying to leave her behind, but somehow she keeps sneaking into the luggage bins. She makes a hell of a drink, too."

"We have a full bar," Pamela said.

"I will have a drink. Could you make it a mojito with brown sugar crushed onto the mint leaves with Malibu, the coconut rum not the Bacardi."

Pamela paused. "Of course. Right away. Sir?"

"The same," Charles replied.

Moments later the drinks were served.

"A toast," Charles said, holding his glass in the air.

"A toast," I replied, mocking his motion.

"To living in the moment," he said.

I took a sip; it was perfection. Just what the doctor ordered, a mind-numbing intoxicant to unwind my tightly clenched nerves. A few minutes later a silver cart came reeling out, with two large, round silver plates covered in glass. It was nothing like any airline I had ever flown. Lifting the lid, Pamela ran down the meal. There were lamb chops with creamy polenta and warm wilted spinach leaves with pine nuts.

Dinner was served, and more drinks were poured. Finally it was time for dessert. A finely whipped custard.

"If there's anything else I can get you, just press the button on your left," Pamela said as again she disappeared into the back.

"You should relax your eyes for a bit. In a few hours we'll be hitting the ground running. You'll need all your energy and more. There's a lot of Paris to fit into a day," he told me. Reaching into his briefcase, he pulled out several stacks of papers, a set of custom wireless reading glasses, and began to immerse himself in his business at hand. Taking his advice, I figured I'd recline my seat slightly, take a quick nap, and then fiddle around with a movie or music or something until we landed. Slowly I closed my eyes, finally at ease and at peace. If once in a lifetime really only did happen once, I could at least lay my head to rest knowing I was headed for mine.

Fifteen

I WAS AWAKENED to the voice of Pilot Watts. "The Champs-Elysées to your right, the Eiffel Tower to your left, and as far as the eyes can see—there's only love. We'll be on the ground in fifteen minutes."

Looking out of the window it was so. We were in Paris. Pamela rolled out a tray with a warm cloth for the face and a basket full of almost every toiletry item a person could need.

"We're meeting my friend at the Hotel Meurice for lunch. We have a day room there where you can freshen up and relax for a moment until he arrives. His boutique is right around the corner from the hotel, so if you'd like we can start there first."

The plane pulled up to what was obviously a private section of an airport with several other private planes nearby. Again the voice of the pilot rang: "You kids enjoy yourselves and we'll see you back here at nine o'clock. Five after nine and it'll be one hell of a long gondola ride back to Philadelphia," he said laughingly. "If I'm lucky I'll be alone due to the fact that my wife has fallen in love with a Frenchman. The husband of the French lady that I had minutes earlier fallen for myself."

"Ouch!" That was the sound coming from the intercom as his wife had obviously had enough of his one-liners. The doors flung open and in the distance it looked like a Hallmark card. The air reeked of romance. And though that was not my intention for coming, still I paused to inhale deeply. Hoping to fill my lungs with that which had evaded me for so long. Again I inhaled. And again, still I inhaled.

Reaching for my hand, he uttered the words "carpe diem."

"Let's seize the day. There's so much to see and so little time to see it," he said, guiding me down the stair unit and into an awaiting Mercedes Benz, with the funny license plates.

Even the license plates were sexier than ours. There was a driver wearing a black Pepe Le Pew hat and a thin mustache waiting to greet us.

"*Bonjour,*" he said.

"*Bonjour,*" I replied.

We were off. Leaving the airport suddenly it was as if the skies had opened up, the clouds all moved to the sides and a bright light shone through, bouncing off what had to be the most beautifully crafted old world buildings. There were bridges and towers and people on bicycles.

"So, what do you think? Do you like it?"

"What's not to like? I love it. I never imagined I'd be here."

"Life is full of surprises. You just have to learn how to stay out of the way and let them happen," he said as the car continued to fly through the city.

"Look there," he said. "That's the Eiffel Tower. All the books and movies and magazines paled in comparison to the real thing."

Really, it was hard not to be inspired in Paris.

"Here's the hotel," he said. "But first we'll go around the corner to find you something to wear for the day. Though most people speak English, a limited use of their language is always appreciated. '*Merci*' means 'thank you.' And '*oui*' means 'yes.'"

Right about now I was beginning to feel like I rode the little yellow bus to school, but it didn't matter. I was a willing pupil and thankfully Charles was a more than accommodating teacher, never making me feel at any time uncomfortable or out of place.

We arrived at his friend's shop. A quaint boutique with clothes lining every nook and cranny of the adjoining rooms. There were shoes and belts and purses and dresses. Like a couture catalog. Any moment I expected Naomi Campbell, or Alek Wek to appear from behind the dressing room curtain draped in one of these elegant outfits. From the back an older woman greeted me with a string of French phrases.

"*Oui?*" Looking at Charles, he smiled and mouthed "*oui.*" To the lady I replied, "*Oui.*" She reached for my hand and for the next half an hour or so I felt like a supermodel during fashion week at the Prêt-à-Porter. There were silks and linens and gabardines. Pinks and blues and oranges. Pantsuits, dresses, and gowns.

Finally I chose the most simple yet elegant black halter dress, black Louis Vuitton pumps, and a rabbit fur wrap. Reaching for my purse, I leaned over into Charles's ear and whispered, "Do they take American Express?"

"Don't worry about it." He smiled, reached for my several bags of clothes, turned to the lady, and offered softly, "*merci.*" She returned the smile. Following suit, I smiled and offered my own *merci.* He reached for my hand and we continued to the hotel, which was like an old cathedral church that had been converted. Rich and regal architecture framed the stained, beveled glass windows and castle-size doors swung open as a host of smiling helpers rushed to serve us.

"*Merci. Oui.*"

"*Merci,*" I said.

They smiled, sensing that I was at least honoring their language. Charles pulled out his identification at the front desk and we were almost immediately handed a key to a room. I stopped next door at the lingerie store for some intimate apparel, and then we were off to our room. The massive nine-foot double doors opened to what had to be a five-bedroom suite with beautiful tapestries hanging from the windows and the chairs. And a sparkling chandelier hung from above.

"The east wing is all yours," he said. "I'll take the west wing. We'll meet back here in half an hour." He checked his watch.

"Yes, in half an hour," I said. I made my way through the hall and into the master suite, a king-size canopy bed covered in silk and velvet, deep gold and burgundy spread, full pillows. See-through silk draping swayed in the slight breeze flowing through the room. In the bathroom, thick burgundy rugs covered the custom marble floor and a mural of the entire city framed the sunken tub. I could have easily spent thirty days in the bathroom alone, but thirty minutes was all I had. I ran my water, sprinkled in the perfume-scented bath crystals that filled the room with a soft vanilla fragrance, almost melting me away as I soaked in the tub for what seemed to be an eternity.

Like clockwork, half an hour later I exited the bedroom, fully dressed, fully revived, and ready to take in a day of discovery. I was determined to enjoy this day to its fullest.

"*Très magnifique,*" he said, as I entered the front parlor. "It means 'this is magnificent.'"

"You're not too hard on the eyes yourself," I said, as I admired his midnight blue, two-button suit, a crisp white shirt with deep pink stripes, and a raspberry-colored tie with of course his patented monogrammed S hanging just slightly from his shirt.

"My friend Pierre is waiting downstairs. So he said." He reached for my hand. "If it be the pleasure of the lady . . ." he continued as I extended my hand to join his.

Together we exited the room and into the elevator, and then to the lobby, where an older dark-haired Frenchman was standing in a more subdued custom black suit, with at least two carats worth of ice lodged in his left ear and a matching two-carat diamond in a simple platinum setting on his right second finger. He was attractive. Regal. The French version of Ed Bradley. His smile broadened and eyes brightened the closer we came.

"*Bonjour, mon ami,* so good to see you. And who is this vision of art standing beside you?" he said, reaching for my hand and then holding it gently between his own.

"This is Morgan. A very special lady who was so kind to accompany me on my journey," he said. Did I sense a man marking his territory?

"It is my pleasure indeed," he said, locking into my eyes. "If I would have known you traveled so elegantly, I would have invited you to France a long time ago," he said, raising my hand to his lips and kissing it gently. "This is an associate of mine," he added. "Her name is Michelle."

"*Bonjour,*" she said. She was a tall slender woman, with a beautiful face, model-like proportions, and dark, rich hair. Obviously she was more than the "associate" that he had claimed she was. But then, I thought to myself, that was probably what she was thinking about me, so at least we were even. I complimented her on her striking blue-green scarf she was wearing, to which she murmured "merci" softly.

"I have reservations for lunch at the Champs-Elysées restaurant, overlooking the Arc de Triomphe. It's old world, but it's quaint. And the dining is *très magnifique.*" Having hours earlier enrolled in French 101, I knew that meant that the food was going to be the bomb!

We arrived at the restaurant, where I was given a brief history of the city. I listened to Charles and Pierre begin calmly and friendly enough, small talking business and finance. Toasting to this and toasting to that. Like me, Michelle was reserved, sitting mostly still as her hair swayed in the breeze. She was clearly used to this and made herself content to enjoy the moment for what it was. My eyes and ears were full of the atmosphere and aesthetic majesty of our view of the city.

For lunch we were served roasted quail with wild rice, dried fruits and nuts mixed in the rice. To wet our whistle, a white wine from the Baron Phillipe de Rothschild vineyard. Pretty soon their once polite conversation escalated, shifting from lighthearted banter to hardcore business. That lasted no more than a half an hour and then, like clockwork, they shook hands and the conversation was over. Pierre stood up, reached for my hand, holding it again in his, kissing it once.

"If you get sick of this man, I'm but a phone call away," he said, winking and then smiling. "*Au revoir,*" he said, taking Michelle's hand and walking away.

With business having just wrapped, Charles and I were completely alone for the first time. Looking at his watch, he said, "It's three o'clock. Which gives us almost six hours before we're headed back. I hope those shoes you bought are comfortable, because I plan to show you the beauty of thousands of years in less than six hours."

"I'm up to it," I replied, taking a deep breath, more than ready for the games to begin. Charles hailed a cab, and after slipping him several large bills, we secured a driver for the day.

Our first stop was the most obvious, the Eiffel Tower.

"You simply can't come to Paris and pass it by," he said. It was more than I had imagined it would be.

It was clear to me now why this was one of the most famous structures in the world. The view of all Paris from the top was breathtaking.

"And to think this is one aspect of man's stroke of artistic mastery. There's more. To the Louvre!" Charles shouted to the driver.

"The Louvre," he said when we reached our destination, "is one of the most famous museums in the world, home of one of the most famous paintings in the world," he said, pausing again. "And that painting would be?" he asked.

"*Sugar Shack*?" I replied. "By Ernie Barnes? The one at the end of *Good Times*? For real."

After a moment, he burst into laughter.

"No, silly. An even more famous painting than that. The Mona Lisa," he said.

My mouth dropped. "*The* Mona Lisa?" I asked.

"That's right."

"Nat King Cole's Mona Lisa?" I continued, still needing clarity.

"How about Leonardo da Vinci's Mona Lisa?" he countered.

I gave a half smile, remembering the last person who called me by that name, and hoped the thought didn't wear on my face and cloud the elation of the moment I was currently in.

For the next hour we wandered the hallowed halls, viewing other famous works such as the *Venus de Milo, Winged Victory of Samothrace,* and *The Coronation of Napoleon.* And then finally we arrived at the Mona Lisa. Arguably the most famous painting in the world.

"The artist was none other than Leonardo da Vinci, born in the mid-fifteenth century, the illegitimate son of a notary from the small Tuscan village of Vinci near Florence," Charles kindly offered, having obviously taken the tour on more than one occasion.

"That means this painting is almost . . ."

"It's more than half a millennium old. In the sixteenth century, the Mona Lisa became the property of the French King François I, who was an acquaintance and admirer of Leonardo da Vinci."

"How much is it worth?"

"Who knows."

"Somebody has to know."

"It's priceless."

"She's owned and her value insured by the country of France."

"She's insured by a whole country?"

"Yep."

By the time we left the museum the sun had set, casting a warm glow over the entire city. On the way to our next stop we passed the famous Cathedral of Notre Dame. Then past the Place de la Concorde that housed Egyptian treasures more than three thousand years old. Then finally to what Charles labeled the most romantic street in Paris. One that he saved for our final moments.

"It's not only romantic," he explained, "but it's also the final leg of the Tour de France bicycle race. We'll grab a quick bite near the Arc de Triomphe. It's an arch that was commissioned by Napoleon. From atop you can see the entire view of the Champs-Elysées."

Once atop we ordered a light meal and talked about lots of everything and a little of nothing. It was one of the most engaging conversations I had ever had. Then just as it was getting good, the clock sounded. I looked at my watch, which by now had been spinning out of control, and just as I had feared, it was a quarter to nine. Time to remove the glass slipper and return to reality. As we arrived back at the airport and into the plane greeted by Pilot Watts and his wife, Pamela, it was as if I had been inside a picture book. A children's fable. A love story. And whatever was to come or was not to come, for one extended moment I was living a fantasy. I was a princess and Charles was my prince. A knight in shining armor with access to a flying chariot with wings of wonder. I eased into my seat, reclining it all the way back, looking out of the window as the plane ascended into the clouds and the city grew faint in the distant darkness. In this one day I had experienced enough adventure and romance to last this Philly princess a lifetime.

Eight hours later we were back in the States. Out of the plane and into the car where we drove through the snow back to my apartment. Like the perfect gentleman that he was, Charles walked me to my front door, where we both stood for that always awkward end-of-first-date moment.

"So," he said, as the moisture of the air melted from the warmth of his mouth.

"So . . ." I replied, locking my eyes into his.

"You'll tell your mother that I behaved myself and took real good care of you?"

"Yes," I said, smiling.

"And that I was the perfect gentleman for almost the entire time," he continued.

"Almost?" I said, thrown by his words.

"Almost," he continued, holding my face in his hands, leaning in slowly, kissing me once lightly. The heat of his mouth, the warmth of his lips in that one single moment melted away all feelings that were frigid, emotions that had been iced over by the past. For what seemed like forever we kissed, and we kissed, and even more we kissed. Then finally, he leaned back his face.

"Try to get some rest. I'll call you tomorrow to check on you," he said as he walked his gentle body back to his car. From the distance he spoke the words "au revoir l'amour." Then he hopped inside his car and zoomed off as a trail of steam followed behind leading all the way to my heart, warming it from the inside out as I entered my apartment building and up the flight of stairs.

For almost the entire day, Sunday, I stayed in bed flipping through the channels in search of any and every old movie with a glimpse or glimmer of Paris. Never once answering the phone or the door or anything. I wanted the fairy tale to last at least till the next morning. And it did.

Sixteen

IT WAS MONDAY morning and I was still on a high. I skipped out of my apartment and into my car. Swerving and curving my way through the traffic into the garage of my office building. Up the elevator.

"Good morning, Morgan."

"*Bonjour,*" I replied. Tess stared for a moment, not knowing what to say or how to react. "It means 'good morning' in French," I said.

"But we're in Philadelphia."

"Our bodies, yes, but our hearts, Tess . . . our hearts are in Paris," I said, with a widened, Cheez Doodle grin on my face.

"I guess," she said.

Reaching my office, I fell into my seat, spinning it round and round and round and . . .

"You want us to believe that you went all the way to Paris with a man that looks like Blair Underwood and he didn't once try to get some?" Suddenly my fairy tale had ended with the poisonous pessimism of Ophelia, destroyer of dreams, joy zapper, glee slayer. She was standing dead in the doorway, with her big arms crossed.

"Good morning, Ophelia."

"Save it."

"Paris? Who says I went to Paris?"

"Who else?" she said, as peeking behind her over the side of her shoulder stood Altima.

"It sort of slipped out."

"Yeah, and it kept slipping for almost the next hour," Ophelia added. "I know you're not trying to tell me nothing happened."

"I'm not trying to tell you anything," I said, not wanting to give her any room to muscle her way into the joy of my day.

"You're not telling me anything, 'cause I'm not buying it."

"Good, Ophelia," I said, "because I'm not selling it."

"This is the most romantic thing I've ever heard in my life," Altima said with a tissue in hand. "Charles is a throwback to the days when things like romance and chivalry ruled. When men were men."

"You mean, he's a throwback to the days when men were getting with men," Ophelia said.

"What is that supposed to mean?" I asked.

"It means if he took you all the way to Paris and didn't try anything, then maybe it's because he likes what we like—dick."

"God, Ophelia, do you have to be so crass?"

"Crass? I could have said he likes ass. Would that have been better?"

"He's not gay, Ophelia. He's a gentleman."

"He can be a gentleman and still be gay."

"He's not gay," Altima said.

"Girl, please. After my girlfriend turned me on to that Down Low book, I found out everything there was to know about the homosexual underworld. They're *all* gay until proven straight. They got gay boxers. Gay football players. They even got gay gangster rappers. So why couldn't he be gay?"

"Because he's not, that's why."

"Okay, then he's getting it from somebody else."

"Why couldn't it simply be that he was being a gentleman?" Altima asked. "Is that so far from the realm of possibility? Does it bother you so much to see someone floating?"

"Not at all. I'm just providing the net for when she does stop floating, and reality sets in, so she won't go spiraling to the ground and break every bone in her body.

"Contrary to what you project Cinderellas may think, keeping it real is providing service. Dreams of a never never land of princes, white horses, and glass slippers is doing a disservice. That's all I'm saying."

"Well, could you say it the hell somewhere else, Ophelia? Like in your office, 'cause a woman, especially a black woman, doesn't have that many chances to have a fantasy, so even if her prince turns into a frog, which I doubt he will, at least let her enjoy him before the transformation begins," Altima countered.

"You know what, Altima? I'm getting real sick of you."

"That makes two of us," Altima countered, as in her usual furious state she pulled out her jar of Vaseline while my door swung open and two taps sounded from the door.

"I hate to be disturbing anything, anything like, oh, I don't know . . . work, maybe." It was Michael Sampson. "Morgan, could I speak with you for a moment?"

"Sure."

"You weren't disturbing us," Altima said. "We were just talking . . ."

Ophelia quickly kicked her in the shin.

"Aaaaah, 'bout work. That's all."

"Nice suit, Mr. Sampson. Blue is my favorite color," Altima blurted.

"Thank you."

Feeling the stare from Ophelia, they both exited, leaving us alone.

"So," he said, in his usual no-nonsense tone. "Good morning."

"*Bonjour*," I said, not realizing that I hadn't yet left Paris alone.

"Did you just say '*Bonjour*'?"

"No. Did I?"

"Yeah, you did."

"Oh," I said softly, then clearing my throat. "So, what did you want to speak with me about?"

"There's a case that the partners threw my way this morning. It's between our client, Preston Monroe, C.E.O. of Monroe Enterprises, and the city of Philadelphia. Turns out, Monroe Enterprises, owned by a black man, was given a contract worth over twenty-five million dollars by the city to create low-rent community housing in North Philly and they were just notified in writing that the city opted instead to award the same contract to the Johansson Brothers, a white-owned and operated company, to build the same housing in a . . ."

"In a white community?"

"You guessed it. Now, this has ACLU, NAACP, and every other civil and racial angle written all over it."

"So, why doesn't Monroe just cry racism? Seems like a much easier way to get the leverage he needs without ever spending a dime in attorney fees," I said.

"That's exactly what he doesn't want. If he pulls the race card, it'll scare off any future business in the private sector for fear that if anything in the slightest were to ever go wrong—he'd wave the race card."

"So, what is he going to do?"

"He's going to hire the sharpest lawyer in Philadelphia to make what is obviously a case that's full of color lines seem colorless. And Philadelphia's sharpest trial lawyer has added as his lead counsel someone soon to be known as Philadelphia's top contracts lawyer."

"And that would be?" I said, hardly able to control my excitement.

"Who else," he said. "You!"

"Oh my God, I can't believe it. *Merci, Merci, Merci*!!"

"Morgan, what is it with you and the French today?"

"I don't know. Oh my God, Michael, this is incredible."

"No, this is the thing that partners are made of," he said. "We bring in this case, and you'll have a feather in your cap the size of the state of California. Trust me."

"Michael, I don't know what to say."

"Just say thank you. Or rather, *merci,*" he said.

"Ha ha."

"This is going to mean a lot of overtime, undertime, and every other kind of time. I hope you're up for it."

"Oh, I'm up for it. Why wouldn't I be? It's not like there's anything else in my life occupying my time."

"Excuse me, Morgan . . ." It was Tess on the phone's intercom. "You have a package that just arrived for you at the front desk. It's a bouquet of flowers in the shape of the Eiffel Tower," she said gleefully. "It's got a note that says, '*Est-tu occupée ce soir.*' What does that mean?"

Looking at Michael like I had just been caught with my hand in the cookie jar, I stood expressionless.

"It's French for, 'Are you busy tonight?'" he said. "I took a class last year before I visited there. So, what's your answer, Morgan?"

"My answer to what?"

"To his question."

"*Oui?*" I said, with a smirk.

"*Oui, oui,*" he said. "I'm headed out to a meeting and I'll see you back at the office at seven. *Au revoir,*" he said with a smile.

"*Au revoir,*" I replied.

Seventeen

FOR THE NEXT week there were late nighters at the office with Michael and me and even later nights spent on the town with Charles and me. The kisses grew longer, wetter, and more intense. We must have gone to every hot spot in Philly. Michael wondered why I was so cheerful, given the fact that I had logged enough overtime to match my entire year's salary.

But it didn't matter. Law was my passion. And besides, this case was for a good cause, and years later, I'll consider its win a turning point in my career. And it didn't hurt any that Michael was sharp as a tack. His own passion was contagious as I saw in him the mirror image of what it means to be young, gifted, and black. He was a role model for me. Not only was he talented, but he was committed. The next week came and went and there was much of the same kind of schedule for overtime hours spent on the case, dissecting and interjecting my own expertise. Because he respected me, it made my respect for him grow larger than its current size. Meanwhile each week with Charles was different from the last. We hit a couple back-to-back 76ers home games, where he seemed to know almost everybody in the entire building. Either he had sold the whole town a car, or his two-year stint as a point guard, though short lived, had long-term impact. Either way, it was fun being with him. He was a public kind of man that didn't seem to mind having his spot blown up by having one woman dangle from his arm. And the good-byes got longer. His kisses were now joined by his drifting hand, which spent a disproportionate amount of time rearranging the junk in my trunk. He was an authentic black man, infatuated by my backside.

Thanks to my momma, I was well endowed in that category. I didn't mind, because occasionally my hand drifted downward, caressing his package ever so slightly. For us both, it was getting good, the good kind of touchy-feely from high school. Another week went by and it was pretty much more of the same. More late nights. More hot and steamy moments that now ended up in the car, with windows fogged, radio turned to the slow jams on 103.9.

It had been almost three weeks since our first date and I had made up my mind that it was time for us to graduate from touchy-feely to more grown-up games. In other words, I was gonna give him some. I called Altima and as usual she agreed to whip up one of her specialties. I wanted to feed him in every way possible. He had earned it.

Rushing out of the elevator and into my apartment, I had a little over an hour to prepare myself for my evening with Charles. Gently pulling the keys from my purse and easing them into my door, just as my door had opened . . .

"Well, look what the wind blew in. A little lovebird swooping down to her nest just long enough to snatch some threads and then fly away, fly away wherever the winds of love and romance may blow. That was original, you know."

"Hey, Andre."

"I'm surprised you remember my name, it's been so long since I've seen you," he said with a lollipop in his mouth, wearing a wife beater T-shirt and drawstring pajamas. "You've been gone, what, about three weeks now? Get home late, leave right back out, on the phone till the wee hours in the morning. You're lucky you got a roommate that cares about you."

"Andre, we are not roommates."

"You got somebody new in your life, don't you? You ain't got to tell me. 'Cause I know. You got 'new man' written all over you. Like it's a neon light embedded in your forehead, flashing 'new man—new man—new man.' So, what's it been about—three weeks? Y'all done had some good sex by now. Some chandelier-swinging, got-my-bell-ringing kinda sex. Tell the truth."

"Who says we had sex?"

"Who says you had sex? Come on, now. You been seeing a brother for three weeks. I would assume he's a brother and that you haven't sold us out just yet."

"Yes, Andre, he's a black man."

"Does he have a job?"

"He owns a car dealership. He don't just have a job, he owns the job."

"Is he good-looking? Not that it matters, 'cause a job prioritizes over looks."

"He's very attractive."

"Well, hell, there it is."

"There what is?"

"A black man with a good job and good looks got too many options to be waiting around for three weeks without getting some. Trust me, I know. I'm broke. No goals. No money. My grille is all jacked up and the only piece of furniture I have in my entire apartment is a bed—and I don't wait more than three days. If he ain't getting it here, and he ain't getting it there, he's getting it somewhere, okay? But he's getting it. Believe that," he said, as his words for a moment raised a flag.

"Don't hate, Andre," I said quickly, shrugging him off.

"Unless, of course," he continued, "you made him sign one of them crazy-ass contracts you were talking about."

"No," I said, having all but removed that thought from my mind.

"No?"

"No. And I've gotta go. I'm expecting company."

"Tonight," he said. "Over here?" he said as his eyes brightened. "Over here? Oh, it's on tonight, huh? I got some company on the way myself. Tell me around what time and maybe we can achieve climax together."

"Good night, Andre," I said, turning to enter my apartment.

"Well, if you change your mind, just tap on the wall."

Inside, his talk of the contract almost weighed me down. But no,

I thought to myself. I'm not going to let it get to me. I'm not going to let one bad apple spoil the whole bunch. Seconds later, the intercom buzzed.

"Girl, it's me."

Moments later Altima barrelled through the door with a brown bag wrapped in more brown bags with clear bowls covered in tin foil. The food's fragrance alone was filling me up. Baked catfish stuffed with crabmeat and shrimp. Fresh plantains and black beans. And for dessert, a chocolate fondue.

"Girl, I hope I didn't make too much food, but I didn't want you to run out on your big night. So, this is the night," she said, eyes sparkling, smile widening.

"Yeah," I sighed, "this is the night."

"Well, girl, he's earned it, so you two have a good time."

"I'm sure we will," I said.

"And you don't think twice about Marcus or Kevin, or Terrance, or any other of your past boyfriends that broke your heart. Don't even think twice about how they lied and cheated and pretended to be somebody that they weren't. Just put away, all the hurt, the pain, the nights you cried yourself to sleep—that's all in the past."

"Thanks, Altima," I said. "Thanks for painting such a vivid picture of my past just minutes before a date with my present."

"You're welcome," she said, not even realizing what she had done to trigger even more bad thoughts. "So, I'll call you tomorrow so you can tell me all about it. And don't leave anything out. I want to know it all. From first position to last, I want to know everything. And handle your business, girl. You representing North Philly. And don't warm up the food too long, because it'll start to dry out." We transferred the food from her pots to my pans, her Tupperware to my tableware. "And remember, when he asks you the recipe, just say—"

"A chef never tells," I said, knowing too well the drill.

"That's right. Well, I guess that's it," she said.

"I guess so."

"Call me tomorrow."

"I will."

"Thanks again, Altima," I said. The phone started ringing as she exited the apartment. "Get the phone and call me tomorrow," she said, closing the door behind her. Checking the caller ID, I saw it was my mother.

"Hey, Mom."

"Hey yourself."

"Mom, I really can't talk right now; I'm about to have company over for dinner."

"That's nice."

"Altima cooked again."

"That's nice. It's good to have friends with strengths in areas where there's weakness. That was what made your father and I such a strong couple. When I was weak he was strong, and vice versa. We were the perfect team. A match made in heaven."

"Momma," I said delicately, not wanting to interrupt her mid-stride down memory lane. "I'm kind of running."

"Oh, that's right. You did say company was on the way. Is it the man who took you to Paris? You'll have to tell him thank you for the lovely T-shirt. I wore it to the third Sunday brunch and you should have seen how they reacted. You could cut the jealousy with a tooth-pick, it was just that thick. You make sure you tell him I said thank you."

"I will."

"He's a nice man. At least from what I can tell on the phone. And he's got good hair, too. You know your father had good hair. Take your time with this one, Morgan, you hear me? I said take your time. Remember, now, hunger is the best sauce. You hear what I said, didn't you? A happy man is a hungry man. Remember what I told you, now."

"I will."

"I'm going to pray for your evening to be everything you want it to be. That finally you find somebody that will treat you like your father treated me. With respect. And honor. With integrity. I'm going to pray on my own once we hang up the phone since I know you're in a hurry."

Buzzzz.

"Momma, that's the door. I love you."

"I love you, too. I'll call you after service on Sunday. It's Pastor's Appreciation Day so it'll be late. Sometime around . . ."

Buzzzz.

"Momma . . ."

" 'Bye."

" 'Bye."

"Hello," I said, racing to the intercom.

"Hello. It's Charles."

"I'm in apartment Two C," I said, as I placed my hand on the button, buzzing him in, all the while thinking about what Andre said. Then Altima, and finally even my mother. Still I removed all thoughts of my past, I was poised to enter my future. Terrance was Terrance. Kevin was Kevin. Marcus was Marcus. And Charles is Charles. There's no reason for me to punish this man because of what other men did. The doorbell rang. Taking one last check in the mirror and quickly straightening up what I had already straightened up moments earlier, I opened the door, still thinking to myself, Marcus was Marcus and Charles is Charles.

As usual he was dressed to perfection, in a chocolate brown suit, a caramel tie with wine pinstripes, chocolate suede square-toe shoes, his patented cufflink-adorned shirt. Marcus was Marcus and Charles is Charles. His suit draped perfectly off his chiseled frame. He was like a king-size Snicker's bar that I would soon be peeling ever so slowly, taking my time to ensure that I honored every inch of its delicious terrain. Marcus was Marcus and Charles is Charles.

"Good evening," he said, leaning over, laying a soft, gentle, moist kiss on my cheek, then from behind his back he pulled a purple orchid. "This is for you, Mona Lisa," he said as my heart nearly dropped to my feet.

"What did you just call me?" I asked, unnerved.

"I called you Mona Lisa."

"You called me Mona Lisa? Why? You never call me that," I said as my voice cracked, my thoughts unraveled.

"I called you Mona Lisa because . . . you look as stunning as you did the day we spent in Paris when we went to see the Louvre. I just thought it sounded cute," he said, as for a moment he looked pensive. "Is that a problem?"

"Is that a problem? No. I just . . . I just would like it if you called me by my name, Morgan."

"Not a problem," he said, as the once dead thoughts of Marcus I was trying so hard to suppress were now alive and well, sprouting wings and hovering in my mind, Charles is Marcus. And Marcus is Charles. Damn. Throughout dinner Charles became every man who had ever done anything remotely rude or foul, fake or fucked up. I watched closely as he cannibalized every crumb from his plate. I watched as his mouth was moving ever so gently, never once taking his eyes off me. Worse things and worse thoughts now began swirling in my head.

"Dinner was incredible," he said, clueless to the thoughts that had been overtaking my mind. "I've been all around the world and I don't remember having a meal as satisfying. You'll have to let your mother know she did one hell of a job raising you," he continued as small beads of sweat slowly formed on my lip.

"She'll be pleased to know that," I said, taking the napkin and patting my face. "All of a sudden it's gotten kind of warm," I said. "Are you warm?"

"Yeah, but not from the temperature of the room," he said.

"Oh," I said, knowing full well the innuendos that were no doubt leading to the dessert. And not the chocolate fondue. "Are you ready for dessert?" I asked.

"I feel more like I'm ready for a workout," he said, "after eating all that food."

"Well," I said, sensing the perfect segue to the moment at hand,

"I suppose we could make the workout the dessert." I walked over to him and undid the top button of his shirt, loosening ever so slightly the noose of his tie. "That is, unless you have a problem with that."

"Is the dessert ready?" he asked.

"There's only one way to find out," I replied, as I clicked off the light switch on the wall and took him by the tie, leading him back to my bedroom, all the time thinking to myself that there was no way in hell that what happened last time was going to happen this time. Passionately he began kissing my ear, then my neck. He was in full heat, setting the stage for what in his mind was sure to be a night of total pleasure.

He laid me down on the bed first, then climbed on top. Slowly I began inching myself back little by little, closer and closer to the nightstand on the left side of my bed. The nightstand where I had stored the contract. More kisses came as he slowly unbuttoned my bra and even more kisses continued over my breasts and down past my stomach, where I could now feel him throbbing firmly against my thigh. Still I inched slowly and slowly, now only inches from the nightstand. With it just in arm's reach, I flipped over, turning him on his back, slowly unbuttoning his shirt, kissing his neck and then down past his stomach I continued, undoing his belt buckle, unsnapping one snap at a time, then gently caressing over the terrain and the strain of his Calvin's.

In his mind, no doubt he was sensing what was to follow. If there was a perfect time, this was it. He was at full attention as I continued slightly and gently rubbing and touching and—

"Damn, you feel good," he moaned as he shifted and turned his body, making sure it was completely accessible and available. Slowly I licked from his neck to his chest, down past his navel and to the rim of his Calvin's and back up slowly to his ear, where I whispered, "Charles . . ."

"Yeah, baby," he replied.

"Charles . . ."

"Yes, baby . . ."

"Is that what you want?" I asked. "Charles, you want me to . . ." I said, with my hand still rubbing and gliding gently over and under.

"*Oui,*" he replied.

"*Oui, oui,*" I returned. "Could you do something for me? Just one thing. One small thing that would make me feel real good about making you feel even better," I whispered into his ear.

"Whatever you want," he said.

"Anything?" I whispered, with wet kisses licking his ear.

"Anything," he said, as slowly I pulled the contract out from the drawer.

"I want you to sign something."

"Sign what?" he asked, still caught in the moment.

"Sign something that will guarantee you a night of the best sex ever. Would you do that for me? So I can do something for you?" I asked.

"What do you want to do for me?" he said, in a soft, still relaxed tone.

"Whatever you want me to," I replied, never once removing my hand from his Calvin's.

"Would you do that for me?"

"Yeah, baby, I'll do that for you," he said, as I reached into the top drawer of my nightstand and pulled out a pen, handing him the contract. In the still of the night as the moonlight poured into my bedroom window, I watched him in one swift motion sign on the dotted line. Almost instantly, I was liberated. Freed from the emotional shackles within. My heart was full. My mind at ease. It was about to be on like never before.

Slowly he turned and placed me on my back as every stitch of clothing fell to my hardwood floor as I watched him in one swift motion slide on his protection. Slowly he began easing his . . . damn, he was huge . . . slowly he penetrated me with his . . . entering me deeper and deeper, he entered into spaces untouched, hit spots that sent chills through my marrow. He was vibrating my vertebrae.

Abandoning recklessly my inhibition, I was bending and shifting, contorting my body in crazy positions. Ways that I had never known or tried. He sighed, I sighed. He was getting it his way, and I was giving it my way.

Climax after climax, we continued into the wee hours of the morning and into the next night it seemed, and into the next and the next and the next as the days merged into the nights and the nights merged into the next nights, as it seemed like we were never not making love. It was an intense two and a half weeks of whatever-is-clever kind of sex. He was exploring and I was ignoring any perceived dos, don'ts, can'ts, or won'ts. I was determined that this man would have no need go unfulfilled. I wanted to give it all to him, things that he didn't even know he wanted. I wanted to take him places that he didn't know existed. No deed went undone, no thought unspoken. It was all good.

Eighteen

AT WORK I COULD barely contain myself from sharing with everyone and anyone who would listen. I was on cloud nine. I had been taken to the moon. There I was, dangling among the stars, free to try again. Free to take chances. Just the freedom of freedom was all the freedom I needed. There were even occasional surprise visits to my job, like today.

"Morgan, you have a visitor at the front," Tess would say. "It's him—and he's got flowers," she whispered into the phone, letting out a giggle of her own. Then, like clockwork, it was Altima and Ophelia rushing into my office.

"Girl, it's him again," Altima cheerfully alerted.

"Yeah, it's the ghetto prince charming making another chariot run," Ophelia blurted.

"Ophelia, don't hate, just 'cause she got a man and we don't."

"We? Speak for yourself; I got a man," Ophelia said.

"In your dreams, you got a man," Altima said.

"And that's where he's gonna stay until I can find someone in real life to match the high standards he's set in the make-believe world where he exists. So, mind your business, okay."

"You mind *your* business."

"I'm minding my business, watching you minding it for me."

"Mind this," Altima said, as she lifted her fist in the air. While they continued their fussing and fighting, I eased out of the office almost undetected and into the front waiting area where he stood, with what had now become his signature purple orchid. He could have just as easily been a model for some fashion magazine.

"You were on my mind," he said, "so I figured since I was in the neighborhood . . ."

"You work ten miles away."

"Damn, the neighborhood just keeps growing and growing," he said with a smile. We headed for lunch downtown. I was the belle of the ball, the toast of the town. I was like that magic ballerina inside the globe, constantly twirling and spinning on her toes. This was definitely working for me. From the midday stop-bys to the late-night drive-bys, it's like he was craving me, and likewise I was craving him. At times I felt we were junkies, hooked on the natural high. We inhaled each other, night after night and day after day.

"I've got to go out of town," he said, one night when he met me after work at a restaurant not too far from my job. It was later than normal, so as a courtesy to me, he made dinner as close as he could so we could spend as much time as possible.

"You're going out of town? Where?" I asked, almost feeling like it was summer break in high school and he was about to go out of town to visit his grandmother in Georgia for the summer.

"It's Pierre. My friend in Paris. He's ready to close the deal, so I have to go there to wrap things up."

"Paris, you're going to Paris!"

"Yes."

"When?" I asked.

"Tonight."

"Tonight? For how long?" I asked, as I had begun in my mind working out an excuse to take time off from the job, which was almost impossible, given that we were ankle-deep in preparation for a trial.

"Just a weekend. He just called me today. Otherwise I would have said something earlier."

"I wish you had. Then I could have at least had time to think of an excuse so I could go with you."

"It's all right. I'll be in back-to-back meetings all day anyway. Paris isn't going anywhere. And neither am I, and neither are you."

"I'm going to miss you," I said.

"Not nearly as much as I will be missing you. Look, my plane leaves in about an hour, but I just had to see you before I left."

"I'm glad you did," I said, stroking his hand in mine. "Well, be careful, and call me as soon as you get there. And tell Pierre I said hello."

"I will," he said as he leaned over the table and kissed me gently, rose from the table, and left the restaurant. I sat there thinking to myself, I'm really, really liking this man. And I can't wait for him to get back in town, ready to pick back up where we left off.

Nineteen

THE NIGHT CAME and went and thoughts of Charles filled the warmest parts of my heart. Vivid images of him creeped into every corner, every crevice of my mind. Over these past few weeks he had made the kind of impression that would leave no room for doubt, no question or fear or moment to pause. He was exactly that which he had represented himself to be and, despite everything I had been through, he had slowly and surely begun mending the broken pieces, stitching my heart back together with threads of kindness, consideration, and care. He was a straight-up kind of man. The kind of man that finally *was* a man. These thoughts continued to race through my mind as I drifted off into the most peaceful slumber, praying to God that His arm of protection cover Charles and at the appointed time return him safely back home. To me.

The next morning I awoke to another long day of contracts, clients, and cases. But I made sure to check in with Tess every other half hour on the hour for the call I was expecting—no call. I suspected the time had gotten away from him. From his back-to-back-to-back meetings, he was obviously tied up and tonight he would call. He was sure to call me when I was nestled in bed, with just the right words to send me off into another night of peaceful rest. The night came and went and there was no call from Charles. I was getting worried. Still trusting and believing everything was okay. It would take more than a day's missed call to rock me from the pedestal I had claimed to be on.

The next day came and went. Calls to the front desk, now every half hour on the hour, and still nothing from Charles. The night was pretty much the same as I still had faith. Praying to God this time to make whatever excuse he had for not calling a good one. And I put in an extra prayer for myself: Lord, please help me to find words other than the ones floating in my mind for when I do eventually speak to him. God, please remove the words like, "What took your bitch ass so long to call me." Amen I said. Amen again. And the night came and went.

The next day I checked every fifteen minutes and still no call from Charles. Now it had been more than the three days that he claimed to be gone. Another night came and went and still no word. This time God was the last thing on my mind as the flashbacks of men gone bad haunted me. By now the devil was busy as my mental hard drive had downloaded almost every negative thought I could find and deleted the good times, the walks, the talks, the late-night dinners turned desserts. I was going through it, preparing myself for the worst, accepting the fact that we had come full circle—our relationship, our sparkle, our connection had ended in the same place it had begun—Paris. At the office the next day it was business as usual. Altima appeared in my office.

"Hey, girl," she said tentatively, knowing me too well not to have noticed the seismic shift in my universe.

"Hey."

"I tried to call you last night, but when you didn't answer, I thought maybe you were talking to Charles," she said. "You were talking to Charles, weren't you?" she said, hoping a yes would come from my mouth.

Looking up momentarily from my work, the look on my face was just the answer she had feared.

"Well, he's probably just busy. France is a big place. He's going to call. Watch. Just when you least expect it. He's gotta call. And will call."

Immediately the doors swung open. And it was Ophelia, standing with a smirk on her face.

"We were having a private conversation," Altima snorted.

"In a public workspace. Impossible," she said, as she walked closer to my desk, placing on it from behind her back a miniature pumpkin.

"It's a gift."

"For what?" I asked. "Halloween is almost eight months away."

"Oh, it's not for Halloween," she said. "It's symbolic."

"Of what?" I asked.

"Of the clock having struck twelve, and your white horse having transformed into a pumpkin."

"Ophelia, you evil, gooney, goo-goo-looking bitch. How could you do something like that?" said Altima.

"Oh, please. Better I say it than somebody else who doesn't even care."

"And you care."

"Yes, I care that she's been setting herself up for this ever since she sashayed back from Paris using broken French every day."

"I don't care what you say. We owe it to her to keep hope alive."

"No," Ophelia countered, "We owe it to her to pull the plug and let hope die. It's been on life support ever since he left."

"How 'bout I pull the plug, then wrap the cord around your thick-ass neck and choke the shit out of you with it. How 'bout that?!"

"You know what, Altima . . . ?"

"What?"

"I'm just about sick of you. You want some of me?"

"Yeah. All three thousand pounds of you."

"Morgan . . ." Tess chimed in, "you have a visitor in the lobby. It's him," she whispered over the phone's intercom. Instantly their arguing came to an abrupt halt.

"What am I gonna do?" I said.

"What you mean, what you gonna do? You're gonna go out there and get him.

"Girl, it's like *Mahogany*. Remember when Billy Dee went all the way to France to get her? Well, he came all the way from France to get you. That's even better," she said as she looked at Ophelia, who was staring with a look of bewilderment on her face.

"Girl, this is soooooo romantic. Wait a minute; let me fix your face. And your outfit, let me check you out. Okay, you're cool. Now, go get your man. Or let your man get you. Girl, just go get got!"

Taking a deep sigh, I walked out of my office, all the while thinking of a million scenarios in my own mind that he would use to make it right, or that maybe he had stayed over, gotten laid over, and fell in love with some Frenchwoman and he's here to bid me a French farewell. That's it. That's it. That's it.

Rounding the corner, there he was, standing with his purple orchid, looking like he leaped off the cover of *Fortune* magazine. His smile was as warm as July.

"Morgan," he said, "I missed you so much."

"So much that you couldn't wait to call me," I said as the lines to the office rang off the hook. Tess was obviously too engrossed in our conversation to answer them.

"I wanted to call."

"Then why didn't you?"

"I don't know. Everything was happening so fast. I guess I just needed some time to be sure this is what I wanted. That you were who I wanted," he said.

"And? Are you sure?" I asked, as by now Tess had a Kleenex in her hand and sniffles in her nose.

"As sure as the air that I breathe. As sure as the sound of my heart that nearly burst from my chest each time I thought of you. Is that enough sure for you?"

"Yes!" It was Tess blurting out her own emotion, then pausing to quickly adjust her glasses, regain her composure, and resume answering the now more than ten calls she had placed on hold.

"So," he said with a smile, "it's obviously sure enough for the receptionist. So, what about you?" he asked tentatively, but still confidently. "Am I sure enough for you?" Out of the corner I could see Altima nodding her head for me to say yes, while Ophelia, who was standing right beside her, nearly shook her head from her shoulders motioning no.

"Yes, Charles. It's sure enough," I said. "Just don't let it happen again."

"I won't. I promise," he said, with a look of sincerity and conviction.

Twenty

ANOTHER WEEK went by and sure enough, it happened again. He was missing in action. Our get-togethers were random at best. Afterthoughts. Penciled-in quickies to steal a moment there, grab a bite to eat here.

Nothing remotely like the ferocity or frequency that had grown to become the norm over the past four weeks. Ever since his return trip from Paris, things seemed to change. According to Altima our relationship, like a house, was just going through its settling period. A time where there's bound to be a few cracks. According to my mother, grumbling makes the loaf no larger. In her words, half a loaf is better than no loaf at all. And, according to Ophelia, he's only merely communicating what he's always been communicating.

The only difference is now, without the sound of my heart beating, the mute button is off and I can finally hear the real deal loud and clear. These were thoughts that jockeyed for mental position as I left from work and headed home for a much-needed break from preparing for the *Monroe v. the City of Philadelphia* case that was almost a month and a half away. Into the garage and up the stairs I was weighing and balancing the suggestions, admonitions, and premonitions that were swirling about. I had heard almost every opinion, every angle, every theorem, postulate, and old wives' tale from almost every person in my life who mattered. And in Ophelia's case, even those who didn't matter. I had just about heard from everyone in my life except . . .

"Sex in the City."

Except Andre. The most socially irrelevant, romantically deficient person on the planet. Which is probably just what the doctor ordered, given that I was making neither head nor tail of my current state of affairs.

"Hey, Andre," I said in an unusually welcoming tone. "How are you today? I like your outfit."

"It's shorts and a tank top," he replied, looking suspicious.

"To some maybe, but to you, it's image. It's art. It's fashion."

"Morgan, have you been smoking?"

"Why would you ask that?" I said with a look of bewilderment.

"Why? Oh, I don't know . . . 'cause you're acting strange again. Which means you're either starting yet another strange relationship, ending a strange relationship, or on the cusp—dangling between the two. Which one is it?"

"The latter," I said.

"How did I guess?" he replied. "Well," he said licking his lips gently, changing his posture, shifting his voice several octaves lower. "You know what they say."

"No, Andre, what do they say?" I replied, setting myself up for an obvious curveball.

"You can go all around the world trying to find your perfect someone, just to find out that he's been right up under your nose, living right next door to you—all along," he said.

"Figuratively speaking, you're probably right."

"No, literally. Right next door. Apartment Two B. The home of a man who cares. And even if he doesn't and kicks you out of the bed like all the other men, at least you won't have far to go," he said with a grin that slowly faded from his face as he noticed my usual returned grin or giggle or laughter was nowhere to be found. "Get it? Next door. Mo? You didn't laugh."

"I get it," I said, half-involved, half in my own world of distant thoughts.

"No chuckle, or nothing. Wow. You must be really going through it. What's up?" he asked.

"I don't know. It's the guy I'm seeing. Charles."

"Charles is the one after Marcus?" he asked, scratching his head.

"Yes."

"The one after Terrance?"

"Yes."

"Who messed you over before Kevin got a crack at it. Who ran mad game on you before Calvin hit the scene, shattering almost every hope you ever had of being happy. Before him it was—"

"Andre!" I said, cutting him off.

"I was just making sure I had the proper chain of pain. Now, what's up with this one? What's his problem, baby momma drama? In between jobs? What?"

"None of that. He's a good guy. Has a great career. Treats me right. I don't know. Everything was flowing just fine and all of a sudden—I don't know. He just got silent all of a sudden. I mean, we have a lot of fun together. The sex is incredible. I don't know what it is."

"What about the added value?" he asked.

"I just told you. We have great fun. Great sex. How much more value needs to be added?"

"A man can get fun and sex anywhere. That's not saying much. I'm talking about added value. What are you giving him that he can't get anywhere else?"

Noticing a puzzled expression on my face, he elaborated.

"Okay, so peep game. Say a woman has a man that has money. But he doesn't make her laugh. That's where I come in. I make her laugh. Tell her jokes, do stupid stuff, and all the while she's giggling, panties is sliding down her ankles. Why? Added value. I gave her something she wasn't getting at home. Or conversely, say a woman has a man who makes her laugh and he has money, but he's not spending any time with her. That's where I come in. I start leaving her 'just because' messages. Didn't want nothing. Didn't really say nothing—I called her just because. Pretty soon we're eating lunch together. Pretty soon she's over the crib and we're watching *Oprah* together. And then before you know it, I'm laying mad pipe. Why? Because I listened to her. Made her believe her opinion mattered. Now, say a woman already has a man that listens and makes her laugh, but he's broke—what do I do?"

"You give her money," I said, following the obvious pattern.

"Hell no! I move on the next one. Added value is giving some-body something that you have—follow me here. Added value is try-ing harder. Bringing more to the table than just the napkin holder and the cups. It's creating an atmosphere or an environment con-ducive to getting some real shit done. A brother's shoe a little dusty—take them to get shined. Shirts a little wrinkled—drop 'em off at the cleaners. Hooking a man up with what he needs before he even realizes that he needs it—added value."

Added value, I thought to myself. "I never thought of it like that. Thanks, Andre. That helped out a lot," I said, leaning over and kiss-ing him on the cheek, and then turning to my door.

"Whoa—wait, wait wait."

"What?"

"My name is Andre, not Oprah. That shit ain't free. That's valu-able advice into the mainframe of a man's mind. I tapped you into the real shit. Took you behind the veil. Gave you the inside track. Violated the code. Betrayed the brotherhood. And all I get is a kiss on the cheek? A dry one, at that. You could have at least licked your lips and made 'em a little moist. Something."

"I was just taking your advice. Giving you something that you're not getting from all your other women—rejection. Good night," I said, leaving him standing there dumbfounded.

"That's where you're wrong," he said, shouting through the door. "I get rejected all the time! What do you think about that?!" he said, as I heard his door slam closed. I sat there thinking to myself what added value would would I bring to Charles's life.

Twenty-One

FOR ALMOST that entire night I meditated on Andre's added value advice and what I could do to differentiate myself. To even further distance myself from the pack of his past or the lack of his present. Shortly after we met, I remembered he mentioned needing to adjust his warrantee contracts to stay competitive with current market standards. Since that specific area wasn't my specialty, I just listened, deciding not to pry. But given my most recent conversation with Andre, this might be just the added value added.

That night, after yet another late-night session with Michael and the Monroe case, I called ol' faithful—I called in Altima. As usual, she arrived with brown bags filled with tin pans, Tupperware bowls, biscuits, cakes, pies, and every other edible delight, as together we began downloading miles of files, researching the automobile industry. For the next several nights it was a crash course in the world of cars.

"Girl, do you want to learn about preowned dealerships or open one of your own?" Altima asked. For even more nights we continued, only taking a break for an occasional sidebar gossip session about what was going on in the firm. Who was hiring who, firing who. What new cases and clients were circling about. Altima convinced me that the Monroe case was still top priority at the firm and all eyes were still on Michael and me and our ability to quench the fires of what had the potential of igniting a political firestorm throughout the city. Michael was depending on me and even though I was burning the candle at both ends, still I was sharp, on point, and all signs seemed to point to the fact that he was more than pleased with my performance.

Now with more than enough research on the automobile industry, I gave Charles a call and set up a time to stop by the dealership. As was the case lately, he was overly busy, which signaled to me that he was underly interested. Still, I pushed forward and made a surprise visit. Looking by absolute best, of course.

"Hey," he said, leaning over and kissing me on the lips and then walking away as I stood there for a moment, marinating in my pensive feelings. "I'm glad you stopped by; I'm in the middle of inventory getting ready in two weeks for my biggest shipment ever. You remember my friend Pierre who you met in Paris?" he asked, as he almost never took his eyes off of his paperwork.

"How could I forget?" I responded. "He was with that very beautiful Frenchwoman in the blue-green scarf."

"Wow," he said, "you remembered what she had on? Anyway, we closed the deal and he's exporting five hundred of his finest low-mileage preowned luxury cars. So, we're in the process of clearing out the old and making room for the new."

"That's good news, right? You should do well."

"Oh, we'll do well. We'll probably have a line wrapped around the block, full of people who can't wait to get into the cars."

"Sounds like even better news."

"It is, only for one problem."

"What's that?" I asked.

"The federal government just passed a new regulation forcing preowned automobile dealerships to provide new buyers with a ten-page report fully disclosing past automobile repair and maintenance history. Which, of course, most preowned cars don't have. Pretty much they come in as is. They cost less, but the risk is more. That's been the game before I got into the business and it'll be the game long after I'm gone. The difference now is, because of the new regulation, either we provide the detailed reports, or we're forced to change the terms in the warranty that more closely match the ones the new car dealerships provide. It's a mess. And two weeks before the biggest shipment of the year arrives."

"Well, what happens if the cars arrive and the warranties aren't in place?"

"Well, then any buyer that has any problem can invoke the lemon clause, which means either I replace the car with the same or its equivalent, or I give a full refund—which will mean the end of my business as we know it," he said, letting out an uncharacteristic sigh. Obviously this had been weighing heavily on him. And because of my now greater grasp of the business, it was the perfect segue into my added value.

"That just means you have to whip up a new warranty that combines the necessary government standards with your necessary margin of profit."

"Yeah, but in less than two weeks that would take a small army of high-priced lawyers."

"Or, one very motivated, and highly incentivized, female lawyer, who's been doing her own set of research for the past week on warranties, guarantees, and the nature of the preowned automobile industry." His eyes grew wide.

"Are you serious?" he asked, as all the rumbling and rustling of his paperwork came to an instant halt.

"Serious as the heart attack you were apparently having a minute before I walked into your office."

"But how would you know about preowned automobile contracts?" he asked, curiously.

"Oh, well," I said, in my mind generating the quickest and most bulletproof lie I could think of. "One of the clients who was divorcing was trying to figure out a settlement for the nine cars that they owned. I was asked to assess their value, and so that's when I began researching cars and contracts. The more I got into it, the more interested I became, and since I said . . ." now myself turning away for dramatic effect, "since I knew this was the business you were in, I figured maybe what I was learning might one day come in handy for you. It looks like that one day is today, huh?"

"Looks like," he said, as his expression changed, his mood warmed up, and almost instantly the Charles I had first met reappeared.

"I can't ask you to go through all of these contracts."

"You're not asking. I'm offering, How 'bout that?" I said as from my periphery I noticed a sparkle in his eye.

"And you're serious," he said. "You'd do this for me?"

"Why not," I said. "You're a smart businessman who's used to assessing worth and then assigning the proper value. I'm sure you'll make it worth my while. And if not," I said, slowly turning and locking his eyes in mine, "I know where you live. I know where you work. I'll just stalk you until you make it right."

"Well, that's assuming there was ever anything wrong in the first place," he said as the room began to get slightly warmer with each step closer. "In the automobile business, it's what we call preventive maintenance," he said.

"Is that right?" I replied, in full play. "And how does one assess whether it has been properly maintained or not in the first place?" I said, feeling myself melting into the moment.

"Probably the most accurate way is for one to simply check under the hood," he said, as his hands began sliding across the small of my back.

"Or take it on a test drive around a block or two," I added with my hand now on his tie, pulling his face down closer to mine.

"I might need more than just a block or two," he replied.

"As long as you keep the tank full, you can drive it as long as you want," I said, as we could both no longer control ourselves. Passionately he kissed me. Just like the first time, he kissed me. And the next day we kissed. In between work, we stopped to play, and still we kissed. Late-night sessions in his offices from one stack to the next, from computer to printer to copy machine, we kissed. It was better than ever. Some nights kissing led to rubbing, which eventually led to cuddling on his office couch. Night after night we continued. And even though my body no longer knew or even cared to know its limits or its need for rest and refueling, in my mind my mission was accomplished. My man was back in pocket. Now, beyond the shadow of a doubt, I was assured that my value had been added.

Twenty-Two

IT WAS MONDAY morning and there was extra pep in my step. I had spent almost the entire weekend in sweet and peaceful slumber, taking a break from the feverish pace that had defined my last several weeks. Ringers turned off, cell phone shut off, and in my hand was the remote control to guide me to my favorite television pastime—black-and-white movies. I left the bed only to bathe and for an occasional trip to the front door to pay the food delivery man. Before I left home, I retrieved the completely full set of messages from my answering machine: my mother, Altima, and even Charles had left a couple of messages, thanking me and looking forward to making good on his promise of a reward. In my mind, the only reward was knowing that things were back to normal. Moving forward. Climbing higher. I was one step closer to a quid pro quo relationship. I was in a good space.

I bounced into the office, noticing Tess staring, her eyes glossy, starry, looking right through me. The look that could only mean there were—

"More flowers," she said. "They're in your office." I had obviously interrupted the vicarious romantic moment she was enjoying.

Heading back to my office—

"Good morning, Morgan."

"Morning, Morgan."

"Morgan, good morning." All the greetings were kind, and I couldn't wait to reach my office, feeling that at this very moment it couldn't possibly get any better.

Finally I opened the door, and there was a fabulous arrangement of exotic flowers on one end of my desk. Hovering over the other end was, of course, Altima, with the card from the flowers in her hand.

"This is so romantic," she said. "He wants to spend a surprise evening with you. Tonight," she said, handing me the note to read for myself.

Charles had invited me for dinner at an undisclosed restaurant for that evening. He ended the note with: "Looking forward to making good even better."

"Things must be back to normal," she said.

"Back and better than ever," I said, in almost mid-celebration, as the door swung open to reveal . . . Ophelia.

"Not so fast," she said.

"Not so fast what?" I asked.

"You know what. The dinner with Charles tonight."

"You read the note?"

"Of course I read the note. But don't get too happy too fast. Some information has leaked out to the press regarding alleged sexual improprieties that were going on up in the mayor's office while he was on the clock. I was in the break room looking at the news and that's all they're talking about. His office is covered with reporters," said Ophelia.

"But what does that have to do with me?"

"Yeah. It's not like she leaked any information. It's not her fault he couldn't keep his hormones under control. That's his problem," Altima continued.

"Grow up, Altima. This firm is handling his divorce. If he's got a problem, this firm has a problem. And more specifically, you got a problem."

"I don't have a problem," I said. "I'm committed to this firm, but I have a life, too, you know."

"No, you don't. Law is your life."

"No, my life is my life. Law is what I do, it's not who I am," I said.

"So, that's what you're going to tell Michael if he were to walk in here right now?"

"That's right," Altima said. "She ain't no punk and she ain't selling her soul to the firm, like some of us. She's her own woman. She had a life before here and she'll have a life after here."

"Excuse me, ladies." The door swung open and it was Michael Sampson, looking a bit undone.

"Big problem," he said. "I don't know if you've been watching the news, but the mayor's in the hot seat and guess who's got to find a way to cool it down. We have an emergency session with him tonight. Bring your pillow," he said as he turned and walked away.

"But I can't," I blurted out as both Ophelia and Altima's eyes popped out of their heads. Slowly Michael turned with a look of confusion.

"Can't what?" he asked.

"I can't work tonight," I said, awkwardly.

"What do you mean, you can't work tonight?"

"I mean, I had plans," I said. "It would be almost impossible to change them at this short notice."

"If this case continues to escalate because we weren't on top of our game, and because of it, the mayor's political future is jeopardized, one of us will have all the time to make all the engagements in the world. You know why? Because one of us will be unemployed. Do you have any idea which one of us that is?"

"You?" I asked, coyly.

Shaking his head as he chuckled softly. "Guess again."

"Me?" I asked.

Nodding his head he confirmed. "So, tonight, I suggest you make the impossible happen. Are we clear?"

"Crystal," I replied.

"Ladies," he said, as he once again headed for the door. Pausing he turned and said, "Oh, and nice flowers. You should send a dozen back along with a rain check for sometime next week." He winked and then closed the door behind me as I thought to myself, No way my dinner would be delayed more than a day. Two at most.

Twenty-Three

IT HAD BEEN two weeks of dinner delays. Every night, even the weekends, it was either a meeting with the mayor himself, his aides, or his assistants; one night we even met with his chef. Everybody jockeying for position, hoping their testimony would add some clarity here or lessen the severity there. Everyone seemed of one mind and on one accord. It was as if they had all read the same script. Rehearsed the same part. Like they were all cast for the same role for the same film. No doubt there was a mayoral mandate to squash any and all allegations affecting the mayor—their meal ticket.

By now I was thinking, Damn their meal ticket, what about my own? Each night I called Charles to cancel and he gracefully understood, keeping his calendar open as we penciled in only to eventually cancel one dinner date after the other. He never once made me feel bad. Always encouraging me to handle my business. Still, the better part of me couldn't help but to wish that this case would swiftly come to a close. But each day came with yet another layer of deception, alleged corruption, and the reality of the downside of a man just being a man.

As counsel I was duty bound to look at the facts and weigh the evidence toward my client, and in that respect I was giving it my all.

Steadfast and on point, I was. As a lawyer, I had his back. But as a woman, it was another question altogether. I could see why his wife was suing him, threatening him, ruining him. The mayor wasn't the most considerate man on the planet. He was arrogant. Self-centered. Controlling. It was as if the world revolved around his schedule and his desire to protect his political and financial future, both of which he would need to cover the bill that as of now was nearing the hundred thousand-dollar mark. Even more nights continued when, to my surprise, Michael pulled me aside.

"It looks like we're finally getting this under control," he said. "You're doing a great job. Take a few days to catch your breath."

"You mean," I said almost in tears, "I can go home and not come back."

"That's right," he said. "But don't get used to it. We still have a long way to go," he continued.

Like a runaway slave I fled, barely allowing the words "good night" to escape from his lips. In record time I was in the elevator and into my car, not giving him time enough to change or shift or alter his mind. It was 6:30 P.M. Time enough for me to make a beeline to my apartment, take off my work clothes and put on my play clothes. Hopefully in the not too far distant future I'd be free of all my clothes, wrapped up, tied up, and tangled up in Charles. The receptionist at his office said that he had left work early, that he seemed to be coming down with a cold.

Right away I called his home, where after three rings the answering machine came on. On his car phone and cell phone it was the same. I had left messages on every phone and was home waiting for his call.

The phone rang, and in mid-first ring I answered. "Charles?" I said.

"No, girl, it's me."

"Altima, I can't talk now."

"Why not?"

"I'm waiting on a call."

"You have call waiting," she said.

"I know. But sometimes the call you're not waiting for comes in at the same time the call that you're waiting for comes in, then you're stuck on the phone talking to the person that you don't want to be talking to while the person you want to be talking to goes straight to voicemail because instead of waiting for the call you wanted you answered the call you didn't want."

"Morgan," she said.

"Yeah."

"What the hell are you talking about?"

"What I'm talking about is I can't talk to you right now. I'll call you later."

"Morgan," she said, raising her voice.

"What?"

"Calm down, girl. He's gonna call you."

"I know, but . . ."

"Morgan. There are no buts. Relax. You left a message for him, right?"

"I left five messages for him on all five of his phones."

"Morgan."

"What?"

"Don't leave another message for that man, okay? He's probably just wrapping up some business and when he's done he's gonna call you. Now relax, okay?"

"Okay," I said as the phone beeped, signaling another call coming in—it was a blocked number, probably him calling.

"Altima, I gotta go. That's a call coming in. It's probably him."

"But, girl—"

"No buts, I love you, 'bye," I said, clicking over.

"Charles?" I asked, eagerly anticipating his voice.

"I just got in from church tonight, I was calling to check on you." It was my mother. "It was missionary jubilee and Pastor Bryant out of Baltimore came in and preached. He's a good-looking young man. And single, too. I asked him if he was seeing anybody and he just smiled and shook his head no. I showed him your picture and he said the next time he was in town he'd love to meet you," she said, as usual never taking a breath or pause. "I told him that you were a member here at the church; even though you haven't really been in over a year, once a member, always a member, that's what I say."

"Momma," I said, cutting her off, "I don't mean to cut you off, but I'm expecting a really important call. Can I call you back?" I asked.

"You know you can always call me back. I didn't want much of nothing, you know, I was just calling to check on you like I always do when I come back home or when I'm gone away, I don't know, I guess it's just a habit of mine and you know what they say about old habits, sometimes old habits are like an old cough—they just seem to linger and before you know it, you wake up one day and—"

"Momma, I really have to go. I'll call you back. Okay?"

"You don't have to call me back, I'm okay, I'll talk to you tomorrow morning before I get my hair done. You know I have an appointment—"

"Momma."

"That's right, baby, you said you have to go. Well, you just call me tomorrow and we'll catch up. You tell that man of yours I said hello."

"I will."

"He's a good man. You tell him I said so, too, and to take care of my baby."

"I will. I'll call you tomorrow. Good night, Momma," I said.

"Good—"

I hung up the phone in the middle of the words "good night" for fear the words might lead to another run-on sentence, leading to another run-on paragraph where, before you know it, you're in the midst of another run-on conversation.

Looking at the clock on the wall it was 7:45. Flipping through the television channels, it was 8:45, and flipping through even more it was 9:45, then 10:45, and then 11:45, and . . . nothing. Before the clock struck twelve I was fast asleep. The next morning I left five more messages from my office, and still nothing. His assistant at the office offered the same bit of generic information that he was out sick and periodically checking his messages from home. I was starting to get worried about him. Maybe he was too sick to pick up the phone and call. Like most men he's probably curled up in bed, roughing it out with leftovers, TV dinners, Pizza Hut and a Coke. He's probably over there needing a little TLC and a home-cooked meal. So why not just swing by and drop off one? It was the perfect idea. One that I was sure Altima would agree to.

"Are you out of your mind!" she said into the phone.

"What's the big deal?"

"The big deal is that he doesn't know you're coming. You never, ever drop by a man's house unannounced."

"I'm not dropping by unannounced. I'm bringing him some soup, that's it."

"That's it?"

"That's it."

"That's it?"

"That's it," I said. "What?"

"You know that's not it. You may be going over there to drop off some soup, but you're also going over there to snoop. Something you promised you wouldn't do. Remember?"

"I'm not snooping, okay? I'm souping," I said. "That's it."

"That's it?"

"That's it. I'm on my way."

"What for? I'm not going with you?"

"I don't need you to go with me. I need your soup to go with me."

"I'm sorry, Mo, I can't make you any soup."

"Why not?"

"One, because I have a lot of work to do and I could use the overtime. And two, that would make me an accomplice."

"To what?"

"To snooping."

"I'm not snooping," I screamed into the phone. "I'm just dropping off some soup. That's it."

"That's it?"

"That's it. Now, either you're going to give me some of your soup, or I'm going to drive by a restaurant and pick up some of theirs. Either way, I'm souping."

"I still think this is a bad idea."

"And I still think it's a good idea."

So I stopped into a restaurant that Altima recommended, grabbed some of their "just like Momma's" soup and crackers and a piece of cake. Back in my car I was on my way to Charles's house, where my only agenda was goodwill for a good man. That's my story and I'm sticking with it.

Twenty-Four

THE SCENT OF CREAM of chicken soup filled the insides of my car as through the winding roads of Mount Airy my car bobbed and weaved its way to Charles's house. Regardless of what Altima was thinking, I wasn't snooping. Really, I wasn't. I was doing for him what I would hope he would do for me. It's no big deal. I was gonna just drive up to his house, ring the doorbell, drop off the soup, and leave. That's it. No sting. No stakeout. No FBI investigation. I was just going to drop off the soup and leave. No big deal.

For some reason, my heart started beating out of my chest when I rounded the last corner. All of a sudden I started feeling guilty. But for what? I was just souping, not snooping. That's it. All of a sudden little sweat beads formed on my forehead. It's no big deal, I kept repeating to myself. It's no big deal. I turned down the radio and turned off my lights. There was no need to wake up the rest of the neighborhood, I thought, parking nearly a hundred feet from his house.

As hard as I tried to fight it, my womanly instincts kicked in—I was no longer souping, I had officially begun snooping. This is ridiculous. I took a deep breath, cleared my head of Altima's warning, grabbed the bag of soup, and walked to his house like I was a woman with good sense, intending for the only thing stirring up to be the soup.

The lights were dim, only the faint flicker of a television filled the second-story bedroom window. With one hand on the doorbell, I took another deep breath and pressed it softly. After a few moments, there was no response. I pressed it slowly again. Still no response. Maybe he was asleep. From my cell phone I dialed his number, where from outside I could hear it chiming through the house. No luck again as the answering machine came on.

I rang the doorbell one more time and then decided to leave and maybe just try it again tomorrow. Just as I was hitting the end of his walkway I heard the door open, and it was Charles, standing in a robe, slightly disheveled, like he had just awakened.

"Hey," he said.

"Hey," I replied from a distance as an awkward silence filled the air.

"I tried calling you, but couldn't reach you."

"Yeah, I've been kind of under the weather for the past couple days. I figured I'd just take a few days off and get some rest."

"That's a good idea. I did the same thing myself last weekend, you know."

"Yeah, I know," he said, as again there was silence.

"Anyway, when I called your office and found out you weren't feeling well, I whipped you up some homemade soup since you probably haven't eaten anything healthy lately, being locked up in the house and all. I figured I'd come by and drop it off. So, that's why I'm here," I said, holding the brown bag up in front of me.

"You didn't have to do that," he said.

"I know. I just figured, you'd do it for me, right?"

"I would."

"So, why not do it for you?" I said, walking up to his door, handing him the bag.

"Thanks," he said.

"You're welcome," I replied, as there was even more silence. "So," I said allowing it to linger.

"So," he replied with a linger of his own. "I would invite you in, but I should probably get back in the bed."

"Right. No, I wasn't trying to come in. I was just snooping—souping, I mean. I was just souping," I said as in the corner of my eye I noticed a woman's blue-green scarf dangling from a table in his foyer.

"Is something wrong?" he asked, obviously noticing my pause.

"No," I said. "I was just noticing the scarf on the table. Funny," I said, manufacturing a chuckle, "it looks like the scarf Michelle was wearing that day we met for lunch in Paris."

"While I was in Paris I was staying with Pierre, his housekeeper must've packed it in my bag by mistake."

"Right," I said. "So, I guess I'll call you tomorrow so we can set a dinner date that I've been missing for the past couple weeks."

"I can't wait," he said.

"Yeah, neither can I," I said, now feeling slightly uncomfortable. "Well, I hope you feel better."

"Me, too."

"Good night."

"Good night. And thanks for the soup. I'm sure it's just what the doctor ordered."

"Good night," I said again as I turned and began walking to my car thinking, Why did I bring up the scarf? Stupid, stupid, stupid. Now he probably thinks I was snooping. From behind me I heard the door close. I couldn't wait to get into my car and away from his house. I turned on the car and noticed on the passenger's side floor the crackers and cake were still there—they had obviously rolled out of the bag and onto the floor during the roads filled with curves and swerves. I sighed, weighing whether I should give him the crackers and dessert or go home. If I give him the crackers and dessert, he'll really think I'm snooping. If I don't, he'll know I was snooping because nobody in their right mind brings over soup without bread or crackers. This is ridiculous. I'm going to give him the crackers and the cake and stop making something out of nothing. This time I even drove up to his house, got out of the car, and again rang the doorbell. After a few moments the door opened.

"Hey," he said.

"Hey, Charles, I'm sorry, on the way up to your house, the bag must've fallen over and these fell out," I said holding the crackers and cake. "No soup is complete without crackers and no meal is complete without dessert. I brought you some homemade upside down pineapple cake."

"Thanks," he said.

"You're welcome," I said. "So, I'll call you tomorrow and check on you."

"You better," he said. "Drive carefully."

"I will," I said, turning to leave. "Charles, I have to be honest."

"About what?" he replied.

"My intention for coming over here was to bring you the soup. That's all. But on the way I just got a little crazy thinking that you might think me coming over here was me trying to check up on you or something. But it's not. I trust you. And I just wanted to do something to make you feel better."

"Well, you have," he said. "So . . ."

"So . . ." I said, as I noticed the sound of the television disappeared.

"Oh," I said. "Your television just cut off."

"Yeah," he said. "It's on a timer. I thought I'd be asleep by now and didn't want it to stay on all night," he said without pause.

"Right. I do the same thing myself sometimes."

Then suddenly I noticed a light shining down the stairs. Noticing that I had noticed it, he stared for a moment, frozen. "So, call me tomorrow," he said. "And thanks again for the soup."

"Do you have company?" I asked.

"Why would you ask that?" he said, looking confused.

"A light just went on upstairs."

"I thought you said you were souping."

"I am," I said.

"Then why does it feel like you're snooping?"

"I'm not snooping, Charles, I just wanted to know if you have company. Is that too difficult a question?"

"Yes, I have company. I had a friend fly in from out of town for a couple days. To save them money, I let them stay with me."

"A friend?"

"A friend."

"Charles, could you bring me something to drink?"

It was the voice of the woman from France whose scarf was on the table.

"Is that who I think it is?"

"It depends on who you think it is," he said, unaffected.

"Is that the woman we met together with Pierre? Did the housekeeper accidentally pack her, too," I said.

Silent, he stood never uttering a word.

"Charles, what's going on?"

"What's going on is it's late, I'm not feeling well, and you stopped by my house uninvited and now you're jumping to conclusions," he said.

"Jumping to conclusions?" I said. "Conclusions," I repeated, my voice getting louder. "You think I'm stupid. Is that what you think?"

"No, I think you're being too loud, that's what I think. I live in a nice neighborhood. Could you please keep it down?" he said.

"Could I keep it down?"

"Yes."

"Could I keep it down? Ain't this about a . . ." Not believing what was going on, I just stood for a moment in awe. "So, that's why you didn't call me from Paris, 'cause you were with her. You know what, Charles, that's real fucked up. Here I am worrying about you and you got some French bitch up in your bedroom. So you don't have nothing to say," I said.

"Seems like you've got enough to say for us both."

"You know what . . . ?" I said, too angry for words. "This is real fucked up, Charles," I said, turning and walking to the car, rolling down all my windows and turning the music as high as I could, going no miles per hour and leaning on the horn from his house around the corner and out of his neighborhood as nearly every house and every light lit up, giving his nice neighborhood a taste of ghetto love gone bad.

Twenty-Five

ON MY WAY to work the next morning, I was in an all-too-familiar state of mind. I tossed and turned the night away, scanning for clues, hints, or anything close to a sign signaling we were heading where we were obviously heading. After spending almost the entire night shifting back and forth between both casting the blame and taking the blame, I had once again resigned myself to the fact that given time and opportunity, a man will no doubt be a man. Once again, I found myself racing to work, my only safe haven. My sole escape, where I would once again dive heart first into miles and piles of clients, cases, and legal mumbo jumbo. Like never before, I desperately needed to distance myself as far from my pain as I possibly could.

First step was to remove all traces of Charles. Erase the thought, the scent, light a candle, burn incense, open the windows—whatever I could to somehow return to myself BC—before Charles. I swiftly rushed past Tess, barely giving her room for her daily greeting.

Past the lawyers' office and into my office. First things first. All cards in the garbage and flowers one by one, branch by branch, followed flying into the can. Prying open my one jammed window, I ushered in the frigid air. Out with the old and in with the new. The candle was lit and there I sat in my office, lights off, behind my desk, as the wind whipped through the room and the candle's stem flickered, swaying back and forth—healing had begun.

The door swung open slowly, causing an air vacuum that sent the papers from my desk flying across the room. It was Altima.

"Hey, girl."

"Hey."

"Are you all right?" she asked.

"Why wouldn't I be all right?"

"Maybe because you're sitting in a dark office with a candle burning, at nine o'clock in the morning."

"What's wrong with that?"

"Nothing, if you're about to get your palm read. Aren't you cold? It's freezing in here."

"No, I'm okay."

"Well, I'm not," she said, flicking on the light switch, blowing out the candle, and going over to the window and pulling it shut.

"Mo, I'm worried about you."

"Well, don't. I'm all right."

"You're not all right."

"I *am* all right."

"Maybe you should take a day off," she said.

"And do what?"

"Whatever," she said. "I mean, after last night . . ."

"Last night was last night. I'm over it. Shit happens, right? I've moved on. I'm over it."

"You're over it?"

"I'm over it."

"Well, maybe you should call him."

"For what?"

"Yeah, for what?" The door swung open and it was Ophelia. "Time for talking is over. It's time for getting."

"Getting mad?" Altima said.

"Getting even," Ophelia said.

"What are you talking about, Ophelia?"

"What am I talking about?"

"Yeah."

"Duh? You have a contract, right? Sue his ass. Do what the mayor's wife is doing."

"Ophelia, I'm not going to sue him."

"She's not going to sue him," Altima added.

"Why not?"

" 'Cause she, unlike you, is not crazy, that's why not."

"Crazy is letting a man get away with a crime without making him do some time. Crazy is coming to work after catching a man cheating on you with another woman, and moving on with your life like nothing happened. Crazy is discovering a cure to end an epidemic and doing nothing with it. Morgan, the contract is the cure. You can end the epidemic. You have the power to make a difference. To right every wrong for every woman that's ever gone through or is about to go through what you're going through. You have the power to change history. To send a message to any man who's ever cheated on any woman that lying, cheating, and breaking hearts is a crime. A crime that because of you will be punishable in a court of law."

"I can't take him to court."

"Why not?"

"Because I'd be the laughingstock of Philadelphia."

"Or you'd be the Joan of Arc of America," Ophelia said. "That's a gamble I'd take. And besides, this would be a lawyer's dream. To set a precedent. This could be the biggest case since Brown versus the Board of Education. Plessy versus Ferguson. This is bigger than O.J. There's not a lawyer on the planet that wouldn't die to try this in court."

"Like who?"

"Like who? Like me," she said.

"You?" Altima said.

"Yeah, me. Why not?"

"Why not, 'cause you've never tried a case on your own, that's why not," Altima said.

"Not because I'm not good enough to, but because I'm a woman working in a male-dominated world. I could litigate circles around half the partners in this firm. I've been working under one of the sharpest divorce lawyers in the state for the past five years. Hell, I write most of his arguments. Do most of the research. *We* can do this."

"I don't know, Ophelia, I hear what you're saying, but . . ."

"But what?"

"But it's a bad idea, that's but."

"But I guess it was a good idea for your man to fly some woman halfway across the world to get something he could have gotten from a woman not even halfway across town," Ophelia shot like daggers.

"Two wrongs don't make one right," Altima countered.

"Yeah, but in this case, one right can stop a whole lot of more wrongs from happening."

"I mean he could have at least apologized, admitted to it—something. He just stood there like I did something wrong. He didn't even say he was sorry," I said, as quick flashbacks of his emotion-free glare raced through my head.

"Of course he didn't. 'Cause he wasn't. What man ever is? Do you know how many women would love to be in your shoes? Do you know how many women would love the chance for emotional retribution?" Ophelia said.

"You mean revenge," Altima added.

"I mean retribution. A make good. Emotional parity. Altima, this is bigger than Morgan. Bigger than you and even bigger than me. Mo, you have an opportunity to level the playing field."

"I wouldn't even know where to begin," I said, as her words started hitting home and making sense.

"You start off by picking up the phone and giving him a chance to settle out of court."

"You're not serious?" Altima asked.

"As a heart attack," she said.

"Settle what out of court?"

"Your damages. You gave him everything you had for almost four months. You tell me, where in the world, postslavery, can you give your services to someone for four months, they fire you without notice or pay, and you have absolutely no recourse."

"I can't think of any place," I said.

"Because there's not a place. Not since Lincoln signed the Emancipation Proclamation. This contract emancipates you."

"But . . ." Altima chimed in.

"But nothing," Ophelia interrupted, cutting her off. "Call him and say that you want to talk about what happened last night and see what he says. If after the conversation you feel better, then I'll leave it alone. But if after you talk to him you feel even worse than you did before you called him, then we move forward. Is that a deal?"

After a moment, "It's a deal."

"This is a bad idea. I can feel it," said Altima.

"It's not a bad idea. What does she have to lose? It's nothing more than a conversation to test the waters. Even if you decide not to pursue any legal action, at the very least it'll make the bastard sweat a little. He at least deserves to do that. Give him a call," Ophelia said, with the receiver in hand.

I looked at Altima for a second.

"Don't look at me. You know what I think," Altima said.

"It's just a call," I said, taking the phone from Ophelia and dialing the number.

"It's just a call. Hello, Charles Sealant please. They're transferring me to his office. Yes, this is Morgan Chase. Hi. Is Charles available? He's not? Could you tell him it's me, please. And it's very important.

I'll hold. Thank you." After a few moments, Charles came to the phone.

"Hello."

"Hey."

"After last night, I certainly didn't expect to hear from you."

"That's why I called. I wanted to talk to you about last night."

"I tried to talk to you last night about last night, but you cussed me out at the top of your lungs, then leaned on your horn, turned up your radio, and flicked your high beams into every house on the block."

"I know, but can you blame me? I came over to bring you some soup and I catch you with another woman after I was worrying about you for the past two days because supposedly you're in bed sick."

"Look, what happened happened. You said what you had to say last night and I heard you loud and clear. The whole neighborhood heard you loud and clear. So, if you don't mind, I'd like to get back to work."

"So, that's it?"

"Is there more?" he said.

"So, you're not going to even apologize or anything."

"Apologize for what? For being harassed at almost midnight in front of my own house because I had company? Is that what you want me to apologize for?"

"Charles, we had a contract, that's what, and you broke it. That's what I want you to apologize for."

"Yes! Let his ass have it!" Ophelia whispered.

"Mo, leave it alone," Altima prayed aloud.

"Oh, so what are you going to do, take me to court? Morgan, please tell me you're not that desperate to think that threatening me with some silly little contract is going to make me want to be with you, because it's not. We hooked up, we hung out, it was good, but it didn't work."

"Tell him, you're willing to discuss a settlement to keep this from going any further," Ophelia whispered, nudging me on.

"Don't tell him that," Altima replied in her own stringent whisper.

"I want to talk about a settlement and maybe we won't have to go to court."

The phone went dead.

"What's he saying?" Ophelia whispered.

"Nothing," I said, covering the phone.

All of a sudden a burst of laughter shot through the phone.

"You know this is ridiculous, right? Okay, so what if you could take me to court, which you can't. Even if you did and you won, you'd still lose because what you want is me and you can't have me."

"So, you're not willing to discuss a settlement."

"It was settled last night when you drove through my neighborhood acting like an ass."

"So, you're not willing to discuss a settlement. Yes or no."

"Hell no. And if that's it, I'd like to get back to work."

"That's it."

"Good. And delete my numbers from your phone book, please. Good-bye."

"Good-bye," I replied, hanging up the phone.

"Let me guess," Ophelia said. "You didn't get the apology."

"No, I didn't," I said. "It's like he just flipped as soon as he heard my voice. It's like that wasn't even the same man I had been seeing for the past few months."

"So how do we move?" Ophelia asked.

"How do we move? We move forward," I said, extending my arm, shaking her hand, and setting in motion a series of events that would no doubt not only change my life, but hopefully the lives of every woman everywhere.

Twenty-Six

BY DAY'S END, even Altima was on board, having been worked over by Ophelia throughout the morning and then at lunch, during all three coffee breaks, and then finally as we walked through the garage headed to our cars. It was now official. Ophelia had already begun writing her opening statement and preparing herself for what she labeled "the most important stride for women since the push-up bra." Even my mother was for it, after she got over the fact that I had fallen from yet another relationship, especially since I had put Charles on such a pedestal. Still she advised me to forge ahead. There's three kinds of people in the world: those who build bridges, cross bridges, or burn bridges. She was proud to have raised a daughter with the courage to build one.

Still, I was restless. I ran through almost every scenario as it related to the outcome of the case. Charles's last words—"even if you win, you'd still lose"—kept ringing in my ears. The last thing I wanted was to be labeled as some embittered woman out to make every man pay for what one man owed. Why couldn't he just say something? Anything. Why do relationships always have to end in some drama? God, I was tired of drama. And the thought of an actual trial meant nothing but drama. I'd taken a few days off but sitting at home, racking my brain, was doing me no good. So I decided to head back to the office, hoping to catch up on this week's work and get a jump-start on next week's. I threw on some sweatpants, hopped in the car, and minutes later I arrived to an empty office where for the next hour and a half I worked. It was just the medicine needed as I had almost forgotten about the case upcoming. Until I got a visit from Michael.

"There's a rule, you know, when you get to a certain amount of overtime it starts working in reverse and you actually start owing the firm."

"I didn't know that," I said with a smile.

"It's true. Why do you think I'm working so hard? I'm just trying to get back to even," he said, shooting his own. "Can I come in for a minute?"

"Sure. I was just finishing up some filing. Reviewing a few cases for the staff meeting next week. And you?"

"I don't know. Just bored, I suppose."

"Bored? You? 'Bored' is not an adjective I would have imagined would describe you. I imagine you living in some swank penthouse apartment with women waiting at your beck and call."

"It's amazing how you can work with someone and yet they know so little about you."

"Come on, now," I said. "Are you trying to tell me that's not your reality?"

"Does it make a difference?" he said. "You know what they say, perception is nine-tenths of reality."

"I guess the difference would be if you were the one-tenth or the nine-tenths."

"I'm the one," he said. "But I'm happy to be the one. My woman is my work. Has been ever since I can remember. Whenever I found a woman that interested me, I always felt as if I was cheating on my work. It was only a matter of time before the 'you're not spending enough time with me' tugs of war began. And then soon after, she was gone. How about you? What's your excuse?"

"That men are crazy. They don't know what they want and when you show them what they want, they usually take the advice and choose somebody else."

"So, that's where all the Bitterade went in the break room cooler. You drank it," he said, standing with a grin on his face.

"Ha ha," I said. "I'm not bitter."

"Who said you were bitter?"

"You did."

"I said your bladder was bitter."

"What's the difference?" I said.

"The difference is it's only in your system temporarily. You can get rid of it any time you want. If you want."

"And what if I *am* bitter? Working here every day where we watch marriages end every day isn't exactly the best form of positive reinforcement."

"But it is the best form of research on what not to do. Either way, it's a gamble."

"What's a gamble?"

"Love," he said. "That's what makes the pursuit of it so intoxicating, given the probability of striking out, it's worth the chance that just one time you'll step up to the plate and hit one clean out of the park."

"That's assuming that the pitcher is playing fair and not throwing you curveballs when you're expecting them to be strikes."

"I didn't say love was fair, I said it was intoxicating."

"Well, you'll have to forgive me, but I'd much rather go into love sober," I said.

"Even sober is scary."

"Yeah, tell me about it," I said in midponder as I flashed back to my most recent events revolving around Charles, the Frenchwoman, and my contract.

"Tell you about what," he said, curious as to what thoughts were swirling about in my head.

"Oh, I don't know, I was just thinking about this friend of mine."

"Oh," he said leaning onto the door. "What about this friend?"

"She used to be the kind of woman who stepped up to the plate with every intention of smacking it clear out of the park. Then after a few innings of curveballs, knuckleballs, sliders, and sinkers, even a walk or two, she decided that the best way to swing was to swing at one you could see coming in slow motion, a mile away."

"And did knowing the pitch help this friend of yours to hit it out of the park?"

"She still struck out. Only this time she had proof that the pitcher had shaved the ball, making it almost impossible to hit. And not only did she have proof, but she had a signed document from the pitcher guaranteeing that he would only throw strikes. And if he did throw a curve, he would let her know. So now she has a case that she's planning to take to a higher court to insure that justice is served and that pitchers like the one she faced will never, ever throw another curveball to another batter again."

"And does this friend of yours really believe that her guarantee will hold up in this higher court, especially given the fact that pitchers have been throwing curveballs since the beginning of time?"

"I don't know, would it hold up?" I asked, as by now we were both more than aware of exactly what we were both saying but not saying.

"A better question would be, would your friend be able to hold up? And if she did go through with such a case, how would the league react to something that would no doubt turn into a media circus? I'm curious to know whether or not your friend has really weighed the cost. You know, Hank Aaron and Babe Ruth both held the record for the most home runs, but a little-known fact is that they also hold the record for the most strikeouts. Winning big sometimes means first losing big. I have a great bit of advice for your friend. He who swings and runs away lives to swing another day. Leave it alone, Morgan. Tell your 'friend' I insist on it."

"I will."

"Morgan . . ."

"I heard you the first time."

"Good. Well, I better be going. It's the bottom of the ninth and I'm worn out. Should I wait a few minutes to walk you to your car?" Michael asked.

"Thanks, but there's a good chance this game's headed into extra innings. Have a good evening."

"You, too. And tell your friend what I said."

"I will," I said, as he winked and left the room.

Twenty-Seven

AFTER DAYS OF DEBATE and deliberation, I finally embraced my destiny. I accepted my calling. My purpose. My life's mission. My conscience was clear. In my mind I was secure that in suing Charles, I would be freeing others, who like myself were haunted by the ghosts of relationships past. In moving forward with a suit, I would be doing more good than bad, shedding light to fight the darkness. I was taking a *Jurassic Park*-size step in ridding the world of its trickery, deceit, and romantic decay. That was my story and I was sticking to it.

And for the next several days over at my apartment I was meeting with Ophelia the man hater, and Altima the food caterer. We all agreed that it would be to our benefit not to mention the case at work. Except for my family, this would be kept top secret. Under wraps. And undercover. Mum was the word as we planned, plotted, and devised a strategy of attack that would win us the war with as little bloodshed as possible. Our lips were sealed. We were clear that the element of surprise would be our most powerful weapon.

Then came that morning when I walked into the office. Michael was waiting in the reception area with a look of disgust and disappointment on his face. His look obviously signaled the end to the element of any surprise.

"Good morning, Michael. Tess."

Tess just waved, never uttering a sound.

"Can I talk to you in your office, please?" he said in a no-nonsense tone.

"Sure," I said. "I just need to return a few calls first and then . . ."

"They can wait," he replied as he motioned his arm for me to go first.

"You're the boss," I said as I began making my way through the hallway where there were no open doors, good morning waves, nor greetings to greet me. Finally inside the office, I began hoping to lighten the moment.

"That's a nice suit," I said, noticing his light gray suit with even lighter accenting pinstripes. "You know, pinstripes are in again," I said sensing that a conversation about pinstripes was the last thing on his mind.

"Please, tell me you're kidding, Morgan."

"Kidding about what?" I said.

"You know what. The case you're working on."

"What case?" After a moment of pause. "Oh . . . that case."

"Yeah, that case," he said.

"How did you know?"

"If Altima knows, the world knows."

"She told you?" I asked.

"She didn't have to. The walls in this firm aren't thin just for aesthetic purposes, you know."

"Well, it's no big deal," I said, hoping to brush it off. "It's just a little something I'm working on."

"You're suing one of the biggest minority car dealers in Philadelphia, that's *not* a 'little something.' And you're suing him because he broke your heart?"

"No. I'm suing him because he broke his promise."

"Morgan, is there something I'm not getting here? You were in a relationship with someone and that relationship didn't work. So, you move on. You weren't married, you weren't living together, and you weren't even together that long. There are no laws that protect broken hearts. If there were, every courtroom in every city in every state would have a waiting list the size of the Empire State Building with someone suing someone. Who knows, maybe someday someone will pass a law or create a contract that guarantees that a . . . oh no," he said pausing in midrant. "Morgan, tell me you didn't."

"Didn't what?" I said in a high-pitched shrill.

"Please tell me you didn't," he said, shaking his head, holding his brow with his hand.

After an extended pause, that was all the answer he needed.

"And he actually signed it?" he asked in utter disbelief.

Nodding my head slowly, I responded, "Yep."

"Well, his dumb ass deserves to be sued. And you developed this document all by yourself or was there some sort of broken hearts tribunal that assisted you?"

"Morgan, I just got off the phone with the court clerk . . . Oh, Michael, I didn't know you two were in a meeting. I'll come back," Ophelia said, attempting a beeline out of the office.

"No, Ophelia. Stay. Please."

Next barging through the door was Altima. "Mo, I went online and checked for precedents and . . . Mr. Sampson. Good morning. Good-bye," she said, turning herself and trying to swiftly exit.

"Altima."

"Yes, sir."

"You can stay, too."

"Oh, it's not a problem, I can come back."

"Altima, come in."

"Really, it's . . ."

"I insist," he said.

"Oh, well, if you insist, I'll come in. You're the boss. At least one of them. But since you're the only black boss, I really consider you my boss. Not that I have anything against white people. 'Cause I don't. It's just that, you know, sometimes white people—"

"Altima," I said, cutting her off. "It's okay."

"Look, ladies . . ." Michael said.

"It was Ophelia's idea," Altima blurted out. "I didn't want to have nothing to do with it. And neither did Mo. She started talking about the problem with men and women and communication. I was just fine not communicating with my man and so was Morgan. Weren't you, Morgan?"

"It was all our idea," I said.

"The concept was mine," Ophelia added, looking to present herself as the lead counsel she had long hoped to become. "And most of the research and strategic planning. Case analysis, precedents, and—"

"I get it," Michael said, cutting her off. "I just hope you all realize the can of worms this could potentially open and the battle it could eventually bring."

"We are aware. But we're cautious. We've done nothing crazy or rash. Every step is carefully planned and strategically positioned. We haven't even sent the man a summons," I said.

Ophelia cleared her throat.

"Ophelia, what did you do?" I said, hoping that she hadn't done what I feared she had done.

"I did what you're supposed to do when you're suing someone—"

"Act crazy and rash," Altima chimed in.

"No, you serve them papers."

"You served him papers?"

"Yes."

"Where?"

"Where else, to his job," said Ophelia.

"When?" I asked, not believing my own ears.

"They went out first thing this morning," she said. "I told you I was sending them out."

"Yeah, but you didn't say when you were sending them out. Do you know if he got them or not?" I asked.

"Excuse me, Morgan . . ." Tess interrupted. "You have a call on line three. It's Charles Sealant. He says it's urgent that he speak with you."

"I believe 'yes' would be the proper answer to your question," Ophelia said meekly.

"What are you going to do now?" Altima asked.

"I'm going to pick up the phone and see what he wants, right?" I asked, turning to Ophelia and Michael.

"Right," Ophelia said.

"Sounds like a good idea to me," Michael added.

Boldly I picked up the phone, not wanting to give any sign of fear or regret.

"Hello," I said nonchalantly into the phone, as if what was happening wasn't really happening.

"You want to serve me with a summons and try to sue me for some shit that every man does every day? You must be out of your got-damn mind. Okay, so you want to play hardball with the big boys. I promise you, you're going to regret this day for the rest of your life. Expect a call from my attorney, Miles Milner. See you in court, you crazy-ass bitch."

I calmly placed the phone down on the receiver. All eyes were on me.

"So, what did he say?" Altima asked.

"Word for word—it's admissible as evidence," said Ophelia.

"He said I should expect a call from his attorney."

Michael stood shaking his head in disbelief.

"Okay, so we'll hear from his attorney," Ophelia said. "That's what he's supposed to do. He probably hired somebody who's already on payroll. We'll eat him alive."

"He hired Miles Milner."

"Who's that?" Altima asked.

"I've never heard of him," Ophelia added.

"I have," Michael said, chiming in.

"Who is he?" I asked unaware.

"I assume you've all heard of the saying, 'Fighting fire with fire.'"

"Sure," we all said.

"In hiring Miles Milner," he said, "Mr. Sealant's fighting fire with a towering inferno. I suggest you all invest in some flame-retardant business attire. Morgan, I'll expect a detailed report on the progress in the mayor's case—the one you're getting paid to work on—on my desk by noon. You ladies have a productive day. Your employment depends on it," he said with a deadpan smile as he walked out of my office.

"Now what do we do?" I said, looking at Ophelia.

"We . . ." she said, heading for the door. "This was your idea, remember?"

Twenty-Eight

AFTER A FEW more days, the late-night sessions with the mayor resumed and all seemed back to normal, at least for the time being. Michael and I were back to our usual late hours with Chinese food, Thai food, and an occasional deep-crust pan pizza. I opted to bury myself in other folks' drama rather than drown myself in my own. The mayor's last attempt to arrive at a settlement was denied and, like it or not, he would soon have his day in court with not only his livelihood at stake, but his candidacy and reputation, as well. Though it was probably the wrong emotion for me to be feeling at the time, given my state of romantic affairs, in a lot of ways I empathized with his wife. Though I never met her, I could understand her pain and what caused her to go after him in the way that she had.

Still, it was my job to somehow help the mayor keep his job, his money, and his reputation intact.

"That's just about it for the evening," Michael said, as he began clearing the papers from the conference room table. Even after a thirteen-hour day he was still sharp, shirt still crisp, he was ever-poised and focused on accomplishing whatever he set out to do.

"Get some rest," he said.

"Thanks," I replied. "You, too." I grabbed my folders from my end of the table, heading toward the door.

"I'm worried," he said, never lifting his head as he continued gathering his files. Pausing in silence, I turned, allowing him to finish his thought.

"There's already a rumor floating around the partners about your case and how it might negatively impact the firm."

"Is that what you're worried about? The firm?"

"The firm? The firm is like the rock of Gibraltar. It's going to be just fine. Ruffling its feathers a bit might actually do it some good," he said with a slight chuckle. "The firm will be fine. Time has proven that."

"Well, if you're not worried about the firm, then what are you worried about?" I asked, unsure of his direction or tone.

"You, silly. I'm worried about you," he said, finally lifting his head. "Miss I'm Every Woman, It's All in Me. I worry that we live in a world where you can order a hamburger and a marriage certificate both in a drive-thru window. A world where you dissolve that same marriage quicker than you can digest that same hamburger. A world where you're more surprised to hear about a relationship working than you are it ending. A world full of breakups, breakdowns, lying, scratching, and clawing for a materialistic thread to mend an emotional scar. I'm worried that the eager, aggressive woman with bright-eyed optimism who I met a few years ago now has eyes that have grown a bit dim. That's what I'm worried about."

"That's just a tint," I said with a chuckle. "It's so bright, I'm just trying to protect it."

"Protect it from coming in or going out?" he said.

"Okay," I said, walking back into the room. "Is this Michael the partner talking?" I said, sensing the line between business and personal having blurred out of focus. " 'Cause I'm confused."

"No, this is Michael the man," he said. "Did that help?"

"Michael the man."

"That's right."

"Giving me advice on relationships and the trappings of cynicism? Advice that you just, what—forgot to listen to yourself," I said.

"Oh, okay . . . a brother tryin' to caution a sistah, and she attacks."

"Not an attack. Just an observation of the obvious," I said.

"And that is . . . ?"

"That I've never once seen you with a significant other. I mean, there's the Christmas party that you show up at with the obligatory arm piece. But five minutes later she's spending more time drinking gin and blending in, because her quote-unquote date is nowhere to be found. And if you ask me, the dates weren't even that cute."

"Wait a minute, my dates were cute."

"Last year, your date was bald-headed."

"She wasn't bald-headed. She was wearing a natural hairstyle."

"They don't call that a style. They call that a bad perm that made your hair fall out," I said, laughing.

"Okay, so is this the lawyer talking?"

"No, this is a woman who's been going to the hair salon since she was eight. I see it happen all the time."

"Okay, you got me. My cousin set us up on a blind date."

"You said the date was blind, or your cousin was blind?"

"Okay," he said. "So, you got jokes, huh? All right, so maybe I'm not the best person to speak on relationships. I just don't want to see the circumstances of your present dictate the romance of your future," he said in a warm and surprisingly intense tone. His words were the sweetest I had heard in some time, touching a place in my heart and causing me a moment of pause. I sighed, and then, catching my breath, for the first time I saw Michael in a different light.

"Thank you," I said. "That was a sweet thing to say."

"You're welcome," he said for a moment, looking as if there was more he wanted to say, but dared not.

"So," he said.

"So," I replied.

"So . . . it's late," he said. "I'm tired."

"I'm worn-out."

"We should probably be headed home," he said.

"It is pretty late," I said.

"Yeah, probably too late to hang out and get a bite or anything like that," he said.

"I'm not really all that sleepy," I said.

"Neither am I," he added. "You want to hang out and grab a bite? Kenny Garrett's playing at Warmdaddy's. The manager was a client of mine."

"Don't tell me—divorced?"

"How did you guess? Two tickets shouldn't be that much of a problem."

"That depends on whether or not he came out a winner or not."

"If he was a client of mine, winning is a given," he said.

"Sounds like someone's a bit conceited."

"Or convinced," he countered.

"Either way, if you look at the root word, it's still a con," I said, laughing.

"Oh, you're good," he said. "Either way it's a con. Very funny. You know at the club tonight, maybe you can come onstage and tell jokes. I could hook that up for you, if you like," he said, as we both laughed. "Or we don't even have to leave for a bite. I could just offer you half of the sandwich that I ordered not too long ago. It's after eight and I'm trying to watch the carbs."

"Sure," I said. "Carbs are the least of my concerns right about now. What kind of sandwich is it?"

"Chicken steak sub loaded with everything unhealthy that you could think of. Green peppers, hot peppers, mounds of fried onions and cheese. And to top it off, a couple cans of ice-cold Coke . . ."

"Sounds delightfully decadent," I said.

For the next hour or so we laughed, drank soda after soda, and chowed down on what had to be the best chicken steak sandwich in all of Philadelphia.

"It should be a crime for a chicken sub to taste this good," I said, taking the last crumb from the wrinkled wrapper and putting it in my mouth.

"It is. Rumor has it they sprinkle a little cocaine on top for that extra added high," he said, laughing.

"Is that right?"

"No, that's rumor."

"Uncorroborated evidence!"

"Conjecture!"

"Hearsay," I said. "But if it pleases the court," I said, now up and out of my seat, pacing the floor. "I'd like to further investigate this alleged chicken steak sub as to the origin of the alleged substance."

"Objection," he said. "Counselor is badgering the sandwich by eating the sandwich," he said as we both lost ourselves laughing in the absurdity of it all.

"You are crazy," he said.

"It takes crazy to know crazy," I replied. "I blame it on the artificial intoxicant."

"The *alleged* artificial intoxicant," he said.

"Whatever," I said laughingly. "It's the sub's fault. One more late-night snack at the office and I could get addicted," I said, still laughing.

"Yeah, not to just the sandwich," he said, still caught in the fun of the moment.

"What does that mean?" I said in half chuckle.

"What does what mean?" he said, taking a last sip from his soda.

"What you said. You said, 'not just the sandwich I would be addicted to.'"

"Did I?" he said, feigning confusion.

"Yeah, you did."

"Oh, then I did."

"Okay," I said, not willing to let him off the hook that easy. "What else would I be addicted to?"

"I don't know," he said. "Maybe that one piece of leftover chicken crumb dangling from your bottom lip," he said with a grin. "As hungry as I am I was tempted to wait till it fell so I could eat it myself."

"I'm sorry, but I'd have to fight you for this crumb," I said jokingly as I tried to wipe it from my face. "Is it gone?" I asked.

"Not yet," he said as still I continued wiping it.

"Gone?"

"It's still there. It's embedded deep into the bottom lip. It's like a Janet Jackson mole," he said. "I could help you with it, but on one condition."

"And that condition would be what?" I said.

"That the crumb belongs to me," he said as he took one step closer, placing his hands to my face. "Deal?" he asked in a soft, warm tone.

"Deal," I replied, equally as soft.

"Deal. Okay," he said, gently wiping my lip with a napkin.

"All gone?"

"Yep, all gone," he said. "Though I can't blame the crumb for hanging as long as it could," he said. "If it were me resting on your bottom lip I wouldn't be in too much of a hurry to leave, either," he said. "That is, judging from the evidence presented to the court."

"And that evidence would be?"

"That your lips are always moist and wet, Your Honor."

"Is that right?"

"Oh yeah, that's right," he said.

"Okay," I said, myself now fully in the moment. "So if you were that crumb, based on the evidence given the court, would you just hang there, or begin further and more intense cross-examination of the evidence?"

"Only if it pleases the court," he said, making his way closer and closer.

"The court insists on being pleased," I replied.

"So, you're saying the witness is all mine?"

"The witness is all yours," I said, taking my own step closer and closer and . . . the conference room door opened. It was the overnight janitor.

"Will you be much longer," he asked.

"No," Michael replied. "I think we've both been here long enough," he said as he gathered his briefcase and walked his fine self out the door.

Twenty-Nine

MY HEARING DATE was finally here. Ophelia, Altima, and I made our way into the downtown Philadelphia Municipal Court Building and into the chambers of hard-nosed Judge Bernetta Bean. She was set to retire, but when this case came across her desk, she decided to take it as a final farewell. Almost seconds before our scheduled appointment with the judge, the doors swung open. Greeting us first was a wood-fragranced cologne.

"That's Charles's lawyer," Ophelia whispered into my ear. "Miles Milner."

"Damn, he's fine," Altima whispered into the other ear. "You think he's single?" she added.

"He's the enemy," I replied.

"Not mine," she said, feeling my stare pierce through her body. "Well, he ain't," Altima said, rolling her eyes and shooting him a smile that he was all too eager to return. He was cleaner than the board of health. A throwback to the Harlem Renaissance days, his suits were straight out of the Cotton Club: soft cream pinstripes warmed up a caramel brown–colored suit. A pair of two-toned brown-and-cream Stacy Adams covered his feet, and the softest, silkiest pomade dressed his charcoal black, glistening hair.

We had done our homework on Miles and found out almost

everything there was to know about him. He was forty-two. A graduate of Howard University. Legend has it, that like Johnnie Cochran, he's prone to rhymes, metaphors, clichés, and an occasional Baptist whoop and holler.

"Don't let the smooth taste fool you," Ophelia again whispered in my ear. "There's not a trick, stunt, or card that he isn't willing to deal from the bottom of the deck or under his leg—whatever gets him to a victory."

"Good evening, ladies," he said, flashing a smile brighter than a baby grand.

"Good—"

"Hello," Altima chimed in, cutting us both off.

"Why hello?" he asked.

"Why not?" she replied, nearly melting in the grasp of his hand.

"Take a seat, counselor. You were ten seconds from being late and five more from being in contempt. Good for you," the judge said, entering her chambers.

"You're looking lovely as ever, Judge Bean. Did you dye your hair?" Miles offered with a smile.

"Save it for the schoolgirls, counselor. We're all busy." She continued, "So let's get down to the brass tacks of it. Counselor Clarke, there is absolutely no precedent for this case in a court of law. You are aware of that?"

"Yes, I am, Your Honor, but—"

"Yes or no is all that's required. Are you aware of that or not?"

"Yes, Your Honor."

"And Counselor Milner, are you here to dispute that the signature on the contract is not the signature of your client?"

"Your Honor, I'm here to state that—"

"Yes or no, counselor."

"No, Your Honor," he replied.

"My decision is that given the rather compelling and unique nature of this case, I will allow it to go to trial."

"Yes!" Ophelia mouthed to herself, grabbing my hand and nearly squeezing the life from it.

"Your Honor, you can't be serious. My client is one of the city's most prominent businessmen. Do you know what this could do to his reputation?"

"Hopefully, what it will do is cause him to be more careful with what he signs."

"Your Honor, I'm requesting that you allow me a moment to—"

"My decision is final. And I do warn you both to be on your best behavior. Keep the arguments pertinent to the case and not some 'he say, she say' cat fighting match. My courtroom will not turn into an episode of *Jerry Springer*. I will have order. Otherwise I'll throw this case so far out of court you'll need a telescope to find it. Are we clear?"

"Crystal," Miles replied begrudgingly with a smile.

Judge Bean said, "Jury selection will begin immediately and the case will begin two weeks from Monday. Good luck, counselors," she said as she exited the room.

Days later the jury was selected, which, after much debate, we were finally able to settle upon: half men and half women. Miles, of course, tried to slant it male, believing that no man on the planet would dare break the code of brotherhood and render a verdict of guilty. Our strategy was the same, feeling that there's not a woman on earth who wouldn't feel a sense of camaraderie. With that out of the way, our first court date was only days away. Days that felt like years.

Thirty

"ALL RISE AS THE Honorable Judge Bernetta Bean enters the court."

Finally, it was here. It was our moment of truth. We had taken the two weeks off that we would need to try and win the case. As we stood side-by-side, Ophelia and I had bonded, joined forces to fight the enemy of loss, of love gone bad, and of shattered dreams and broken promises. We had all but buried the hatchet between us. We were a united front being driven by the desire to right a thousand wrongs. And we weren't alone, having been joined by my mother and her two friends from church, who drove in from Baltimore to lend their support both morally, as well as spiritually. We stood as Judge Bean entered the courtroom.

Dressed in a freshly steamed black robe, her hair was whipped into a short flip and her nails were freshly French manicured. Obviously she was prepared in the event of any media attention.

"You may be seated," the bailiff proclaimed.

"Counselor Clarke, you may begin with your opening statement."

"Well, that's us," I said slowly. "Go get 'em, girl."

"Thanks," Ophelia said, as she remained seated.

"Counselor Clarke," Judge Bean continued.

"That's you," I said, sensing a blank expression cover her face. "Ophelia, are you all right?" I asked.

"I'm fine," she said. "Okay. Here goes," she said, rising from her seat.

Clearing her throat, she approached the jury bench, pausing for a moment and then beginning.

"Ladies and gentlemen of the jury, the case you are about to hear will in many ways shake the very foundation of what you think you know about our judicial system. About justice. About law. You probably have in your mind that this case is about an affair. A broken heart. A somebody-done-somebody-wrong vendetta. Though those are all very flammable emotions that would no doubt make for a hot and steamy, made-for-TV movie, I'm sorry . . . but I'm not a Hollywood producer, this is a not a television set, and we are not actors."

So far so good, I thought to myself. She was doing her thing, holding court as even Altima began nudging me in surprise at how well she was doing.

"This case is about love," she continued. "About lies. About a lawsuit. All of which began with a contract. A legal and binding instrument enforceable in a court of law. A very detailed and well-constructed document layered with conditions, consideration, and yes . . . consequences.

"The conditions were the defendant's promise to be faithful, loyal, forthright, and honest. All the things one would expect in a committed relationship. The consideration in exchange for his commitment was my client's affection. Her deepest and most intimate affection. And her consideration was considerably considerate, because the sex was good. So good that he kept coming back for more and more and more.

"Now . . . I know what some of you may be thinking. This sounds like a sophisticated form of prostitution. And you know what, in theory, I would agree," she said as several members of the male jury began nodding their heads in affirmation. "But then really . . . if we're really honest with ourselves . . . haven't we all been prostitutes in some way or another?" she continued as the court began to slightly mumble and groan. "For something we loved? Someone we craved? Something we longed for? For prostitution is merely a form of exchange—a barter of goods for services. And not just for those single among us. Some would argue even married men and women have engaged in some form or another. A new dress, a bigger diamond ring, a credit card with a higher limit. Or, maybe a big-screen TV with an all-day, get-out-of-chores pass for an uninterrupted Sunday afternoon filled with food, fellas, and football—an exchange.

"But for a moment, I'd like to shift focus and turn our spotlight on the pimp," she said, turning and looking at Charles. "Because that's exactly what he is," making her way closer toward him. "Now, he may not be wearing the traditional purple hat with a pink feather, or sporting a diamond-encrusted pinky ring. Those are merely distractions. You see, the new millennium pimp is known by his actions."

By now Altima was pinching my leg. "This bitch better work," she whispered.

"How he slings hope," Ophelia went on. "How he peddles promises. How he deals dreams of a tomorrow. And then ultimately, and unapologetically, how he steals the soul of women who innocently cling to their dream of a future with him. A pimp.

"And why did she fall for him? Why did she trust him? Because he gave her his word. But not just his word, also his signature. His stamp. His seal of approval, which was reflective of his honor, his integrity. He gave her his word only for her to later find out that it was no more valuable than the paper it was written on. Why? Because like the used cars he pawns, he's overhyped, overpriced, and usually lacking an adequate warranty. He's a hustler. A snake oil salesman with a penchant for fine-print loopholes. But not this time. This time in his lustful and hurried haste to have her, he gave her something better than a warranty. What he gave her was a legal and binding contract of commitment.

"And now I'm going to prove to you, ladies and gentlemen of the jury, that the defendant had no intention whatsoever of honoring his warranty or his word. I'm going to prove to you, the men and women of this jury, that the defendant willfully, and without regret, broke his bond of commitment, thereby breeching the contract which he signed. Oh yeah, he's guilty. He committed a crime. And for that crime, my friends, we must set an example to the entire world and ensure that he does indeed do the time." Back to her seat, she turned and sat down as she placed her sweat-drenched hand in mine. "How'd I do?" she asked.

"Like you've been doing it all your life," I said.

"I have," she said as suddenly we three sighed a sigh of relief. Regardless of the outcome, it was evident that our preparation would make beating us no easy task. Our celebration came to an abrupt halt when we heard the words, "Counselor Milner, you may begin."

Thirty-One

AS ALL EYES LOCKED on Miles, slowly he rose from his seat, fixing his silk hanky inside the lapel of his custom-made suit. Relaxed yet poised, comfortable in his own skin, he walked over to the stand, leaning on its wooden frame and, after pausing for a moment, turned to the jurors and flashed his million-dollar smile.

"Moments like this," he said, "make me proud to be an American. A land where regardless of race, creed, or gender, we are guaranteed the presumption of innocence. "Now," he said slowly, beginning to pace, "unlike my esteemed colleague, I come before you, ladies and gentlemen of the jury, not to defame, degrade, or spin a bunch of slanderous and hateful allegories about the woman who brought such unfounded allegations about my client.

"To the contrary, I come to you today, not to denigrate her. I'm here to celebrate her. That's right," he said, clapping his hands together slowly. "I come before you today to celebrate a woman who truly epitomizes the dream of America. Your America. Our America. My America. 'My country 'tis of thee, sweet land of liberty, of thee I sing' America. Land of the free, home of the brave, and playground of perception. A land where if you can conceive it, you truly can achieve it. America . . . the salesman's sanctuary. Where quick, slick, and flashy celebrity-driven endorsements drive what we want, what we crave, and ultimately what we're willing to reach into our pockets to purchase. A land where what we need is manipulated simply by what we see. A land where we'll actually spend money on things that are free.

"Like drinking water, for example. But not just plain drinking water, Rocky mountain spring, clear, crisp, tasty, fresh, healthy, drinking water. Water. They drip-drop a chemical here, design a fancy bottle there, and all of a sudden what you could simply hop out of the bed, walk in the kitchen, turn the faucet on and get for free, because of perception and those that stand to profit from it, we're now willing to drive halfway across town, stand in long lines, and pay a premium for it. America—'land where my fathers died, land of the Pilgrims' pride'—America, a land where bigger is better. Excess is no longer the exception but the rule. A 'where's the beef?' society. Where if it can be packaged, it can be positioned. And if it can be positioned, it's almost guaranteed to be patronized.

"Ladies and gentlemen of the jury, what happened to the dream of America? I often ask myself that very same question. Soon we'll be selling air. But not the air that just anybody can breathe, no— we'll package and sell you the good air, guaranteed to keep you breathing longer and fuller and deeper. 'Our air is better than the tap air you can get for free.' America . . . 'oh beautiful, for spacious skies, for amber waves of grain'—what happened to the dream of America? I'll tell you what happened. Hype happened. Hype—a four-letter word that has changed the fabric of our society to a paradise of perception. Yes, ladies and gentlemen of the jury, hype happened. But why? Where did it come from? How did it get here? Was it always there? In the beginning, God created the heavens and the earth. It was without form—void—darkness moved upon the face of the deep, and God said, 'Let there be light.' And then He looked at that light and said it was good. He transformed a vast nothingness into an infinite somethingness and He simply called it good. Not off the hook, the chain, the register, the meter, or the hinges. And then this same God—the almighty, the great and everlasting all powerful, the Great I am, the maker of all things breathing, living, moving—made man and woman. And again, He looked at his work. How He connected the anklebone to the leg bone, the leg bone to the hipbone, created cells, chromosomes, the heart, the brain, and the blood running warm in your veins, and still the word God used to describe His work was "good." God didn't need perception to drive His reality, because His reality *was* reality.

"What happened to the dream of America? Hype happened to the dream. Which is really why we're here today, aren't we? This isn't really about a contract, as the prosecution would have you believe. It's not about love, lies, trickery, or even a man being slippery. This, my friends is about hype. This is about a woman who, in writing, proclaimed to possess the ability to provide a man with his ultimate sexual experience. To be more specific, as she labels it in her own words, she 'guarantees to give a man the best sex ever.' 'Unrivaled, unequalled, and unparalleled,' as she puts it. The best sex ever. Now, God, when He made the heavens and earth, He called it good. But the prosecution would have us believe that her client's sex was more than just good. It was the best ever. Did they see the lightning flash? Could they hear the thunder roll? At the point of penetration, was there some sort of cosmic collisions of the constellations? Was there a meteor shower that rained down like Fourth of July fireworks outside the bedroom window? Did the earth move, the Red Sea part, did it rain for forty days and forty nights? The 'best sex ever' is what she guaranteed my client. Ladies and gentlemen of the jury, what happened to America is the same thing that happened to my client—hype happened. Overpricing and overvalue happened. And then when my client was no longer willing to buy into her hype, anger happened. Revenge happened. Why? Because the very thing that my client perceived was valuable enough to drive halfway across town, stand in long lines to purchase, was no better than the tap water he could get for free.

"My friends, the only thing my client is guilty of is living in and loving America—the land of the free, home of the brave, the haven of hype. And if he's guilty, then we're all guilty. Why? Because every day of our lives we buy into the very same thing. We participate in it, revel in it, and ultimately reward it. But this time, ladies and gentlemen of the jury, this time I urge you, don't believe the hype. Don't honor the perpetrators of perception. Don't reward the relegators of reality—do not believe the hype.

"In closing, I stand before you believing in reality and not the perception of what our great country was built on. I stand before you believing in a land where truth and justice prevail. A land where my client, the victim, will become my client, the victor. I stand before you today proud to be an American. For what happened to the dream of America? You happened to the dream. Each and every one of you happened. Because today you and you alone have the opportunity to restore the dream. And you have the power to return our great country to a land where reality is the rule and perception the exception. My client is innocent. Like each and every one of you is innocent. And in freeing him, you will in turn free yourselves. God bless you. And God bless America!"

Instantly the jury broke out in thunderous applause as the judge's gavel fell, calling for order in the court. Immediately we looked at one another, sharing the same sentiment. We were in for the fight of our lives.

Thirty-Two

AFTER A BRIEF recess, we were back in court and ready to begin.

"Counselor Milner," the judge offered, "you may call your first witness."

"Who do you think he's going to call to the stand?" I asked Ophelia, leaning into her ear.

"I don't know, but whoever it is, he's got to get warmed up first."

"Your Honor, if it pleases the court, I'd like to forgo the usual formalities and get right to the meat of the matter. Your Honor, as my first and maybe even my last witness, I'd like to call to the stand my client, Charles Sealant."

A hush fell over the courtroom.

"He called Charles? First!" I whispered to Ophelia in disbelief. "If this is getting warm, what's getting hot?"

"He's just bluffing, trying to throw us off balance, that's all."

"Well, he's doing a good job," Altima said.

"Do you solemnly swear that your testimony is the truth, the whole truth, and nothing but the truth, so help you God?" the bailiff questioned.

"I do," he said, shooting me a nasty look and easing into his seat.

"I'm not feeling too good about this," I said into Ophelia's ear.

"It's going to be fine. He's just bluffing. It's a smokescreen. Trust me."

"So, how exactly *was* the sex, Mr. Sealant?" he asked.

Again, we all three looked at one another as it was now clear that Charles's testimony was to be anything but the smokescreen we had hoped.

"It was good," he said.

"It was good. 'Good' meaning adequate, above adequate, meeting your expectations, exceeding your expectations, exactly what do you mean when you say it was 'good'?"

"Objection," Ophelia blurted. "He's badgering the witness."

"But it's his own client, counselor," the judge replied with a twisted look on her face.

"Oh," she said to herself.

"Oh, indeed. Overruled."

"Of course," she said, whispering under her breath as she shrunk back to her seat.

"What was that all about?" I asked.

"It's strategy?"

"If your strategy was to make yourself look like a dumb ass, you've succeeded," Altima shot to Ophelia under her breath as Ophelia's eyes rolled and the questioning continued.

"The sex was adequate."

"Adequate, meaning 'the best'?" Miles asked.

"Adequate meaning it was good. It was nothing to write home about," he said. The court began to murmur. "Unless you just didn't have anything better to do and just wanted to write," he said. "It was acceptable. But then, all sex is acceptable."

"All sex?" he asked.

"Sure. You ask any man, and he'd likely say the same thing. What makes sex above average doesn't have really much to do with the physical at all as much as the mental. That's where most women get it wrong, they think they can hook a man by how many tricks they can perform, or how many positions they can contort their body into. That may catch a man, but it won't keep a man."

"So, what you're saying is that physical prowess, accessibility, and availability of the sexual exchange are not important to you?"

"It's important. I'm not saying that. I mean, no man wants an uninspired woman in the bed. But what I'm saying is that how a man feels about the woman that he's having sex with is what raises the bar and makes it what she would call the best sex ever," he said. I noticed my mother's mouth began to slowly open in amazement.

"So, in your mind, based on what you call the mental and not just the physical, did she have the capacity to offer you the best sex ever?"

My heart began beating out of my chest as I could only imagine his response.

"Oh yeah," he said. "She definitely had the capacity," he continued confidently and respectfully. I watched my mother's mouth close and eyes brighten as she turned in pride to her two church friends. I sighed deeply in relief.

"She's a smart woman. And she's intelligent. When she walked into my dealership, she had every salesman shaking in his boots."

"So, given the way you describe her, it sounds to me like this relationship should have been perfect. What went wrong?"

"I'm not sure, exactly."

"Do you believe it had something to do with your present relationship with her?" Miles asked.

"Not as much to do with the present as it did with her past. Her previous owners, so to speak."

"Previous owners?" Miles asked.

"Oh yeah, you'll have to forgive me; I'm in the preowned automobile business, so it's natural for me to use that lingo."

"Meaning you sell cars that have been previously owned by one, or sometimes multiple owners?"

"Correct. I'm in the business of acquiring something that's been around the block a few times, so to speak. Something that's been handled. May have been banged up lightly a few times, but it's been fixed."

"Automobiles that have been test-driven."

"Or women that have been tested-and-tried-driven?"

"Objection, Your Honor, by referring to my client as an automobile, the defense is manufacturing an unfair impression of my client."

"Sustained. Witness will refer to automobiles as automobiles and women as women."

"So, you were saying, Mr. Sealant," Miles said.

"I was saying that I'm used to handling automobiles that have been broken in," he said. "It's not factory fresh, but because of the care and attention of the previous owner, by the time I get to it it's still in pretty good shape. It's had its regularly scheduled maintenance, annual tune-ups, necessary touch-ups; it's in good shape. And that's why I acquire it."

"So, what you're saying is you're not predisposed to purchase an automobile that's used."

"I don't purchase used cars. I purchase preowned cars."

"Is there a difference?" he asked.

"Is there? There's all the difference in the world," he replied.

"So, is that what you thought you were getting in Morgan, preowned as opposed to used?"

"Objection, Your Honor!" Ophelia shouted out. "The counselor's attempt to equate my client to an automobile is purely argumentative and has no relevance to whether or not he signed and ultimately breached the contract."

"Your Honor," Miles added, chiming in without ever skipping a beat, "my client's testimony is adding clarity as to who he is as a person, thus giving greater clarity as to why he allegedly did what the prosecution is accusing him of doing in the first place."

"Overruled. Counselor, you may unfortunately proceed."

"If it pleases the court, Your Honor, I'd like to rephrase my question and ask that my client simply elaborate on the differences between the preowned automobile and the used car."

"Probably the easiest way to distinguish the two is that with a preowned automobile, like the ones I sell, it's 'what you see is what you get.' A preowned car usually has had one owner who took special care. A preowned automobile has been kept in a garage. Away from the cold, the rain, the sleet, and the snow. It's protected. It's pampered, always with a fresh coat of wax on it. A preowned car doesn't have a lot of dings and scratches. If there were any scratches, bumps, dings, or pings, they've all been disclosed in notarized documentation. It comes with all the original parts, the proper paperwork, and most importantly, the factory warranty. If later the buyer were to discover that something was wrong with the car that wasn't disclosed, then the dealership is liable and in most cases will fix the problem free of charge. Preowned cars are for educated consumers more interested in a smart purchase over a good deal."

"And a used car?"

"A used car . . . well, a used car can be classified as 'what you see is *never* what you get.' It's probably the worst kind of investment possible."

"It's low cost, I assume?"

"Low cost and high risk. See, you never know how many people have at one time or another claimed ownership. You never know how many different drivers it's had. Or how they handled the car when they were behind the wheel. A used car's been out on the street. Beat down by the elements. The paint's usually a little dull. It's a high-risk proposition at best. But most people know that. It's fast, quick, convenient. It's an in-between car. A tide-you-over, transitional transportation vehicle. It's not the car that you want, but it's usually what you'll take until you can afford what you really want."

"And what kind of vehicle was Ms. Chase?" he asked.

First looking away and then turning to me, he said:

"Oh, she was definitely a used car."

"Your witness!" Miles said smugly.

Thirty-Three

"YOU WERE AN athlete, were you not, Mr. Sealant?" Ophelia asked.

"I was. I played for the Philadelphia Seventy-Sixers."

"And what position did you play?"

"Point guard."

"Point guard. Right. You stood in the middle of the lane with your back turned to the basket, and they lobbed you the ball and without barely looking, you jumped, turned, and slam-dunked it, right? Would that be accurate, Mr. Sealant?"

"No," he said as his chuckles joined the chuckles of the court-room. "That's a center. Centers have eyes in the back of their head. I'm a guard. My job was to see all things at all times. To know where everybody was and where they were going."

"And you were a good point guard, I assume?"

"The best, till my knee gave out."

"You could see the whole court at once. Analyze every move, every action, foresee every reaction."

"That was my job, yes."

"I saw a few of your games on TV. You had skills, as they say. Would you agree?"

"Absolutely."

"And those skills on the court transferred to your skill off the court, I would assume?" she asked.

"Most definitely."

"I suppose that's why you got into the used car business?"

"Preowned automobile business," he said, correcting her.

"Of course. Because your skills . . . rather, your *game* transferred."

"Correct."

"So, you would agree that you have game?"

"Objection, Your Honor, counselor is misleading the witness with a play on words."

"Your Honor, I'm simply communicating with the witness in the vernacular of his former profession."

"Overruled. Counselor, you may proceed."

"Again, would you agree that you have game?"

"Sure, I have game."

"Good at the no-look pass? Could you do that, Mr. Sealant?"

"Without thinking twice," he said.

"And the no-look pass is what?"

"It's when the person covering you thinks you're going to go in one direction and out of nowhere you switch up and go in the opposite direction, leaving him there standing in a cloud of dust."

"And you were an expert at the no-look pass, is that right, Mr. Sealant?"

"One of the best."

"You were the best at making your opponent believe one thing, only to already have decided in your mind that you were going to do another?"

"Objection, Your Honor, the counselor is attempting to mislead my client with his own words."

"Overruled, continue."

"Mr. Sealant, explain to me what the 'cool-down period' means."

"That's the time a buyer has to think about his or her purchase before it becomes binding."

"And what is the cool-down period in the used car business?"

"I wouldn't know. I don't sell used cars."

"Forgive me. What is the cool-down period in the preowned automobile industry?"

"There is no cool-down period."

"The same as the used car dealerships?" she asked.

"I wouldn't know," he said. "I don't—"

"I know. You don't sell used cars. Your Honor, I'd like to admit as evidence the standard used-car dealership policy that shows proof that there is no cool-down period in the standard used-car dealership. So, we find a similarity," she said, and both Altima and I were low-fiving each other under the table.

"She's wearing his ass out," Altima whispered.

"I guess," Charles continued. "There is a slight similarity."

"And why is there no cool-down period, Mr. Sealant?" asked Ophelia.

"Your Honor, I object, she's asking my client to represent the industry for a policy and practice that was invoked before he ever started selling used cars."

"You mean preowned," Judge Bean said, correcting him and raising her brow.

"Yes, Your Honor. Preowned."

"Your Honor," Ophelia added, "whether he created the rule or not is inconsequential to the question, given that the practice of the law is the primary foundation of the sales process."

"Overruled. You may continue."

"Again, Mr. Sealant, why is there no cool-down period?"

"I'm not sure," he said. "I know what you're getting at, but I didn't make up the rules."

"You just play by them, I know, is that right, Mr. Sealant?"

"Objection. Badgering the witness," said Miles.

"Sustained."

"Would you agree that the reason why there is no cool-down period is because you don't want to give the buyer a chance to change his mind and spoil the sale, is that right?"

"Objection."

"Overruled."

"Is that right, Mr. Sealant?"

"I suppose it is. When you give people too much time to think they usually make the wrong choice."

"Wrong for whom?"

"For me."

"For you, but right for them?"

"They want a car, I sell them a car. They want some quick transportation, I give them that. Otherwise they would go to a new car dealership and get themselves tied up in a five-year lease."

"Unlike the new car dealership, you're a quick fix? Is that right Mr. Sealant?"

"I guess."

"Like an in-between car."

"You could say that."

"A tide-you-over transitional transportation vehicle. You're not the man that she wants, but you're the man she'll take until she can afford to have the man she really wants. Just like a used car," she said.

"Objection, Your Honor. The counselor is putting words in the mouth of the witness."

"Sustained."

"No more questions for this witness, Your Honor." Ophelia returned to her seat to our smiles and low-fives under the bench.

"We'll take a recess and return at three," Judge Bean said as the gavel fell, and round one had ended. To our surprise we had Charles backed up and leaning against the ropes. Round one goes to us.

Thirty-Four

OVER ALTIMA'S homemade lunch, we had a chance to exhale, catch our breath, and prepare ourselves for round two. My mother was kind enough to make my favorite German chocolate cake, which I was more than happy to share with our troops.

"This reminds me of a John Grisham book," my mother added to the conversation while we were eating. "Do you think they'll make it into a movie? If they do, I want Angela Bassett to play me."

"Ladies, court's in session in five minutes," sounded the voice of the bailiff as we scarfed down what little cake remained, huddled together for one last moment of affirmation and empowerment as off we went for more.

"All rise as the Honorable Judge Bernetta Bean enters the court."

Up then down we went as the gavel fell.

"Counselor Milner, it's your witness."

"I'd like to call back to the stand my client, Charles Sealant."

"You're reminded that you are still under oath, Mr. Sealant."

"Yes, ma'am," he replied.

Miles wasted no time in picking up exactly where he left off.

"So, Mr. Sealant, exactly how long did it take before you and Ms. Chase became sexually active?"

"Too long," he replied, as the court broke into laughter.

"Order in the court," the judge shouted as her gavel fell. "This is not an episode of *Jerry Springer*. The next outburst and someone, maybe several someones, will be held in contempt of court. Counselor, you may continue. Cautiously and very carefully continue," she added.

"She made me wait six weeks."

"Is that the norm?"

"That's the abnorm. Usually I don't wait six days. But I did. I mean, I understand for some women it makes them feel better about themselves if they wait till the day they've prearranged in their mind is the day they should give a man what they wanted to give him the minute they laid eyes on him. I could tell she had just been through a bad relationship, so I didn't mind making the investment because I believed she was worth it and that it would ultimately reap dividends."

"You say you made an investment. Do you mean you took her to dinner, the movies?"

"I mean, I took her around the world."

"Around the world, meaning you took her to the hottest spots around Philadelphia?"

"No, I mean I took her *around* the world. I took her to Paris."

"Paris, Texas?" Miles asked laughingly. "You took her to a suburb of Houston?"

"I took her to Europe. Paris, France," he added. "I took her with me on a business trip on a private plane that my associate chartered."

"I'm sure that wasn't such a big deal. She had already been there, I'm sure," Miles asked.

"Please. She hadn't been farther than South Street. Probably never sat in first class, let alone flown in a private plane. Fine dining to her was a cheesesteak at Ishkibibbles. But I don't fault a woman for where she's been; I try to remain focused on where she's going. Where I can take her."

"So, after the trip to Paris, you had sex right after? Surely such a bout of romance and chivalry was capped off with a night of steamy, hot passion. I mean, what woman wouldn't reward a man for literally broadening her horizons?"

"That was only week one. I still had five more to go."

"You took her around the world, wined her and dined her on a private plane, and never once asked for a romantic reward?"

"Like I said before, I could tell she had just ended a relationship and was a little tentative. I wanted her to know that I was in it for the long haul."

"And what happened on the night of the sixth week?"

"I came over to her house for dinner. I brought the finest bottle of wine I could find and we ate, we drank, and we very merrily made our way to the bedroom to close the deal."

"Close the deal, meaning to make love."

"It takes love to make love. I mean sex. Good, old-fashioned sex."

"And did anything unusual happen?" Miles asked.

"Not at first. At first it was pretty much the usual. The petting, which led to the rubbing, which led to the kissing, which led to us both grinding on top of each other in the bed."

"And how did that feel?"

"It felt good. She's a very well-proportioned woman, obviously raised on a very healthy supply of milk. She was stacked. I couldn't wait."

"You were excited?"

"To say the least. And she knew I was because she had her hand on my . . . you know," he said, looking at the judge.

"And then what happened?"

"Well, right when I'm thinking we're about to get it on, she pulls out about five or six sheets of paper and asks me to initial and sign."

"And what did you do?"

"I did what any full-blooded straight American man would do. I signed it."

"You signed something without reading it."

"Even if I had read it, it wouldn't have mattered. A man has two heads, with just enough blood to operate only one at a time. At that moment, I would have signed my grandmomma's execution papers. And I love my grandmomma. But that night, she would have come up a little short."

"So, you were under duress?"

"Objection, calls for a legal conclusion and the witness is not an attorney."

"Sustained."

"I was in heat." Charles continued. "I was hard enough to chop a cinderblock, and she knew it."

"And still, she asked you to sign a legal document at a time when you were in a compromised state."

"That is correct."

"No more questions, Your Honor."

"Counselor Clarke, the witness is all yours." Ophelia grabbed my hand, squeezed it tight and then released it and approached the bench.

"Mr. Sealant," she said. "So, you were 'in heat'? I believe those are the words you used to describe your state of mind."

"That's correct."

"Would you elaborate on that, please?"

"Heat. Excitement. It's when you want something so bad, you disregard all logic and reason."

"Would you agree that's the worst time to ask someone to sign a binding document?"

"The absolute worst. It's like giving crack to a crackhead."

"So, you're saying sex is an addiction."

"Ask Eric Benet. He had the finest woman on the planet. But that didn't stop him," he said, as again the courtroom began to murmur.

"And how would you describe the mind-set of one of your customers when they enter your dealership? Would you describe them as being in 'heat'?" she asked.

"Not at all," he said.

"How would you describe them then?"

"Like I said earlier, my customer is an educated consumer who makes logical, well-informed, and insightful decisions. My customer knows exactly what they want. The shape, size, and color of what they want. And how much they're willing to pay for what they want."

"Of course they do," she said, pacing as she approached the jury stand with her back to Charles. "Which is precisely why you enforce the no-cooling-off policy that binds this very logical and insightful client of yours to a binding contract the very second they take the car off the lot. In reality, isn't it true that this customer is no more logical than you yourself were when you signed the contract given to you by my client?"

"Objection!"

"Isn't it true that you prey on customers that, like yourself, are also in heat?"

"Objection, the prosecution is leading the witness!"

"Isn't it true that your cars are the crack, and in selling those cars you are no better than the common corner crack dealer preying on an addiction? Is that right, Mr. Sealant?"

"Objection!"

"Is that right, Mr. Sealant?" Ophelia said, now nearly yelling.

"You damn right, that's right! Shit, if I didn't sell it to them, they were just gonna buy it somewhere else. I did them a favor. I gave them what they wanted."

"You serviced their addiction?"

"Hell yeah, if that's what you want to call it."

"No more questions, Your Honor."

Thirty-Five

THE DAY ENDED and the next day began with Charles once again on the stand, discussing the very same thing—sex. Only this time the questions dug deeper and the dirt slung farther.

"And how exactly was the sex?"

"Nothing spectacular. She wanted me to reload it, recharge it, rehit it, and jump-start it all night long. I know I sell automobiles for a living, but it's not as easy as sticking the key in the ignition and slamming on the gas. Sometimes a more advanced engine has to warm up first. I could tell she was used to the gas-and-go kind of model."

I felt my mother shrinking farther and farther into her seat behind me.

"And she was loud. I could tell she was a church girl, the way she kept calling on Jesus all the time with such fervor and intensity."

"Objection! Objection! Objection!" came a shout from the courtroom—my mother stood in protest. The judge's gavel fell and fell and fell, pounding the bench, finally causing my mother to return to her seat.

"And she couldn't even really cook. The greens were always bitter."

"Bitter! My greens ain't *bitter*," Altima blurted out, standing up, then pausing to catch herself as everyone silently watched. "I mean . . . my recipe for greens ain't bitter. That's what I mean. I mean that . . ." For a moment she continued to babble as the judge's gavel fell. Ophelia and I lowered our heads. Altima had just hand-delivered the nail that Miles would use to hammer our contract's coffin closed.

"No more questions for this witness. At this time, Your Honor, I'd like to call to the stand Altima Davis."

Ophelia and I both held our breath, as Altima made her way to the stand.

"Do you solemnly swear that your testimony is the truth, the whole truth, and nothing but the truth, so help you God?"

"I do," she said tentatively.

"So, Ms. Davis, were the greens bitter?"

"Objection, Your Honor," Ophelia jumped in. "Speculative."

"Your Honor, if the chef herself can't speculate on how the greens tasted, then who can?"

"Overruled. Witness will answer the question."

"No, they weren't bitter."

"And you know that, because why?"

"Because it's the way you season the greens. See, most people use ham hocks for seasoning, and maybe even a little hot sauce. I burn a little sugar onto the ham hocks before I add them to the greens, so they never come out bitter. That's how I know."

"Interesting," Miles said. "Just listening to you is making me hungry," he said as the entire courtroom rumbled in obvious agreement. "I'm going to have to ask the court stenographer for a transcript so I can go home and try to re-create those greens myself. Just curious, what other things have you made for your friend?"

"Objection, defense is leading the witness. Witness has not yet stated she has cooked anything other than the greens."

"Sustained. Defense will rephrase the question."

"Ms. Davis, are greens the only thing you've cooked for Ms. Chase?"

"Do I have to answer the question?" she asked.

"Why would you not want to answer the question?" Miles asked.

"Because no matter what I say you're gonna turn it around and use it against my friend."

"Your friend would be referring to Ms. Chase?"

"That's right."

"She's your best friend, is that right?"

"In the whole wide world, that's right."

"A friend that you would do just about anything for?"

"Not *just about* anything—anything."

"And that's why you cooked the greens, to help out a friend?"

"That's right. She's a great person. She'd do anything in the world for anybody. Even people she barely knows."

"And how long have you two known each other?"

"Since high school," said Altima.

"And how long have you been working together?"

"She's been at the job for almost two years. I've been there a little over a year.

"She kept pushing for me to work there. She knows how much I love watching lawyers on television and I was in between jobs. Actually, I'm pretty much always in between jobs. She knew I was going through it, and so she always tells me that dreams can't come true unless you're first willing to take the first step, which is to dream them in the first place. Being around her watching her dreams come true makes me want to dream myself."

"And your dream is to do what?"

"Really, I don't know. I thought it was to become a lawyer, but ever since this case started, and I've been in here watching you, I don't know if I want to be a lawyer anymore."

"I'm curious as to why you would say that. Please clarify."

"I always thought lawyers were there to help people. But it seems like to help somebody, you have to hurt somebody else. I don't want to hurt anybody. And I don't want to see anybody else get hurt. That's why I helped my friend out cooking. Because really, I just don't want to see her in and out of relationships. Me? I'm used to a little drama in my life, growing up the way I did, but Mo's not used to that. She's got a nice family and went to a nice college. I just always thought feeding a man was the first step to pleasing a man, so I figure since she always helps me out, I'd help her out. Everybody love a good plate of greens. Especially a black man. Oh, and not to mention the smothered chicken. I got that recipe from my great-grandmother. And the candied yams, from my grandmother on my mommy's side—the secret to the yams is just the right amount of cinnamon and sugar. And for dessert, the blueberry cobbler with slices of peach on the top." For almost an hour she went on with one recipe after another, as her eyes lit up and her face began glowing.

When the gavel fell, signaling for the end of the day, almost everyone in the courtroom had one thing on their mind—food. I couldn't be mad at Altima. All she really did was tell the truth.

Thirty-Six

BY THE END of week one, our giant step for all womankind had turned into a media circus, and its ringmaster was Miles Milner.

"This case is about more than just one man and one woman," he ranted, while cameras flashed and recorders were perched beneath his mouth. "That's Milner," he corrected. "Miles Milner. M-I-L-N-E-R of Milner, Jackson and Jacobs. This case is about the very foundation of humanity. The fundamental precepts of how we look, touch, smell, how we taste one another. And I for one am proud to be the lead counsel for the defense, as I not only defend this one man, but I defend every man and every woman everywhere who still believes that a broken heart can mend without forcing our great laws to bend. Any additional questions should be forwarded to my personal publicist, who handles my interviews, book deals, and personal appearances. God bless you, and God bless this great land we call America."

My exit from the courthouse was far less eventful. As I had done all week, I slipped out the side door, to avoid contact with the media, which now included not only local and national television stations but the ACLU, the NAACP, and almost every special interest activist group you could name. The case was consuming my every thought and my every move. I decided the best option would be to put my mind on something else. I took the back streets to my office. Since it was late, the office was sure to be empty and I was grateful for the guaranteed moment of calm.

The familiar leathery arms of my office chair wrapped my now worn-and-torn body. I was emotionally drained, physically weary, and mentally taxed. But I was still feeling that what I was doing was the right thing. I rose from my seat and walked over to the wall, where my framed certificates hung. My diploma. My bar examination. I was lost in a back-down-memory-lane moment when a voice from behind me said, "The last time I saw my diploma was the day I graduated."

I turned to see Michael standing in the door frame. The light from the hallway cast a shadow across the side of his face.

"Five minutes after I walked across the stage it was out of my hands, into my mother's hands, and then to the wall in her dining room where it will hang for all of eternity," he said. "Do you mind if I come in?"

"As long as you're not carrying a camera or a tape recorder," I said with a half chuckle, attempting to manufacture some sanity.

"No need, I've already licensed the rights of your story to the Lifetime Channel. They're giving us a six-figure advance and an executive consultant credit. I didn't think you'd mind."

"Not at all. You're smart enough to get somebody to pay for what everybody else seems to be getting for free," I said. "Which, according to Miles, would make you an accomplice to murdering the American dream," I said, finding some fleeting amusement in the lunacy of it all.

"I warned you about him."

"Yeah, you did," I said.

"But I'm not here to tell you I told you so. Though we're real clear on the fact that I did tell you so," he said, giving me a playful look.

"We're clear," I said. "If you're not here to tell me you told me so, then what are you here for? Why are you in the office so late?"

"Well, for one, because someone who I won't mention decided to try her own case rather than assist me on my case—the case that's paying her salary. But let's not go there," he said.

"Let's not," I said softly.

"Do you want to know what the other reason is?"

"I'm scared to ask," I said.

"You should be."

"It's about my case, isn't it?" I asked.

"Yep. There's a rumbling among the partners. Apparently last night one of the partners was flipping through the channels and guess who was front and center on the local news?"

"That would be me," I supposed.

"No. Try someone worse."

"Miles."

"Or as he puts it, 'Miles Milner, the last hope for free love.' Atop his usual soapbox, he was proclaiming that the conviction of his client would be the end of the liberation of love as we know it. And then they flashed a picture of you. The partner wondered why they would flash a picture of one of our lawyers, suing a man for the very same thing our firm has been hired to defend a very high-profile client for. Then today at the board meeting that same senior partner got the other senior partners to start to wonder the same thing. Not good," he said. "Definitely not good."

"Did it start to make you wonder, too?"

"No, because I already know why you're doing it. Because you're crazy," he said. "The only thing I wondered was if it was worth it. Is it worth ruining your career? Your reputation? Your future?"

"Are you asking me if standing up and fighting is worth it?"

"For a social belief, no. But for an emotional relief, yes, I am. I'm asking if your intention is to make a law or to teach a lesson. If it's the latter, I would strongly advise you to leave it alone. People have their hearts broken all the time. And they mend all the time. Every day people hurt, and every day they heal. Sometimes the only way you really appreciate finding love is after you've lost it. Morgan, I've got your back, you know that. I've got your back, your front, and all parts in between, but if this thing drags out much longer, or God forbid, if you're crazy enough to take the stand, they're going to let you go. And you know what that means, don't you?" he said with a solemn face.

"What?"

"No more fried chicken Fridays at the firm," he said with a straight face and then a smile.

"Thanks," I said.

"Don't mention it. You get some rest."

He leaned down and kissed me on the forehead.

Thirty-Seven

ON MY WAY HOME from the office I called an emergency meeting between me, Altima, and Ophelia. After my conversation with Michael, I thought a heart-to-heart was in order. I could handle my job being in jeopardy, but I didn't want to be responsible for Ophelia or Altima losing theirs, too.

"Girl, I was in the middle of some good sleep," Altima said. "But you know if it's for you, I'm here, there, or anywhere," she said.

Within an hour, Ophelia, Altima, and I were all in my living room, sipping coffee and talking strategy.

"So, I called you both here tonight because I had a long talk with Michael tonight when I stopped by the office."

"Is that all you two were doing? Talking?" Altima asked with a mischievous look on her face.

"Yes, that's all we were doing, thank you."

"Don't thank me—thank God, for making such a beautiful creature like Michael Sampson," said Altima.

"Did he comment on the case?" Ophelia interrupted.

"Indirectly, yes. It was more of what the partners had to say. One of them caught an interview on TV and it didn't sit too well. Especially since I'm supposed to be co-lead counsel defending the mayor for almost the same thing we're suing Charles for."

"And?"

"And so, it could get ugly."

"Uglier than being overqualified and underutilized?" she said. "Uglier than working for a man that knows less than you, makes more than you, and the way he rewards you each year for covering his ass and making him look good is a box of holiday Godiva chocolates? Like I need to be eating a damn box of Godiva chocolates."

"If we keep going, it could cost me my job. And maybe even yours."

"That's one cost I don't mind paying," Ophelia said.

"Me, neither," Altima said. "I'm with you, Mo, you know that."

"That's very nice of you both, but I'm serious. You could lose your jobs."

"Or we could gain our lives," Ophelia said. "This is what I was born to do. This is who I was born to be. Because of this case, I finally feel like I'm important. Like I'm more than just a background bookend. I'm in the forefront. The main stage. For the first time in my life, I'm a headliner. And it's because you gave me a chance. Even as difficult as I've been over the years, you still gave me a chance. I will always respect you for that," she said.

"I feel the same way, girl," Altima chirped in. "Ever since I beat that bitch down for you in high school, you've been looking out.

Now it's time somebody looked out for you. And besides, I don't know if I want to do this law thing anyway. What I really want to do is maybe open up a restaurant. Being up on the stand watching everybody's mouth water while I was talking about the recipes made me feel really good. You know, I usually just cook for friends, but after I left the stand, three of the jurors, the bailiff, and the stenographer wanted to order my pineapple upside-down cake. I have nobody but you to thank for that. Forget the job. I'm rolling with you."

"Wow," I said, as my eyes began tearing up.

"Girl, don't cry," Altima said.

"Yes, please don't cry, Morgan. 'Cause it's going to make me cry, and I don't usually show that kind of emotion in public," said Ophelia.

"I can't help it," I said.

"Neither can I," whimpered Altima.

"Aw hell, neither can I!" Ophelia screamed. "I love you guys," she hollered, as we all three hugged and cried tears of joy and camaraderie. Through all the drama, we had formed a bond that would most likely last forever.

"Okay, that's enough hugging," Ophelia said. "We have a case to win."

"So, how are we doing?"

"Fine," she said. "We're doing just fine. We're going to be fine."

"Ophelia . . ."

"What?"

"Come on now, girl. Really, what do you think? Do we have a chance?"

"We have a chance," she said. "Not a good chance, but still, it's a chance."

"It's my fault, isn't it?" Altima asked. "I couldn't just let him sit his pompous ass up there and talk about my greens like that. That was Aunt Ethel's recipe."

"It's not your fault," Ophelia said.

"It's not?"

"No."

"Then whose fault is it?" Altima asked.

"Nobody's. So far they've taken almost every potshot in the world."

"And without a testimony from Morgan, it's going to be hard to convince the jury otherwise," Ophelia said.

"Then she should testify," Altima exclaimed.

"I can't."

"Why not?"

"Because she's a lawyer. It would be seen as compromising her profession and personally it would open her up to public and private scrutiny," said Ophelia. "If she ever plans on practicing law anywhere in this state, it would be like signing her own death certificate. And knowing Miles, he would love to be the one to hand her the pen."

"There's got to be something we can do," said Altima.

"Something short of breaking into Charles's house and finding some dirt, I don't know what," she said. Altima and I looked at each other contemplating the same thing.

"We are not breaking into that man's house," Ophelia intently stated.

"Why not?" Altima replied.

"I don't know . . . maybe because it's a *crime*!"

"It's only a crime if you get caught," Altima replied.

"I am not breaking into anybody's house."

"Nobody's asking *you* to break into anybody's house," I said.

"Then *who* are we asking?" she said.

"I haven't figured that one out yet."

"It would have to be somebody with absolutely nothing to lose," she said.

"Somebody without an ounce of moral fiber."

"Somebody that's unemployed," Altima said.

"Uninspired," Ophelia added.

"Somebody with no life."

"And most of all, somebody that's stupid enough to believe they can actually get away with it," Ophelia added.

Seconds later, we were all three in front of Andre's door. I had changed into one of his favorite outfits, a tight Juicy jumpsuit with the jacket zipper at the base of my cleavage. Altima was standing with a heated piece of her famous pineapple upside-down cake. And Ophelia was there just in case Andre tried to escape.

Before I could barely finish knocking once, the door swung open to the thumping sounds of old school Jodeci.

"Hey now," he said as he stepped outside in a pair of plaid Sean John pajama bottoms and a too-small tank top. "To what do I owe this pleasure?"

"I have something for you. A gift."

"I can see that," he said, eyeing Altima from head to toe.

"Not her?"

He turned, and looked at Ophelia.

"Don't even think it," she said.

"It's a piece of cake," I said.

"It's homemade," Altima added. "I made it myself."

"Is that right?" he said. "What kind?"

"Pineapple upside-down. Try it," she said, sticking her fork into the cake and then into his mouth. Soon thereafter, a smile covered his face.

"That tastes like the cake Morgan makes."

"It is," I said. "She made it."

"She made your cake?" he said confused.

"Yes, it's a long story."

"I got time. Would you ladies like to come inside for a spell? I got a little wine. We could talk a bit and get to know each other. Cuddle up for a warm winter's night. A little grown folks' foray into the wonderful world of indulgence and delight. Like the movie *Trois*. We could make our own movie. *Ménage à trois*."

"That's three people," I said.

"I know," he said counting, "one, two, three. Trois."

"But there's four of us, dumb ass," Ophelia added.

"Oh," he said. "Then you should take your ass home."

"So, Andre," I interrupted, "we need a favor."

"From who?"

"You," Ophelia said.

"What kind of favor?" he asked with his eyebrows raised.

"We need you to help us find something that's lost," Altima said.

"Something like my heart, 'cause I think I'm slowly losing it," he said, staring at Altima. "Any woman that can cook in the kitchen can damn sure cook in the bedroom," he said, licking his lips.

"Andre, get your mind out of the gutter for once," I chastised.

"Why I got to be the gutter?" Altima said.

"I'm not calling you the gutter, per se," I said.

"Then what are you calling her, per se?" Andre said.

"I'm not calling her nothing. Look, Andre we need your help."

"To do what?"

"To break into someone's house," Ophelia said, interrupting me and obviously tired of beating around the bush.

"Did you just say 'break into somebody's house'?"

"Yes."

"Do I look like some kind of criminal to you? Like I don't have anything better going for myself than to risk my future on a petty crime."

"Pretty much," we all chimed in.

"So, what if I am? What's in it for me?"

"The satisfaction of knowing that for once in your life you did something kind for somebody without expecting anything in return."

"Naw," he said. "Try again."

"It would make me feel good," Altima said.

"See, now we're getting somewhere. Whose house is it anyway?"

"My ex."

"Which one?"

"The last one."

"Which last one? I get confused."

"The one I'm suing."

"You're suing somebody? I thought your job was to represent folks that were suing folks."

"You haven't seen it on the news?" Ophelia asked.

"I don't watch the news. Actually, I don't watch nothing since my cable got cut off."

"So, you haven't heard anything about the case?" I asked.

"What case?"

"Look Andre, we need to you to break into my ex's house and help us find something."

"Find what?"

"We won't know till we get there."

"I'm sorry, ladies. I would love to help you out, but contrary to what you may or may not think of me, I'm not that kind of guy. I know those kinds of guys, but I don't frequently frequent them any longer. So, I'm sorry, I would love to help, but I can't."

"And there's nothing we can do to change your mind?" Altima said.

"Unfortunately not, sweetheart."

"Nothing at all?" I said.

"Not even if we paid the bill to cut your cable back on?" Ophelia asked.

Thirty-Eight

MINUTES LATER, we were pulling up around the corner to Charles's house.

"You know, I really shouldn't be doing this," Andre said. "Breaking and entering is a crime."

"We're not breaking," I said. "We're just entering."

"It's the same thing. Hell, even I know that and I didn't have to go to law school. Hell, I barely got out of high school. What if we got caught and I went to prison?"

"First of all, we're not going to get caught."

"But what if we did? I could go to prison. I'm too pretty to go to prison. In prison they prey on pretty. Lay on pretty. And then they have their way on pretty."

"You're not going to jail," Ophelia said as we inched closer and closer to Charles's house. "And besides, if you do, you'll have us as your lawyers."

"We're good," Altima said.

"So good that we're outside a man's house contemplating a criminal act? Great consolation," he said, twisting his face.

"There it is," I said. "That's his house on the right."

"*Damn!* That's his house?" Andre said.

"Yep."

"Just his?"

"Yep."

"All by hisself?! He's not, like, renting some rooms out or nothing?"

"That's all his."

"And you messed that up?"

"No, he messed that up," I said. "He had another woman up in there."

"Okay, so he was a dog in one room. But he got about thirty more to go. He had to have been worth something in at least one of the rooms. What do y'all women want nowadays?"

"For you to shut the hell up," Ophelia said. "That's what we women want."

"See, you ain't got to cuss at me. I don't have to be here. I'm doing y'all a favor."

"He's right. Andre, we're sorry," Altima said.

"You better tell her," he added. "Let her know. I got other stuff I could be working on. Even at home doing nothing is doing something. Tell her to apologize for cussing at me and calling me out my name."

"Andre, come on now," I said.

"Tell her to apologize or I'm getting out the car and walking my about-to-commit-some-illegal-shit-for-a-friend, black ass home."

"I'm sorry, okay? Can we please move on?" Ophelia said.

"Yes, we can. As long as it doesn't happen again," he said.

"It won't," I assured him.

"So, what's the plan?" Ophelia asked.

"The plan is to check around the back and see if there's a window that's cracked, hop inside, and let us in the front."

"And who's gonna implement this plan?" Andre said. " 'Cause I know y'all don't expect me to hop over some fucking fence so I can get bit in the ass by some dog. Y'all got to do more than cut my cable on. Y'all got to buy me the TiVo, too."

"Are you out of your mind?" Ophelia said.

"Yes. It's contagious," he said, looking around at all of us. "It's either the TiVo or hopping the fence is a no-go."

"Okay, Andre, I'll get you the TiVo."

"And the cable?" he said.

"And the cable," Ophelia said.

"And some cakes and pies from my chocolate soufflé over here that she will hand deliver to me once a week for a month?"

"You like my cake that much?" Altima asked.

"Not as much as I like you," he replied, winking his eye.

"Why do I feel like I'm stuck inside a ghetto greeting card?" Ophelia asked as both Andre and Altima gazed romantically into each other's eyes.

"Andre!"

"What?!"

"Come on!" I said, "we don't have all night. You got the TiVo, the cable, and pies for a month. Now get going."

"Okay," he said. "But how do you know he ain't home?"

"It's Wednesday night. He does new inventory at his dealership on Wednesday nights."

Andre reached in his bag, pulled out a black knit cap that he had cut the eyes out of, and slid it over his head.

"What the hell are you doing?" Ophelia asked.

"I'm getting into character," he said.

"You mean, you are a character," Ophelia countered.

"There she go again. Somebody better tell her something," he said.

"Ophelia—" I said. "Okay, Andre, hurry up," we said as he eased out of the car, making his way to the house looking like a mix of James Bond, Maxwell Smart, and Inspector Clouseau all wrapped up in one. After several failed attempts at clearing the fence, finally he made it over.

"He's going to get himself killed," Ophelia said.

"I hope not," Altima said. "I think he's pretty cool."

"Obviously this case hasn't affected your standards," Ophelia countered.

After a few minutes, he again made his way to the car with feline grace and style.

"So, what did you see?" we asked.

"There's a window open, but it's on the second floor. I'm gonna need something sturdy to stand on."

We all looked at Ophelia.

"Why's everybody looking at me?"

"'Cause you're about the sturdiest thing available," Andre said.

"You know what, I've had just about enough of you," Ophelia threatened.

"Ditto," he said.

"You want some of me?" Ophelia said.

"Bring it on," Andre said. "I ain't scared of you."

"Guys, guys, guys, come on, now. Let's focus. We're almost there. All we need to do now is find a way to lift Andre up."

"He should be able to lift himself up with some of that hot air he's blowing all the time."

"Ophelia, can Andre stand on your shoulders so he can get in the window and so we can go home?" I asked as sweetly as possible.

"How am I supposed to get over the fence?"

"Over it? Why not just run through it?" Andre said.

It was obvious that they were going to be at it the entire night. Still, we had a mission and I wasn't about to let a petty squabble throw us off track.

"Andre, is there a latch to open the gate on the other side of the fence?"

"Yeah. I believe it is."

"Then could you hop back over and unlock it?"

"If properly motivated, I supposed I could."

Out of nowhere, Altima leaned over and kissed him on the cheek. "How's that?" she asked.

"Girl, I'll show you how's that," he said as he backed up and ran full speed, nearly clearing the fence in one full leap. From the other side, the gate slowly opened as we three made our way to the back-yard and under the window, where Ophelia moved into position. Andre hopped onto her shoulders and then slowly stood up where he was just about at the window.

"Can you stand on your tippy toes?" he asked. "I need a couple more inches."

Wobbling and wiggling him on her shoulders, he was lifted up on the ledge and then slowly the window raised and he was inside.

"What am I looking for?" he asked.

"Whatever you can find."

"Don't steal anything," Ophelia said.

"I thought that was the purpose," he said.

"Andre, hurry up," I said.

"Be careful," Altima whispered.

"Oh God," Ophelia said under her breath.

Almost seconds after he entered the house we noticed sharp lights seeping through the fence.

"Uh-oh," Altima said.

"That's him," I said.

"That's Charles?" Ophelia whispered in shock.

"I think so."

"What about Andre?" Altima asked.

"What about him? It's only five to ten for breaking and entering. Or ten to fifteen if while he's breaking and entering he unintentionally injures someone, like the owner."

"Andre!" Altima shouted in a loud whisper-shout.

"*Shh,*" Ophelia said, "he'll hear you."

"We can't just let him get caught. We have to do something."

"Okay, how 'bout a pebble. We'll throw a pebble at the window," I said, as seconds later we nearly emptied the entire pebble bed of small stones from the flowerbed. Charles's car door closed just as Andre's head peered from the window.

"What? I'm getting close."

"So is he," I silently shouted.

"He who?" he asked.

"Charles."

"*Charles* Charles," he said.

"Yes."

"Oh, shit. Shit. Shit. Shit."

"I think I heard the door close," Altima said.

"I'ma go to jail. Pretty got problems. Pretty going to the pen. Somebody help Pretty," Andre moaned as the lights filled the house.

"Get out of the window and jump," Ophelia said.

"No, he can't jump, he'll hear us," I said.

"Well, he just can't stay in the house," Altima said.

"Stand on the side of the ledge," Ophelia said.

"And then what?"

"I don't know. We'll take it one step at a time. Just get on the ledge," I said.

"I am not standing on the ledge."

"Andre, please." Altima pleaded. "Stand on the ledge. If you fall we'll catch you."

"Okay, boo, only for you. I'm doing it for you only."

Slowly, Andre climbed out on the ledge just in time, as Charles's shadow filled the room.

"Now what," he said.

"*Shhh.* Give it a minute."

After a few minutes, the lights went dim and another shadow joined Charles in the bedroom.

"Who's that?" I asked.

"Who's who?" he asked.

"The other shadow?"

"I think it's a woman," he said. "Oh, it's a woman for sure. Damn, she got some big titties. And she fine, too," he said.

"Is it a Frenchwoman?" I asked.

"Morgan, are you serious?" Ophelia asked.

"What? It's evidence, right?"

"Morgan . . ." she said.

"Well, I just want to know if it's that same French bitch from before. Is she French, Andre?"

"Ask me if the titty is French, 'cause that's all I can see right about now."

"Is she white or black?"

"She definitely ain't a sistah from what I can tell. Got all that titty and no ass. Uup, there go the titty in his mouth. She could be French, 'cause he's sucking on it like it's French-fried titty."

"That's her," I said. "That's the bitch he flew in from France."

"Uup, there go the other titty. Damn, this is better than porno."

"What are they doing now?" I asked.

"Morgan, don't do this to yourself," Ophelia said.

"I can handle it," I said.

"Is she prettier than me?" Altima asked.

"Prettier than my chocolate fondue? She don't come close," he said.

"Andre, what are they doing now?" I asked.

"You don't want to know," he said. "Damn . . ."

"What?"

"I'ma have to try that position myself. Uup, there go the leg. The leg is perpendicular, uup, now it's parallel. It's at a forty-five-degree angle. Ninety degrees, one hundred and eighty. Damn, She just did a three-hundred-and-sixty-degree spin."

Unable to take it any longer, suddenly the loud crash of a brick through the window ended Andre's play-by-play. A brick that I had just hurled.

"What the hell you do that for?" Andre whispered.

"Jump, baby," Altima said.

"I can't," he said.

"Jump or Pretty going to the pen," Altima soft-screamed in her loudest and most desperate whisper.

Andre closed his eyes and jumped, landing right beside us. We all snuck past the fence, through the gate, around the side of the house, and behind a bush, where we watched a naked Charles come to the window, mouthing obscenities and then walking away. After a moment we rushed to the car and sped off in a cloud of dust, fussing and cussing our way back to my apartment.

Thirty-Nine

"OWWWWWW. My ankle. It hurts!" Andre screamed as we helped him up the stairs and into his apartment. "I think it's broken," he said as Altima removed his sock. "Careful, I'm in pain. Ahhhhh-haaaah! Morgan, you made me break my ankle! I hate you for this. I was supposed to be at this party this weekend. Now I can't dance."

"How bad is it swollen?" Altima asked.

"Aaaaah, don't touch it!" Andre continued moaning. "It's the size of a honeydew melon. Damn. I got five toes wrapped in a honeydew melon. Damn! This is gonna cost you, Morgan. I want the TiVo, my cable bill paid, pies and cakes for a month, and ten DVDs to watch while my ankle gets better. Aaaah, damn! I can't stand the pain. I can't stand the *pain!*"

"No problem," I said.

"Oh, for real?" he said as the pain magically disappeared. "Can we make that twenty DVDs?"

"No," I said.

"Aaaaaah," he resumed moaning. "Damn! I'm hurting. It's more than I can bear!"

"I could rub it down for you with some ice," Altima said.

"Would you?" Andre asked, again pausing his pain.

"Sure. I could rub it down and then we could eat a slice of one of my pies."

"Word?"

"But don't stay too long, Altima. It's late and we have another long day tomorrow," Ophelia warned her.

"I'm really not sleepy," she said.

"Neither am I. Hey, you want to watch a movie or something?" Andre asked.

"Sure," she said, as she began to lightly examine his ankle.

"Aaaaah, owwww, damn. I think I'ma need overnight watch care," he said. "Aaaah! Daaaaaam! Morgan, see what you did to me!"

"Andre," Altima said, "you don't have to pretend you're hurt to get me to stay longer."

"I don't?" he said with a look of bewilderment.

"No."

"Then how am I supposed to get you to stay?" he asked, as for the first time he let down his raging bravado to be human.

"I'll stay because I want to stay," she said. "That's if you want me to."

"Yeah," he said. "I want you to."

"Good. Why don't I go in the kitchen, get you some ice, put your leg up, and we can watch movies till the swelling goes down."

"Shoot, you keep sounding that sweet and that ain't the only thing that's gonna be swole," he said, "if you know what I mean."

"I think that's my cue to leave," Ophelia said.

"Mine, too. You two have a nice and short evening," I said, as Ophelia and I headed out into the hallway.

"Well, Ophelia, what can I say; we gave it our best, right?"

"'We gave it our best'? What's that supposed to mean? Are you giving up? I know you're not giving up. The opera ain't over till this fat lady sings. And this fat lady isn't singing."

"Come on now. You said it earlier, unless we found something incriminating or I testified, it'd be pretty tough to get the jury to deliver a verdict of guilty. We didn't find anything tonight."

"But we still have one more option," she said, giving me a look.

"Oh no," I said. "I'm not getting on the stand. They would eat me alive. They've already made me out to be the town tramp."

"So, then what do you have to lose? Your job? You've probably already lost that. Your integrity? You could never lose that for standing up for something you believed in. You're a hero," she said. "You're an icon. Even if we lose, we've won. Why? Because we did what was right. But I'm not going to sit here and say what I would do if I were you."

"Because it's not you," I said.

"It's not. But if it was," she said, "I'd give him hell. I'd go down with a bang. They'd have to shoot me, stab me, run me over with a truck before I'd lay down and die. It's going to take Evander Holyfield-when-he-whipped-Mike-Tyson's-ass kind of ass whipping. Hell, a Brenda-Ritchie-when-she-kicked-Lionel's-ass kind of I'm-out-in-the-middle-of-the-street-with-curlers-in-my-hair kind of ass whipping. 'Cause anything short of that, we're winning this case! You hear me?" she said.

"I hear you, champ. Get you some rest."

"I will. You, too. We shook up the world," she said as she began bouncing like Ali. "Shook up the world!" she continued as the elevators opened and closed.

I'd just closed the front door behind me and put down the keys when the phone rang. It was my mother.

"I couldn't sleep, you know, so I decided to fix me some herbal tea and give you a call. Your father used to fix it for me all the time when I was pregnant with you. I don't know if it was the tea that put me to sleep or the fact that he was sweet enough to get up at all hours of the night to fix it for me, but either way, I was out like a lightbulb," she said in her usual ramble. "Yeah, I was out like a lightbulb. Speaking of lightbulbs, I was reading today's newspaper and they said that this trial has begun to shed light on relationships all over the world. I was watching CNN and they showed packs of women from all over the globe commenting on the contract. Folks in Asia, Australia, even in Africa. Of course, I wasn't too sure exactly what they were saying in all those places since I don't speak their language, but whatever it was they were saying, they were saying it because of you. That's what I do know. Anytime you're talking about love, you can't help but make an impact. God knows, in the world we live in today we need all the love we can get.

"Pastor Reid was just preaching on love last Sunday. Sure was. Had the whole church hopping and jumping in the aisles, sure did. Love is a powerful thing. Yeah. I think you're doing a service to the whole world."

"Momma, did you know the first time you met Daddy that he was the one?"

"The one and only one," she said with warmth in her voice.

"Did you let him know it?"

"Of course not. I made him work for it. I gave him the opportunity to rise to the occasion. Which is what every man wants to do, if you let him. Most women don't know that. If you allow a man to do just enough, that's exactly what he'll do. Just enough. I gave your father room to be more than the man he ever thought he could be and that's just what he did. He was my king."

"Just when I think I've found a king and I sit him on a throne, by the time I turn around he's on some other woman's throne running some other kingdom."

"Maybe that's because you were too quick to give him the crown," she said. "You know, a throne is nothing but a bench covered in velvet. That's all it is. It's not the throne that makes the king, it's the king that makes the throne. You hear what I said? It's the king. Your daddy was my king and I have every bit of confidence that you'll find yours. And it won't be because of a contract, a crown, or a throne that he's the king. He'll be a king because that's what he is— a king." Letting out a deep yawn, she had counseled herself into the start of a peaceful nights' sleep.

"You get some rest, Momma."

"Oh, I intend on doing just that. I'll see you in the morning at the courtroom. You think about what I said, now, you hear?"

"Yes, Momma," I said.

"I'm proud of you. Shocked at some of your exploits," she said, "but like the Bible says, there's nothing new under the sun. We did the same thing, too. We were just a bit more discreet about it, that's all. Did I ever tell you, your father was a freak?"

"Momma, I do not want to hear about you and Daddy."

"But I had to hear about you and half the men in Philadelphia," she said.

"It wasn't half the men, Momma."

"Okay then, a third," she said.

"It wasn't a third, either," I said with my hand on my hip.

"Well, it was a lot, that's all I know," she said, laughing to herself. "That's what I know, it was a lot." After we said our good nights I sat on the couch pondering her words and what tomorrow would bring.

Forty

THE NEXT MORNING, the courtroom was buzzing with anticipation. It was the last day of testimony in a trial that had been the talk of Philadelphia for the past several weeks.

"All rise as the Honorable Judge Bernetta Bean enters the court."

"In reviewing the documents from the trial and my notes from yesterday, it appears as though there are no more witnesses. Counselor Milner, is that correct?" judge Bean questioned.

"That is, Your Honor. If it pleases the court, the defense rests, believing that it has satisfied its obligation to uphold and—"

"A simple yes or no answer will suffice, counselor," Judge Bean interrupted.

"Yes, Your Honor," Miles replied as he shrank into his seat.

"And Counselor Clarke, does the same apply to you? Have you no more witnesses?"

"Your Honor, if it pleases the court—"

"We would like to call one more witness to the stand, Your Honor—me," I said as the court erupted.

"Order in the court!" the judge shouted as her gavel pounded her wooden perch. "Order in the court!"

"Your Honor, if at all possible, I'd like to request a few moments to confer with my client," Ophelia pleaded.

"You have one minute," the judge replied.

"What are you doing?" Ophelia asked as we three huddled together in an attempt to hear ourselves and drown out the mumbling and rumbling in the courtroom.

"I'm doing what you would do. What Holyfield, Ali, and Brenda Ritchie did. I'm going in the ring and I'm kicking some ass. And if we're going down, we're going down swinging. Ali *bombaye,*" I said softly.

"Ali *bombaye,* indeed," Ophelia softly replied as we gave each other one long embrace.

"Your minute is up, counselor. What's your answer?"

"Your Honor, if it pleases the court, I'd like to call to the stand my final witness, Morgan Chase."

Charles's mouth almost dropped to the floor as I approached the bench to be sworn under oath.

"Do you, Morgan Chase, solemnly swear that the testimony you are about to give is the truth, the whole truth, and nothing but the truth, so help you God?"

"I do," I said as I eased into my seat. From my periphery, I saw my mother smile and nod in approval. At the next glance I noticed Miles licking his chops, barely able to disguise the anticipation for his cross-examination.

"Are you ready?" Ophelia mouthed to me. Taking a deep breath and then nodding slightly, I affirmed that I was.

"Morgan Chase, would you state your profession?"

"I'm a contracts lawyer."

"And where did you attend law school?"

"Temple University."

"And you grew up in the inner city?"

"Yes. But though I grew up in the inner city, the inner city didn't grow up in me. Before my father passed, he pushed me to exceed my expectations. He used to say, 'Morgan, don't listen when they say the sky is the limit. That's people just trying to give you a ceiling. There's something beyond the sky. And the only way you get it is to never, ever stop growing and reaching.'"

"And your mother. What kind of woman is she?"

"Oh, my mother. She's the sweetest woman I know. She raised me in the church. Tuesday night, Bible class. Friday night, young people's night, and all day Sunday from ten A.M. morning service, to noon devotion and praise service, to four-thirty afternoon service and an occasional Sunday evening service. And during the summer, it was vacation Bible school."

"So, it's safe to say that you grew up in a church."

"Yes, but unlike the inner city, the church grew up in me."

"So, given the way your parents raised you, the teaching that you obviously received in the church, I guess the question that's on the minds of us all is, why in the world would you create a love contract?"

"I was raised in a family that believed in accountability. You make a mess in your room, you clean it up. You get a bad report card, you stay in the house with no television or outdoor activity until you bring home a better report card. You break a window with a rock, you knock on the door of whoever owns the house and ask what you can do to work off what it would cost to repair the window. In our house, accountability was the eleventh commandment. It was the fabric of our family and along the way, it became the very foundation of how I approached my life and the people I wanted in my life. That's why I created the contract. Because lately most if not all of the relationships I was involved in were what I call '*my bad* relationships,'" I said, as the courtroom started stirring.

" '*My bad* relationships,' would you explain?"

"Sure. It's Monday, you meet a man who invites you out to dinner on Friday. Monday night, you call all your girlfriends and brag about this new man you just met and how he asked you out to dinner. Tuesday you go through your closet and realize you hate everything you own. Wednesday you go to the mall and spend money you don't have for an outfit you really don't need. Thursday you take off work early to get your nails and toes done and Thursday night you sit in a salon where you wait and wait and wait for your turn with the stylist. And you wait and you wait. Through weaves, swirls, perms, and curls, you wait. One overbooked client after another you wait and you wait till finally she gets to you just to tell you she's run out of your color. Then you wait till she goes to the Rite Aid and finally she does your hair, and by now it's about two-thirty in the morning. You get to work, rush through the day hardly getting any work done because all you're really thinking about is dinner with this man. You rush home, hop in the shower, and put on your perfume, your new outfit, and the phone rings."

"It's him, telling you something has come up and he has to cancel dinner tonight. And how does he account for having you go through a week of what you just went through—he tells you—'my bad.' 'My bad,' he says while you hang up the phone cussing him out. So, that's why I created the contract. I got sick of 'my bad relationships.' I got sick of making an emotional investment and yielding a no-longer-interested-in-being-with-you, no-interest return. They say there's a thin line between love and hate. Well, the contract turned that thin line into one with a Sharpie."

"I have no more questions, Your Honor," Ophelia said, sneaking in a wink as she eased in her seat.

"Counselor Milner, the witness is all yours."

"All mine, indeed," he said, as he rose from his seat, casually walking toward the jury stand. "So, you were brought up in the church, you say?"

"That is correct."

"What kind of church?"

"A holiness church."

"Oh, a Pentecostal church? A Jesus only church, where you were raised, no doubt, on the precepts of the New Testament. How a man born of a virgin died on the cross for the sins of mankind, then three days later He arose with all power in his hands? Then He ascended to heaven, where He rests forever more at the right hand of the Father. A loving, kind God. A God that you believe in, no doubt?"

"That is correct."

"And you live each day to abide by the fundamental precepts of those teachings?"

"That is correct."

"So, you are a Christian?" he asked.

"Objection, Your Honor, counselor is going nowhere, asking a line of questions with no relevance to the case."

"Counselor, get where you're going. And fast. Witness will answer the question."

"Yes, I am a Christian."

"And you've made certain promises to God?"

"That is correct."

"And what happens when you break those promises?"

"Grace and mercy happens."

"Grace and mercy, God's panacea happens. Grace and mercy, the very fundamental foundation of Jesus Christ's teachings happens. And you believe strongly in this grace and mercy?"

"That is correct."

"Then it stands to question, what happened to your beliefs when it came down to my client? Where's the grace and mercy for the transgressions my client allegedly committed?"

"I'm not God."

"You're not God?"

"No, I'm not."

"But yet you sit at the seat of judgment as if you were God," he said. "Is that correct? I mean, you can't have it both ways. You want to judge as if you're God, but you don't want to forgive as if you're God's son. Who are you really?" he asks.

"Objection! Counselor is badgering the witness," Ophelia chimed in.

"The kind of Christian who straddles the fence?" Miles continued.

"Objection, Your Honor!"

"Neither hot nor cold, but a lukewarm believer?" Miles added.

"Objection."

"Who cherry-picks the passages that suit her own agenda."

"Objection."

"What kind of Christian are you really, because I'm confused," he said. "And for that matter, so is the entire courtroom who themselves want to know what kind of Christian you are."

"A Christian who believes in retribution," I shouted.

"Retribution or revenge?" he shouted back. "Hurt for hurt? Pain for pain?"

"An eye for an eye and a tooth for a tooth," I said.

"Which to me sounds less like the Jesus I know of which you profess to follow and more like the crowd of mobs that put Him to death. No more questions, Your Honor," he said as he went to his seat. Miles had succeeded in making me contradict the very foundation of what I believed.

"The court will take a brief recess and return in one hour."

This round went to Miles.

Forty-One

THE HOUR FLEW BY quickly, and in what seemed like only seconds I was back at the stand for my second round of questions. During the recess Ophelia had cautioned me to keep my composure at all costs. Any sign of emotion could sway the jury into thinking that this was just the ploy of a bitter and smitten woman and not the work of a smart, sane, and sound woman seeking to level the playing field.

The gavel fell as again the court was in session.

"The witness is yours, Counselor Milner."

"Praise the Lord," he said under his breath.

"The counselor will kindly refrain from any religious reference," Judge Bean cautioned.

"I apologize, Your Honor. The devil made me do it," he said.

"Counselor, you're pushing it," she said with an eyebrow raised.

"So, Ms. Chase, men need to be accountable," he said. "They need to be honest and upfront. They need to be clear in representing themselves as to who they are and not just what and who they would have you believe that they are?"

"That is correct," I said.

"What you see should be what you get?" he continued. "I believe a popular saying among women of late is, 'Don't just talk about it, be about it,'" he said, flailing his hands and snapping his fingers as the court broke out into laughter. "Is that correct, Ms. Chase?"

"That is correct."

"That's odd," he said. "Because maybe it's just me, but that week you described earlier in such great detail is not about being honest and upfront. The first thing you said a woman does is call her girlfriends to talk about the new man in her life. When really he isn't her man, he's just someone she just met. But almost instantly she claims ownership and professes it to her girlfriends, getting them to buy into the reality of her fantasy. He could be another woman's man. How could she know? She just met him. But to her and anybody willing to listen, it's her man. Two days later you say she goes shopping for an outfit. Why not just go in her closet and be who she is. Wear what she has. Nope. That's no fun. 'I've already been who I was and that didn't get me anywhere. So, this time, I'm going to be who he thinks I am. Who he'll want me to be. And if I can be who he wants me to be long enough, he'll start to believe that's who I really am.' And then she goes to the nail salon and to get her nails done. What was wrong with her nails when they met? They were fine enough for him to make a date. Why wouldn't they be fine enough to have the date? And then the night before this first date you go where every woman goes—the beauty shop, or, as I like to call it, the magic shop. A woman's one-stop shop for trickery and transformation. Because all the stylists are magicians. Weaving their spell, heaving their gel. A place where what you see ain't never, ever what you get. They go in one way, and come out another.

"I used to pick up my girlfriend from the salon," he continued, now pacing the courtroom, "and I'd come early just to observe. I'd see women ease out the car, slip in the back door with sunglasses and floppy hats like they were undercover operatives on a stakeout. Then hours later, some of the scariest-looking women in the world that came in, come out as some of the world's most glamorous. But yet, you want my client to be upfront, honest, and forthright with women when women themselves are diametrically opposed to anything related to such.

"Your Honor, if it pleases the court, I'd like to admit as evidence, from the Victoria's Secret catalog, something referred to as a Miracle Bra. Are you familiar with this, Ms. Chase?"

"Yes," I said, as I saw Ophelia's mouth slowly open and her head slowly begin to shake.

"And what does this push-up bra do?"

"Just what it says, it pushes up."

"Your breasts? It pushes up your breasts?" he asked.

"That is correct."

"Makes them appear perkier? Fluffier, more vibrant and alive? Stands them at attention," he asked.

"That is correct."

"And what happens when you remove this bra in the heat of passion. Do they stay at attention?"

"Objection, Your Honor. Witness cannot speak for the breasts of the entire female population," Ophelia stated.

"Your Honor, allow me to rephrase the question. Have you ever worn a Miracle Bra?" he asked.

"Objection, Your Honor. The personal and intimate apparel of my client is privileged and confidential information."

"Your Honor, it's privileged information that was used to lure my client into signing the contract in the first place."

"Overruled."

"Again, I'll ask. Have you ever worn a push-up bra?"

"Yes."

"And what happened once that push-up bra was removed?"

"The same thing that happens to all women. Gravity happened."

"For the record, the defense would like to note that the witness does indeed speak for all women. Let's turn specifically to the contract in question, Ms. Chase."

Forty-Two

MILES CONTINUED HIS line of questioning. "I'm having a bit of difficulty with this idea of sex and exchange. You have to forgive me because I didn't grow up in the big city like most of you in here, but in the country, where I'm from, that sounds like a sophisticated form of prostitution," Milner said.

"Objection, Your Honor, the defense is attempting to cast a moral cloud over my client by suggesting socially reprehensible behavior."

"Your Honor, I'm not suggesting that at all, I'm only attempting to put in layman's terms the stipulations of the contract that the witness by her own admission constructed."

"Overruled."

"Is this contract your idea of exchange? Is it just a sophisticated form of prostitution?" he asked.

"I prefer to call it quid pro quo. You are familiar with the term, I'm sure."

"Very," he said. "It's a Latin term—it means 'something for something.' A thing that is exchanged for another thing of more or less equal value. A substitute."

"The south couldn't have been too bad if they taught you Latin," I said as the court rumbled with laughter.

"Well, like you, I grew up in the country, but the country didn't grow up in me," he said, laughingly. "So, quid pro quo. Is that how you would define prostitution?"

"What I'm saying is that it's the same thing. Prostitution is the dirty label.

"Barter is the more traditional label," I added. "It's like having sex or making love. One term makes you feel warm and fuzzy while the other is a little dirtier, a little more dangerous, but they're still the same thing. You get a gift. Whether it's in a brown paper bag or specially gift-wrapped at Macy's, once you removed the paper, it's still the same thing."

"So, you're saying the process of courtship is the road that leads to this sophisticated form of prostitution?"

"Isn't it?" I said.

"You tell me."

"No, why don't you tell me? When you take a woman out on a date, you make a choice. You have those you take to the fancy restaurants—that's the Macy's gift wrapping. Then there are those you take to the not-so-fancy restaurants—that's the brown paper bag. Why do you do this? Because a man decides the level of his investment the first time he meets a woman. He decides how much time he's willing to invest and how much money he's willing to invest to get what he wants—sex. A man invests his time and money; a woman invests her body and her emotions. A man talks to a woman just so he can get her to sleep with him. A woman sleeps with a man just so she can get him to talk to her. It's all an exchange," I said. "Men call women gold diggers all the time because they ask for money. But then it's okay for a man to ask for sex. As soon as a man starts talking about sex, a woman has the right to start talking about money. He's trying to get some. I'm trying to get some, too. 'I want to be intimate with you,' he says, again trying to put the Macy's wrapping paper on it. Well, I'm trying to be intimate with you, too. I want to be intimate with your bank account," I said, as the courtroom erupted. "I want to make love to your wallet."

"Order in the court! Order in the court!" the judge shouted as the gavel fell and Miles's mouth joined the gavel, falling to the ground.

"No more questions, Your Honor," Miles said.

"The court will take a brief recess and return in one hour."

During a brief recess, Ophelia whispered in my ear that my talk of relationships seemed to finally be affecting the jury. She felt that we should keep it going into the next session. And that's exactly what we did. Back on the stand for Ophelia's redirect, I picked up right where I left off.

"I have this rule I call the one in five rule," I said.

"Could you elaborate on that?" Ophelia asked.

"It's simple. Out of every five men, you get one who's halfway decent. And to you, he's like the pot of gold at the end of the rainbow. Really, he's the pot. You don't even have the gold, but you're just happy with the pot. It's like going into your grandmother's kitchen smelling the food and not being able to eat until dinner. The only problem with finding the pot is that by the time you find that one good one, the fool has already put you through so much drama, you start believing that the pot of real gold is just like the pots full of fool's gold that you're used to.

"For example. Here's Man Number One. He dates my girlfriend in Baltimore and she had a young daughter. He knows this. It's the end of the summer and school is about to begin. They've been in a physical relationship for a couple months now, making love and having sex," I said as several jurors chuckled. "He asks to spend the night again so they can do what grown folks do. So, she says to him, since school is starting next week, she would like him to go shopping with her and as a gift for her daughter, buy a couple outfits for school before they go back to her apartment. 'Are you serious?' he asks. 'Yes,' she responds. 'Why do you have wrinkles on your forehead?' 'Because it's hot,' he says. And my girlfriend replies, 'It wasn't hot a minute ago when you were asking me for some sex, but now when I ask you for a gift for my daughter, all of a sudden, it's hot,' she says. That's just one out of the five.

"Man Number Two dates my girlfriend in D.C. A very pretty woman with a banging short bob. When they first meet, he's all over her, telling her how she looks like Halle Berry. After two weeks they get together, have sex and make love, and then after two weeks he asks her if she normally wears her hair that short—suggesting to her that maybe she could try to grow it longer. So on the defense, she asks him if he normally wears his hair short. He's like, 'Huh? I'm a man.' He says to her, 'Men don't change their styles.' 'Sure they do,' she says. 'Sometimes it's short, it's faded, when it grows long, it's braided.' So she says to him, 'Look, say what you really want to say.' Then he admits that he really prefers long hair over short and asks if she'd grow it long for him. After dating for two weeks, he asks her to change her hairstyle. Just two weeks ago he was all over her, telling her that she looks like Halle Berry, one of the most beautiful women in the world. He didn't offer to pay not one of her bills. Didn't offer to chip in on not one hair appointment, but now after he got what he wanted from her, all of a sudden he's Vidal Sassoon. That's Man Number Two.

"Then there's Man Number Three. The I'ma-move-you-up-in-my-house-and-give-you-the-key kind of man. The my-life-is-an-open-book kind of man. My girlfriend from Temple was living with this kind of a man. She had an apartment of her own, her own money, her own career, her own identity, everything she has, she acquired it by herself without the help of nobody other than God. But then she meets this man. The if-this-world-were-mine, I'd-give-you-the-flowers,-the-birds,-and-the-trees kind of smooth-talking, to-the-side-walking kind of man. So they meet and begin dating. Pretty soon she's spending more time over his house than she is her own. He suggests that she give up her place and move in with him. 'It just makes good sense,' he says. 'Why waste money?' he says. 'You're always over here anyway,' he says, convincing her that it's all good.' 'My life is an open book,' he says.

"So, she terminates her lease early. She pays the early termination fee, hires the moving truck, and puts her things in storage. She moves in and it's all good. Until the phone starts ringing late at night, but when she picks up, the phone hangs up. She checks the caller ID and asks her man who it is. 'Who knows?' he says. The next few nights the same. Again, who knows? 'My life is an open book,' he says. Then one day he accidentally leaves his phone book at home and asks if she could drop it off to him on the way to work. 'No problem,' she says. So she takes that phone book and puts it in her car. Soon, of course, the natural instinct of a woman kicks in and at a stoplight she opens up the book and sees an unknown woman's name, address, and number. The next night, he's late, and what does she do? She goes by the woman's house and there's his car. She turns around and goes home, not wanting to make a scene. When she questions him about it, he flips and says, 'Now you're acting like my wife. And you shouldn't have gone through my book even though I assured you it was open.' She has a key to his house. She's cooking, cleaning, paying part of the mortgage. She's staying with you, laying with you, but she's confused, thinking she's your wife. It gets heated, he asks her to leave, and she does. Now, she's got no man, no apartment, and suddenly no identity because she lost herself in his. That's Man Number Three.

"Rounding off the list is 'undercover brother.' Man Number Four is the sexually vague man. Like the one my cousin dated. The man, who just likes to, as he calls it, 'experiment.' He's open to it all. Wants you to do little things to him you wouldn't normally expect a man to ask you to do. He's probably 'experimented' with a man before, but he'll never admit it. This kind of man knows exactly what he wants from the relationship—sex. But instead of coming out and saying it, he leaves little hints, makes little statements, and tries to get you to play games, like he asks you about your past relationships, wants to know who you've been with and what you did and why it didn't work. He knows he could care less about your past, but what he's really doing is sizing you up to see how far you'd go with him. And we all know that properly motivated, there's no limit to what a woman would do.

"Pretty soon they started hanging out, having wild sex with each other. 'Experimented' with a threesome. Then a foursome. She wasn't into it at first, but after a while she got into it and started making suggestions on how to push the envelope even farther. How to add a little more spice to the 'experiment.' Oh, but he didn't like it when she took the lead, so he ended the relationship. He said she wasn't the same woman he fell in love with. How could she be the same woman after he done turned her out and got her to do things she would have never thought of doing in the first place? So, he's moved on and now she's a lesbian," I said, glancing at the jury while half eyebrows were raised and half mouths open not wanting to believe a man could really turn a woman gay. "That's Man Number Four.

"I wrote the contract because I just got sick of rolling the dice and playing the odds," I concluded.

Forty-Three

DURING A BRIEF RECESS, Ophelia assured me that my last testimony had hit its mark. We were on a high.

"Let's not celebrate too soon. Miles has one more chance at a cross-examination," she said. "He's going to throw everything but the kitchen sink at you, so be careful. And remember, whatever you do—don't get emotional. No matter what he says or how he says it. Keep cool and I think we can win this thing. I really think we can win it."

"Five minutes, ladies," the bailiff said into our room.

"Are you ready?" Ophelia asked.

"Do I have a choice?" I answered.

"Not really," she said.

"Mo, don't worry, you're gonna be just fine," Altima said, as we all three hugged and prepared ourselves for our final round before closing arguments and the verdict.

"All rise!" the bailiff ordered.

Judge Bean returned to her seat and we were back in session.

"Counselor, the witness is yours."

"The plaintiff rests, Your Honor," Ophelia said.

"Counselor Milner, the witness is yours."

"Mine indeed," he said, taking one long drink of water from his custom crystal glass. "Mine indeed," he repeated, taking his time before approaching the bench. "All I can say is, I'm glad my momma raised me to be the one out of the five," he said as the entire courtroom erupted into laughter. "Wow. Are men really that bad?" he asked.

"They are what they are," I said.

"'They are what they are.' Listening to you, it's pretty bad out there. The pickings seem kind of slim. Listening to you, I'm surprised anybody is happy. Unless of course they've found that one out of five needle in the haystack, as you put it. That pot of gold—but really not the gold, just the pot. Is that how you put it, Ms. Chase?"

"That is correct."

"That is correct, indeed. So, you've dated some real losers, I see. We've dug up just about every man that's ever been in your life and not one of them has been worth anything, according to you. I'm curious. Where did you get such high standards, Ms. Chase?"

"From my father."

"From your father. Dear old dad. Of course. And how is dear old dad?"

"He passed after my first year of college."

"I'm sorry to hear that," he said. "And he loved you?"

"Deeply."

"He's the one who gave you the car that you were driving when you met my client, is that correct?"

"That is correct."

"I believe it was a 1987 Buick Skylark. It was in pretty bad shape, if I'm not mistaken. Being that he was a mechanic, why do you think he would give you an automobile that was in such poor condition?"

"You know what they say. Dentists have the worst teeth. Optometrists the worst eyes, and I guess daughters of mechanics the worst cars," I said as several members of the jury smiled, mouthing "amen" to themselves.

"And lawyers create the worst contracts," he added.

"Objection, Your Honor."

"Sustained."

"And you come from a family where both parents were working."

"That is correct."

"I remember my first car. It was a real lemon. Barely got me back and forth to work. But I was happy to just have a car at all. I was raised in a single-parent household, and that's all my mother could afford. Why do you think he gave you that particular car when he could have afforded better?"

"He was big on responsibility and independence. He wanted me to appreciate the time when I could buy a better one for myself."

"If you were around long enough to ever get to be responsible," he said. "Your Honor, I'd like to admit as evidence the diagnostic report that was done on the car when she dropped it off at the dealership. In this report it shows several cracks in the engine's mainframe. And a malfunctioning fuel injector. Were you aware of these problems when your father purchased you the car?"

"No, and I didn't care. I was just happy to get a car. It really didn't matter."

"Your safety obviously didn't matter, either, because according to this you were riding around in a death trap. A vehicle that could have blown up from the front, back, or either side simply with a collision at the speed of ten to fifteen miles. Your Honor, I'd also like to admit as evidence the report from the Pennsylvania Office of Automobile Inspection stating the facts that when this car was purchased initially, its current condition was the same and noted on the sales invoice."

"Objection! Your Honor, the condition of my client's vehicle is irrelevant to the case."

"Your Honor, it's relevant in the fact that I'm trying to put in perspective the 'four bad men' the plaintiff spoke of by gaining insight into her one good one."

"Overruled. You may continue with the witness."

"Given the fact that your father was an auto mechanic—'the best' as you described him—why do you think your father would place his only daughter—the apple of his eye, as you described yourself—in a virtual death trap?"

"There's no way he would have intentionally put me in danger."

"But you would agree that whether intentionally or unintentionally, dead is still dead?"

"Objection."

"Sustained. Counselor will rephrase the questioning so as to make it more appropriate to the case we're dealing with."

"Of course, Your Honor," he said. I was tempted to reach across the bench and slap the shit out of him for suggesting that my father would do something to hurt me. But looking at Ophelia mouthing "keep your cool" was just what I needed.

"If you would, tell us about your first day at college."

"What's there to tell? It was one of the happiest days of my life," I said.

"I'm sure your family was proud of you. College is a crowning accomplishment. The path to your future. I can see it now. Dad throwing your bags in the trunk of his car, Mom on one side, you in the back, and off you went to Temple University, everyone laughing, singing, just like one happy family. Is that right? Is that picture correct?" he asked.

I paused, looking at Ophelia and then at my mother, wondering how he could know what had happened.

"No, that wasn't the picture at all, was it?" Miles smirked.

"Your Honor, I'd like to admit as evidence the college admission papers from Ms. Chase's first day at college, where you'll notice under guardian it was signed only by Mrs. Chase."

"And why was that, Ms. Chase? Why on one of the most important days of your life was your father not there to see the apple of his eye take her biggest and boldest step toward her future?"

"Objection, Your Honor."

"Overruled. Witness will answer the question."

"How could he miss such a date? In fact, wasn't this the rule for your beloved father, rather than the exception? In fact, isn't it true that you were often accompanied only by one parent to most, if not all of your important events? I'd like to admit as evidence this set of pictures taken at your high school graduation party, where the only face I don't see is your father's. Where was this perfect man? This model of manhood? The measuring stick that you've used to judge the worth and value of almost every man in your life. Where was he?"

"Ask *me* where he was, and I'll tell you where he was!" It was my mother standing up and shouting from her seat as the court began to rumble.

"Order in the court!"

"He was working to support his family! That's where he was! He loved his daughter."

"Order in the court!"

"Don't you stand up there and try to say that he didn't!"

"Order in the court, or I'll have to ask you to leave."

"The one you oughta ask to leave is that asshole who's asking the questions!" Andre shouted. "That's who you should ask to leave!"

"Order in the court!" the judge screamed as her gavel rang over the grumblings in the court.

"Isn't it true, Ms. Chase, that in fact your father was not the ideal man that you would have us to believe he was? Isn't it true that your father was always missing in action?"

"No."

"Isn't it true that since his death you've made him out to be something that in fact he never was? You've created in your mind a man that no man could ever measure up to because no man like the man you would have us believe your father was *ever* existed. Isn't that true?"

"No."

"Objection, Your Honor."

"Overruled."

"Isn't it true that you've never forgiven your father for dying too soon? Leaving you too soon? Letting you go before you could show him that you were indeed good enough for him to attend your high school graduation party. That you were indeed worth him buying you a good car. That you were indeed worth him taking one half hour from his day to be with you as you took the first step of your future. Isn't that true, Ms. Chase?"

Miles's words pierced my heart to the point that all I could find myself saying, silently and then audibly, was, "Yes! Yes! Yes! Yes, it's true!" I yelled in a state of unleashed emotion, "Yes!"

"No, it's not true," my mother shouted. "It's not true!"

"Order in the court! Order in the court!!" the judge again shouted as her gavel fell and fell and fell and my tears followed in a scene that couldn't have been better choreographed if it were on court TV.

"No more questions, Your Honor, the defense rests," Miles softly spoke, as the bailiff reached out his hand to me to exit the stand.

"Wait, but there's more I have to tell you," I said.

"Ms. Chase, you may now leave the stand."

"But he didn't ask me about all the times he was there. And all the other times when—"

"Ms. Chase, you have to leave the stand. Your testimony is over," the judge said, as the bailiff took my hand and led me down as I looked and noticed a stream of tears falling from my mother's face and Ophelia's eyes hanging heavy, worried, wondering if my last outburst had just cost us the case.

Forty-Four

AFTER A BRIEF RECESS, we were back in court for the hearing of our closing arguments. Miles was first, approaching the juror's bench with ease and calm.

"I don't know about you," he said, "but I feel like I've been more of a therapist than a lawyer. I've dealt more with emotional issues than actual evidence. This case has absolutely nothing to do with a piece of paper—this so-called contract—but it has everything to do with a woman in pain. A lot of pain. So much so that she's lashed out at almost every man she's encountered. Men that may or may not have risen to the occasion or, for that matter, even tried," he said as he began pacing.

"But let's say they did try to rise to the occasion. Let's say they did search for the mark—how could they ever hit the mark when the mark is constantly moving? When the bull's eye is forever changing and shifting. The pendulum swinging from one side to the other. From 'you don't spend enough time with me' this day, to 'you're not listening enough to me' that day. 'Why don't we go on a vacation?' this week to 'do you think we go on too many vacations?' next week.

"Ladies and gentlemen of the jury, Morgan Chase is in pain. A lot of pain. But does my client have to be the one man held accountable for the pain caused by many men? Did they have a relationship? Of course they did. Did it go the way they wanted it? Obviously not, or we wouldn't be here. But people break up every day. And they make up every day. 'Break up to make up, that's all we do.' Morgan Chase is in pain. So much so that she decided to create a contract to make men pay for her pain. So, it's my client today. Who's next? Maybe you, male member of the jury," he said, locking his eyes on an older gentleman in the jury. "You own a convenience store. She walks in your convenience store and asks for a bottle of Coca-Cola. You've got a lot of customers in your store and in your haste, you accidentally put a bottle of Pepsi in the bag. An honest mistake. At least you think so. The next day you walk into your convenience store and you've got a notice summoning you to court—you're being sued, but why? Because some man somewhere at some time gave her something other than what she thought she was getting.

"And you, ma'am," he said pointedly to a woman in the jury. "You own a clothing boutique on South Street. A very nice one; Ms. Chase walks in your store and requests a skirt for an awards banquet. She requests that skirt in a size eight, only to get home and realize that the skirt was marked incorrectly and really it's a size ten. You get a call from her and you gladly offer your apologies and offer to exchange the dress and give her a discount on her next purchase. In your mind that's what any good person—any good businessperson—would do. But that's not enough. She notifies you that the next voice you'll hear is that of her lawyer. You're being sued, she says, and then hangs up the phone. Before we know it, we're all getting sued. How can it end? Where does the madness, the mayhem, the misuse of the law, where does it all end? I'll tell you where. It ends here. It ends now. Morgan Chase is in pain. I don't make light of that. I don't deny that. But her pain should not automatically translate into her gain.

"Ladies and gentlemen, I stand before you today still in love with America. Only now I realize that, like Morgan, America is hurting. And like Morgan, America needs healing. And today, I'd like to write a prescription—and on that prescription is one word: 'justice.' On that prescription I'd write 'fair play.' I'd write 'love.' I'd write 'forgiveness,' and on that prescription I'd write 'hope.' Hope for healing. And to administer the medicine to a world that's hurting, all I would need is a signature of a physician. You are the physician," he said, slowly eyeing each member of the jury. "You, ma'am, and you, sir, have the power to heal the world—one person, one woman, one day at a time.

"Ladies and gentlemen of the jury, I ask that you return a verdict of not guilty. I ask that you take a step in curing, in curing . . . rather healing this great land called America. Thank you."

Miles walked away from the jury, ever so poised, to his seat.

"Counselor Clarke," Judge Bean continued. "The court will now hear your closing argument." Grabbing my hand firmly, Ophelia squeezed once real tight and then released. Proud, confident, and alive, she strutted with her head held high as she approached the bench.

"We've learned a lot about contracts," she said. "A lot about the legal process. But more importantly, I've learned a lot about love. So much so that I feel it is most likely the greatest gift of all. Not something to be toyed with, dangled like a carrot, or used as a weapon of mass destruction. But it is to be honored. It is to be cherished. It's to be cradled like a newborn.

"Ladies and gentlemen of the jury, the defendant is guilty. But he's not just guilty of breach of contract. He's guilty of something even worse. He's guilty of not being man to a good woman. And that alone, even outside of the court, should be a crime. It should be a crime morally, spiritually, and emotionally. But what price can you put on a heart? What form of emotional reparations could one enact for such a crime? What would the penalty be for such a perpetrator?" Ophelia asked as she began taking her own command.

"Now, the counselor suggests that my client is in pain. But I would add that so is the defendant. The difference is that my client admits her pain, but the defendant denies his. Look at him for yourself. He's sitting there in his seat right now, looking pompous, arrogant. But if you take a closer look, you'll see what my client saw—and that is that the defense is the walking wounded. Crying out for help. But no one hears him. He's like a puppy that's been hit by a car—he's limping, bleeding, hurting—and he's crying. But no one hears him. That's why he acts the way he acts, he's crying out. 'I'll lie and tell her I love her when really I don't.' He's crying, 'I'll build her up this week and tear her down the next.' He's hurting. Woman after woman after woman,' he keeps crying and crying and crying, but no one ever hears him. My client, Morgan Chase, heard that cry," she said, pausing for emotional effect. "And not only did she hear him, but she created an instrument that would heal him. The instrument to heal all men and all women who are hurting. Who are crying. Lack of communication—they're crying. Broken promises, shattered dreams—they're hurting, they're crying. Can you hear them? This contract hears them," she continued as by now you could hear a pin drop in the courtroom. "This contract heals them. The defense so proudly talks about America, the land of the free and the home of the brave. Well, if in fact those words are true, then my client is the greatest American in this courtroom, because she is the bravest American in this courtroom. Brave because she still believes that good things truly can happen to good people. That not only the strong survive, but so do the brave. That we live in a quid pro quo society of even exchange—a something-for-something, kindness-for-kindness society—a reap-what-you-sow society where if you give love, you get love. A world where your word still means something. And so let it be written, that in this land truth and justice really are for all and not just the sly, the slick, or the wicked. The America that I know is about justice. It's about truth. It's about what's right. The defendant is guilty. He's crying. Can you hear him? He's hurting. He's crying.

"Ladies and gentlemen of the jury, if you want to heal him, I ask that you hear him and return a verdict of guilty. Thank you."

"The court will take a brief recess and return for the verdict," said the judge. The gavel fell and everyone filed quickly out of the court-room only to return just as quickly for the reading of the verdict.

Forty-Five

"ALL RISE AS THE Honorable Judge Bernetta Bean presiding over the Twenty-ninth District Court of Philadelphia enters."

For the last time, she entered with a look of calm on her face as she gently eased into her seat. Under the bench, Ophelia, Altima, and I held onto one another's hands as our hearts raced.

"Well," Judge Bean began, "I must say, this is the most extraordinary and unusual case I've ever tried. As a woman, I'm inspired. As a human being, I'm encouraged. But as a judge, I'm duly bound to hear the verdict and deliver a sentence. So, without any further pause, ladies and gentlemen of the jury, do you have a verdict?"

"Yes, Your Honor," spoke a wiry, thin, elderly, gray-haired black man elected spokesman for the jury.

"Your Honor, we, the members of the jury, find the defendant Charles Anthony Sealant . . ." he paused to take a breath, looking at the several male and female jurors, who all looked on in anticipation. The courtroom was dead silent. From the corner of my eye I saw my mother taking a deep breath, clutching her purse. From the distance I could hear reporters clamoring outside, awaiting the news. My heart stopped as the anticipation had overtaken me.

"We find the defendant, Charles Anthony Sealant, guilty of breach of contract," he said, as instantly the court erupted in a mix of cheers and protest. Ophelia, Altima, and I jumped up, screaming and hugging. Even Andre ran up to us, hugging us and congratulating us on the verdict.

"Order in the court!" the judge screamed as her gavel fell. "Order in the court!"

I turned to my mother, whose tears again streamed.

"Order in the court!" the judge shouted.

"As this is a civil case," the judge began, "and not a criminal case, the court allows latitude for sentencing," she said. "In the case of punitive damages, I fine the defendant fifty thousand dollars."

Again we erupted.

"In the case of emotional reparations, I fine the defendant another fifty thousand dollars to be donated to a women's charity of the plaintiff's choosing.

"And for being an asshole, a man of blatant disrespect and disregard for the feelings of another human being, I hereby sentence the defendant to a thousand hours of community service answering phones at an abuse hotline and women's outreach service. The court is adjourned!" she said, pounding her gavel and leaving the stand.

"Good job, ladies," the judge mouthed to Ophelia, Altima, and I as together we hugged and shouted.

"I hope you're happy," Charles said, having made his way over to us in the midst of our celebration. "You didn't do nothing but make me more of a catch. Women love dogs. After this case you've made me into the definitive dog. Oh, and as far as the one hundred-thousand-dollar fine—I can shit a hundred thousand dollars. Do you hear me? I shit it and then I wipe my ass with it. You hear that, you crazy bitter bitch!"

"You best to raise up, partner," Andre said, by now having heard enough, "or you're about to be wiping your ass with my foot! Didn't your momma teach you how to treat a lady?" he said as Charles grinned and moved on. Together we all celebrated as we left the courtroom, overhearing Miles Milner being interviewed on the steps of the court.

"So, what do you think about the case, Counselor Milner?" a reporter asked.

"I am inspired that in this great country of ours a man is given the chance to be innocent until proven guilty. My job is to make sure he has that chance. I am confident that I have done my job to the fullest of my capability and I am honored to have represented the judicial system established by our fine forefathers over four score and two hundred years ago.

"I'd also like to take this opportunity to announce that I will no longer be practicing law in the public sector. I have a new talk show premiering on Fox, called *I Love America and So Does Miles*. I have a seven-figure publishing deal and I've negotiated the rights for my side of this trial for a made-for-television movie. All questions, comments, and advance purchase of the novel can be directed to my publicist, Samantha Selowane, and my agent, Alan Nevins. God bless you and God bless America," he said as he turned and winked, mouthing to me "good luck."

After at least an hour of reporters and camera crews, we were finally alone.

"So, I guess this is it," I said, looking at Ophelia.

"It for who?"

"For us, I suppose. It's all over now. Now what?"

"I don't know what's 'now what' for you, but what's 'now what' for me is after the verdict, I got a message from the mayor's wife, who wants me to represent her in the case against her husband."

"You're kidding," I said.

"She's the first client of my new firm—Clarke, Chase and Davis," she said.

"Are you serious?" I said.

"As a heart attack, which I don't plan on having anytime soon. 'Cause I'm officially getting back in shape as I work on whipping the mayor's cheating ass! Are you with me?"

"I don't know. Give me a few days to think about it," I said.

"Take all the time you need," she said. "What about you, Altima, are you coming with me?"

"I'll help you," she said. "But law is you guys' thing. Cooking is my thing. With my name and recipes in the newspaper for the past few weeks, I've got over a thousand orders for special engagements and catering. I was even offered my own cooking show on the Food Network."

"Girl, congratulations," we both said.

"But who's going to help you with all that cooking and planning? That's a lot."

"I am," Andre said.

"You are?" I asked with my mouth hanging open.

"Yes, I am. It's about time I got myself together. I'm not getting any younger, you know. I just needed a reason to do better. Altima gave me that reason," he said, holding her close and kissing her.

"Well," Altima said. "All's well that ends well."

"So, what are you going to do?" Ophelia asked.

"I don't know. But the first thing I'm going to do is go clean out my office," I said, knowing full well that by now on my desk was a letter of termination. We hugged one more time and all three hopped in our cars, headed our own way. I took one last glance at the courtroom behind me as I thought to myself—man . . . I actually did it.

Forty-Six

I WAS GATHERING a few of my personal things from my office drawer, took down a few pictures from my desk, and then walked to the wall where my diploma hung. It seemed like it was only days ago that I found just the right spot on the wall for it. Really, given the size of the room, it was the only spot on the wall. I placed it in the box with the other things and for a moment, I stood there reminiscing on where I'd been and how far I was still eager to go.

"It's probably an old wives' tale, but I always thought spring cleaning was in the spring. We're barely into March." It was Michael standing in the doorway, looking his usual best. "I hear congratulations are in order," he said. "Congratulations."

"Thanks."

"I thought you'd be out celebrating somewhere."

"I guess this is how I chose to celebrate. Getting a head start on the rest of my life."

"Did I not get the memo?"

"I'm sure you got a lot of memos," I said.

"Oh, it's not that bad. So you ruffled a few feathers. That's what feathers are for," he said. "And besides, in addition to the obvious good news of you winning your case, there's even more good news."

"I qualify for the full unemployment package?"

"Probably," he said with a smile. "But that's not the news I'm referring to. The mayor and his top aides finally got around to reading your summary on his case. They think it's incredible. The mayor himself said that it's the best summary of defense a man could have from a woman who's suing a man for the very same thing. I read it, too. Cover to cover. It's impressive. It's all bullshit, but it's impressive bullshit. Because knowing you, you don't believe one word of it. You think he's guilty as guilty can be, right?"

"It doesn't really matter what I think. What matters is that I was getting paid to do a job. I was hired to look past the truth. To defend only what the client believes is truth, right? Because that's really the job of a good lawyer, isn't it? To protect and defend, and if none of that works, come up with the best lie, the best trick, pull the biggest joker you can find clear from the bottom of the deck." I said, now questioning my whole purpose for ever becoming a lawyer.

"You take the good with the bad and hope that there's more good than bad. I still believe there's more good than bad," Michael said.

"Do you really?"

"I have to, or otherwise I couldn't wake up in the morning, get dressed, and come here to work. And so do you. Otherwise you wouldn't have done what you did."

"Well, you'll have to forgive me because what I've been through over the past few weeks, the past few years, the past few decades, makes me question that equation," I said.

"It couldn't be all that bad," he said. "There must be a few bright spots that you can think of."

"Let me see," I said, posing in thought. "Nope, not one."

"Oh, come on," he said. "You can't name one?"

"I'm sorry, I can't," I said.

"Not one? There's got to be one," he continued to ask, surefooted and calm.

"Are you not hearing me?" I said, now getting a bit annoyed by his questioning.

"I'm hearing you, but I'm not believing you," he said.

"Well, if you know so much, then name one?"

"Okay, I will."

"Okay, who?"

"You want to know who?"

"Yes. Please, tell me who!"

"You're looking at him, that's who," he said.

"You?" I said with a chuckle. "That's sweet, but you don't have to say that to try to make me feel good."

"How 'bout I say it to try to make *me* feel good?" At this very moment his eyes locked into mine and refused to break their hold as he continued. "I thought blinders were only fitted for horses, but you've obviously cornered the market of your own line of designer frames. Morgan, from the first day we met, from the first time you walked into the boardroom. From the first time I walked into your office and saw you hanging your law degree on your wall. From the first time I smelled the scent of your perfume, or the fragrance of your hair," he said, slowly making his way closer, "I was crazy enough to want to put myself through the torture of watching men walk in and out of your life, one by one, month by month, while I waited. Through Kevin I waited, Carl, and even Marcus, I stood on the side, hoping that you could see me like I see you."

"Why didn't you say something sooner?" I said, not believing my ears.

"I don't know. For one, we were working together, and I didn't want to make you feel uncomfortable."

"So you waited until I got fired to say something?"

"Honestly, that's not the way I intended this to happen, but if I didn't tell you now, I might not ever get the chance to again. Knowing you, you'll leave your job and go start a practice in Alaska or something and fall in and out of love with every Eskimo in town, and then I'd have to wait even longer. Morgan I don't want to wait any longer. I can't wait any longer," he said intently.

"So the other night wasn't just about the late nights and long hours," I asked.

"Hell no," he quickly replied. "The other night was about me starting to do something that I wanted to do ever since the first day I met you. And that's hold you in my arms, pull you close, and tell you that before I even knew you I loved you. And whether you're down the hall or down the street, or atop the equator, it won't matter. I'll find you. And I'll hold you. And I'll love you. Now, unless you have an objection, I'd rather stop talking and start kissing. But only if it pleases the court," he said, now inches from my face.

"It most definitely pleases the court," I said softly, as with the side of his hand he caught a tear as it fell from my face. Softly and gently we kissed and we kissed and we kissed.

"Now, rumor has it that 'ghetto girls' such as yourself prefer a South Street cheesesteak sub. So, I made reservations for two at the greasiest one I could find," he said with his signature smile and chuckle.

"Do they serve Kool-Aid?"

"They serve red Kool-Aid," he said. Into the garage and into his car we were headed to South Street without a care in the world.

RRRRRRRing! It was my cell phone.

"I'm not gonna answer it," I said.

"Go ahead," he insisted. "It's probably someone calling to congratulate you."

"Hello?"

"What the hell did you do to my contract?" a voice came shouting through the phone.

"Charles?"

"I'm at my dealership and it's a line wrapped around the entire lot, full of folks waving a contract, talking about some stipulation they read in their lease agreement that if anything goes wrong with their car, they're entitled to a full refund."

"Oh, you know what? When you asked me to work on your contract, I must have e-mailed you the wrong one. The one where I accidently deleted the original clause that protected you. I was in such a bad emotional state, having just caught you with another woman. Sorry."

"Sorry?! Sorry?!! Do you have any idea how much money this is gonna cost me?" he yelled into the phone.

"I don't know, but I believe you said you 'shit a hundred thousand dollars.' Just take a laxative and you'll have all the money you need. Good-bye," I said as Michael and I headed past the downtown Liberty Bell, as its chime sounded, ringing for justice. Ringing for truth. And after thirty-four years, ringing for love.

Acknowledgments

I admit that fifteen years of writing plays has gotten me a little spoiled. Spoiled in the sense that theater is a collaborate creative effort, where novels are pretty singular. With the plays, I can always lean on my musical director, my lighting designer, wardrobe, hair, and makeup stylists to fill in the blanks when I run into an artistic brick wall. But these novels . . . Good Lord! So, I'd like to acknowledge a heightened level of respect for novelists, because how you folks do what you do at the rate you do it . . . I'll never know!

I acknowledge that though writing a novel is one-on-one, still, there's no way you get it done right without a great support team: My support team is first and foremost, my wife, my buddy, and (after seven years of marriage) still my boo, Lyn Talbert. My manager, Mike Prevett (you really should write a novel yourself, 'cause your notes are that good!). My agent, Alan Nevins (thank you for helping me broaden my creative horizons). My editor, Cherise Davis (this was a tough one, but we got through it!). My lawyer, and one of the smartest brothas I know, Darrell Miller (I'm working on those seven streams!). My former assistant Patricia Cuffie (thanks for keeping it moving for me). Amy and Mindy. My in-house law team of Michael and Mattie Lawson, Relani Belous (yes, I know you're not the audience!). Crazy Karena in Houston, who kept me in stitches as I rambled for months about this story. Lynette in Philly, who helped me with hot drinks and hot spots in her area. Baby Sam (what up son!).

I acknowledge that in a bookstore full of hundreds and thousands of books, to me it's nothing short of a miracle when someone actually purchases your book, let alone takes the time to actually read it. I am deeply grateful for your support of my contributions to the literary community as well as the theatrical community. Thank you to the reader, the theatergoer, the DVD buyer, and the website surfer!

I also learned that the book world is a lot different from the play world. On the book tours I ran into so many people that had either never heard of me or had never seen any of my plays. I also discovered that I'm really a frustrated actor, because I was really getting into those readings. I had the most fun ever out on the road signing books and reading excerpts from my first novel. And since only God knows when I'll be writing another novel . . . I've decided to make this the longest and most all-inclusive list of thank-yous ever! So, you might want to get you a sandwich and a glass of red Kool-Aid 'cause we're gonna be a while! (Hopefully I won't miss anyone, but if I do, email me and I'll add you on the list when the paperback comes out.)

Thanks Emma Rogers in Dallas. Thanks to Pam for hooking me up with the best margarita ever! Thanks to my man James Brusard at Eso Won Books. My folks over at Morgan State University for hooking up an Alumni. My friends at the Howard University Bookstore. My PG crew at Karibu Books! Thanks to Alexander's Book Co. in San Francisco, Marcus Books in Oakland, Black Facts and Hue-Man in New York, Black Horizon in New Jersey, Afrocentric, Afri-Wave Inc., Sylvia Flanagan, Clarence Waldron, and all my peeps at Johnson Publishing Company in Chicago. Thanks to Horizon Bookstore, Barnes & Noble, B. Dalton's, and Ligorius Bookstore Inc. in Philadelphia. Borders in Dearborn, Shrine of the Black Madonna in Livernois, God's World in Detroit, and Black Images Book Bazaar in Dallas. Oasis Bookstore—African Spectrum, Waldenbooks, and Medu Books in Atlanta, and Nubian Bookstore in Marrow. Thanks to African American Book Stop in New Orleans, Mitchie's Fine Black Art & Gift Gallery in Austin, Enoch Pratt Library in Baltimore, Queens Borough Public Library, and Overbrook Library in Philadelphia. To Jim and the beautiful folks at Zahrah's Books & Things for moving a ton of *Baggage Claim* books.

Big ups to Tom Joyner, J. Anthony Brown, Cybil, Lue, and the entire staff and crew of the *Tom Joyner Morning Show.* To Steve Harvey, Rushion Macdonald, Big Lez, and my sis—Shirly Strawberry—at the *Steve Harvey Morning Show* (y'all helped me sell a lot of books!). To my sister Carol Mackey and the Black Expressions book club. To Thomas Owens, Andre Russel, Kevin Nash, and Cliff & Janine and the Hometeam at KJLH. I also want to thank the following radio stations, magazines, and newspapers for supporting a brother: In California, KALI-AM/FM in Los Angeles, *Los Angeles Scoop,* and the *Oakland Post* in Oakland. In Baltimore, WBAL-TV *Weekend Morning,* WEAA-FM *The Morning Journey with Sandi Mallory,* WJZ-TV *Coffee With,* MSU *Spokesman* newspaper, WBFF-TV *Fox Morning News,* Lee Michaels and my folks at WOCA Heaven 600 Radio ("Lee, what can Brown do for you?"), WERQ Radio *Big Phat Morning Show,* WWIN Radio (Magic 95.9), and the *Baltimore Times.* Washington *Afro-American,* DC XM Radio *Too Much Information,* WHUR-FM *Adult Morning Mix Show,* WMMJ-FM, Washington Gospel, WPGC-AM/FM *Joy in the Morning,* and UDC Cable Television. In St. Louis, WGNU Radio. In Philadelphia, WDAS-AM/FM Community Action, KYW-AM, WUSL-FM *Empowerment Half Hour,* WDAS-AM/FM *Patty Jackson Show,* WPVI-TV *Visions,* WPHI 103.9 FM, and WHAT-AM *Mornings with Mary Mason.* In New York, MJI Broadcasting and WPAT/WNSW-AM. In Chicago, WVON-AM *Mo in the Midday,* MTV Radio, *Sophisticates Black Hair* magazine, and the *Chicago Defender.* In Michigan, WCBH-AM *Mildred Gaddis Show,* WDMK-FM *Mason in the Morning, Step Dance TV Special,* and WQBH *Entertainment News.* Thanks to the *Clementyne Review* in Dallas. WHOV 88.1 FM *Gospel Express Morning Show* in Hampton. KRWP-FM *Funky Larry Jones Show* in Houston. And V103 Radio *Frank Ski Morning Show* in Atlanta. To my girls—Frankie Darcell (boy, did we have fun hanging out!) and Jamilah Muhammad at the 92.3 the Mix in Detroit. Also, thanks to Jamie Foster Brown and my friends at *Sister 2 Sister* magazine, *Savoy* magazine, *The Gospel Truth* magazine, *Black Elegance* magazine, and *Dysonna* magazine.

Thanks to Rev. Cecil Murray, Diane Young, and the entire First A.M.E. family in Los Angeles. To my big brother Frank Reid and the Bethel Nation in Baltimore. To my man Bishop Charles Ellis and my Detroit family at Greater Grace. Larry Robinson and my God's World family. To my li'l sis Natalie Case and Kathy "K.B." Brown— you know I got love for you! To Ms. Jeanie "I'm much too sexy for my microphone" Jones, much love. To Prince DeJor, Justine Love, and my folks in D.C. (Justine—when are you gonna do your book?). I'd also like to thank my man Pastor Jamal Bryant and my friends at Empowerment Temple. Pastor and First Lady Browning at Ebe- neezer A.M.E. Church. Metropolitan Baptist Church in Washington, D.C. Mountaintop Faith Ministries in Las Vegas. Also thanks to For Sisters Only Expo, Holy Grounds in Las Vegas. To James Brown, Armstrong Williams, Julian Bond and the gang at *America's Black Forum*. To Ms. Susan Taylor, Michelle Griffin, Gena Charbonet, and my friends at *Essence* magazine and the Essence Festival. Thanks to my sister scribes—Lolita Files, Victoria Christopher Murray, and Kimberla Lawson Roby. Travis Hunter, you're as talented as you are crazy! To Shirley Nichols and friends, Janet Walker and the Reading Group of Sisters and Friends. To Edna Simms and Damien Bruce, Mary "I got me a husband" Moore, Nancy Flowers and Yvette Hay- ward, Rebecca and the S&S publicity crew.

Thank you to my inner circle of family and friends who helped in more ways than I can even express. My mother, Diane Harris, my momma-in-law Sandy Sisson, Karen and Gerald McBride, My father and brother, Pastor Jim Talbert and Rev James Talbert. To Bernard and Shirley Kinsey, Bill and Brenda Galloway. (I think folks came to the signing just to eat some of Connie's good cooking. Thanks a bunch!) To Ms. Cathy Hughes and the entire Radio One family— thanks for rolling out the red carpet and always looking out for your D.C. homeboy. To Kent, Carmen, and Debbie Amos. (Our crowd wasn't too bad for a Sunday when the Redskins were playing. Thanks a million!) Michael and Mattie Lawson, Wayne and Marueen Tucker, Tim and Pam Watts, Reginald and Ivy Carey (though you know you need to give me that velvet long coat of yours), Pastor Zach and Donna Carey and my friends at True Vine (holla at a preacher). Chuck West, Rhonda Elliot (I know that's not your married name, but I can't remember what it is), Ed Hawkins, Rose, Arthur, and Michelle Davis, Edwin and Walter Hawkins and my Love Center Family—thanks for making my signing in Oakland a success! To Ron and Steph Cadet (our Dreamworks is right around the corner), Kelcey and Rochelle Newman. Jacqui, Sha, Enoch, Keith, and Andre at Eclectic Salon in LA. Tracy Nelson, Abe Rafeal, Keneesha Gil, Raye Lynn Russel, Patrice Wilson, Robin Green (I know you got that man hid up under the bed), Veda Brown, Al B. Sure (man, will you please clear out your messages!) Cheryl Wiggins, Chris Best, Thomas Sledd (whether you like it or not, you are the nicest black man on the planet!), Maurice "Bootsy" Wilkinson. The Body Clinic in LA for all those wonderful promotions (and not to mention that massage that was off the hook!).

Finally, a big shout-out to all my folks at the storefront churches, the megachurches, even the pillow Pentecostals like myself who struggle to make it out of bed on Sunday mornings. Thanks for your well wishes, your thoughts, your prayers, and your emails. God gave me this gift. My desire is to write and write and write till either I run out of ink, run out of hardrive space, or run out of inspiration. Neither of which I'd bet on in this lifetime. Love is my inspiration. And I would daresay there's more than enough to last us through this lifetime and the next. We just have to learn how to look for it and how better to treat it once we've found it.

And this just in . . . I'd like to welcome to the world my newborn niece Moriah Diane Harris, born January 7. May your light brighten the world.

Till next time . . .

David
January 2005